SISTERS AND SUNRISES

JULIA CLEMENS

PICKLED PLUM PUBLISHING

CHAPTER ONE

DEB DREW in a deep breath of salt air as she paused during her run along the sand. She lived right next to one of the most beautiful strips of beach in the Pacific Northwest, if she did say so herself, and she often took advantage of the beauty with her daily jog.

She had to start running in place as cold air seeped into the layers she wore to keep warm while braving the beach at close to freezing temperatures. She probably shouldn't have stopped to admire the beauty around her, especially in January, but sunrise on Whisling Island was truly breathtaking—a magical moment that Deb couldn't help admiring.

But even as she tried to warm herself up, Deb could feel the cold continue to push its way in, and she figured it was time to be done for the day. She was rounding the loop that brought her close to her home, meaning she'd only gotten three miles in—she usually strove for running the loop twice—but it was more important to listen to her body than push herself to reach her goals.

Deb continued to run up the beach past her neighbors' homes and finally to the backyard of her own. A rocky pathway led from the beach straight to her yard, her personal little slice of paradise.

Deb paused again, even though her cold body was begging her to press on. She thought she could see a vase of flowers at the end of the path on the very edge of her backyard.

That definitely had not been there when she'd left thirty minutes before.

Deb approached the vase cautiously, unsure of why she was feeling nervous. She ran this very same stretch of beach and walked these very same steps to her home nearly every day. Maybe that was the cause of her caution. The route was always the same, but today, something was different. The flowers.

She looked from side to side as she continued down the path and then crouched when she got to the flowers.

They were absolutely beautiful. Deb had an affinity for all flowers, but as she observed this bunch, she quickly realized they were hydrangeas. One of her favorites. Getting hydrangeas in the dead of winter was near impossible. So why were they here?

Luke, Deb's boyfriend, often sent her flowers, but they always came to her front door. She picked up the vase and realized that, even though the flowers were without a card, they had to be from Luke. No one else was so thoughtful. But why were they back here, and if he'd brought them, where was he?

Deb looked from left to right again, hoping for a glimpse of Luke, but no one was there. Her body finally demanded that she get a move on out of the cold, so she hurried into the house, leaving the hydrangeas on her kitchen table. Well, after she'd admired them for a moment or two more.

The doorbell rang, pulling Deb away from her flowers. *That* had to be Luke. It was just like him to surprise her like this. But as she opened the door, Deb was greeted by yet another vase full of flowers—this time adorable daisies on her doorstep. But again, no Luke. Her gaze stretched down her driveway to the road she lived on and then into the front yard of her neighbors, but no one was there.

When Deb reached down to grab this bundle, she noticed a bit of white paper in the midst of the enormous bouquet, and she hurried inside so that she could set the second bunch of flowers next to the first and take out the card.

Deb

She would've recognized the handwriting on the front of that card anywhere, and Deb smiled as she opened the card from Luke.

Did you know this is the six-month mark since you made the best decision of your life?

Deb tilted her head as she pondered Luke's question. What had she done six months ago? She laughed as she remembered the day in July when she'd gone to her best friend Bess's home and started her online profile on a dating site that had led her to Luke. She'd matched with Luke that very first day, and that day was exactly six months ago. Of course Luke remembered this date, even when Deb didn't. And of course he wanted to celebrate it. He was a true romantic and loved paying attention to the details. That meant many very thoughtful dates and moments for Deb and the man she loved.

She continued to read, *I hope you had a great run, but now it's time for the real sporting of the day.*

Deb chuckled as she thought about the many times Luke had teased her that running wasn't really a sport. She knew he only did it to get a rise out of her—most of the time he talked about how much he greatly admired Deb's athleticism and how hard it was to run the distances she did with ease. But Luke loved to have a good laugh, and getting Deb riled up always made him laugh.

Go to the place where this awesome decision was made for your next clue.

Next clue? Wait, was Deb going on a scavenger hunt? She loved these things. But had she ever told Luke that she loved them? She wasn't sure, but that was Luke for her. He seemed to know what she liked before she said anything and what she needed before she even anticipated it. The man was a gift from God. That was all there was to it.

Deb jumped into the shower, needing to wash off the sand and sweat before going off on this adventure, and then got ready in record time. She'd perfected her hair and makeup routine over the years, one good thing about aging.

Deb was out the door and off to Bess's home a little more than half an hour later, and she smiled at herself for making good time and looking good while doing it. She wore a bright blue sweater, one of her favorites, and black jeans that Bess said made her booty pop. Apparently that was what you wanted your booty to do these days, if Bess's daughter, Lindsey, could be believed.

As Deb pulled up in Bess's driveway, the first thing she noticed was a large bouquet of purple, pink, yellow, and orange tulips on Bess's front porch. The bright colors stood out in stark contrast to the white sideboard of Bess's home, and Deb jumped out of her car to the pick up the bouquet as soon as she was in park.

The colors spoke to Deb's soul, and she couldn't help the huge smile on her face. Luke knew how much she adored color, and even though she loved all the flowers, this bouquet was now her favorite. She realized the vibrant color that Luke's bouquet had brought to Bess's white home was kind of like the lovely color Luke and his sweet daughters had brought into Deb's life. She'd always thought her life complete with her Bailee and Wes, but after getting to know Luke's daughters, Clara and

Grace, Deb felt a love for them she wouldn't have understood without experiencing it. She now loved Luke's girls as her own, and her rainbow of life felt perfectly full.

Deb saw a white envelope peeking out from behind the tulips, and she leaned down to grab it before knocking on Bess's door. This scavenger hunt was fun, but she kind of hoped to find out the end result from Bess without having to go through all of the steps. Deb was the worst when it came to surprises. She loved them, but she also loved figuring them out. It was a conundrum that often left her without any surprises because she ruined them all.

Bess isn't home.

Deb laughed out loud at Luke's first line of the card. He knew her too well.

But if you keep on going, you may get to see her ... or not.

Deb laughed even harder. The man wasn't going to give her any insight into her final treasure, which she highly deserved, considering their track record with surprises. Last Christmas, Luke had tried to fly Deb's sister, Nora, into town without Deb knowing. But while talking to her mom right before Christmas, Deb had thought her mom was acting strangely during the call. It seemed she was trying to avoid all talk of Nora, which was completely unlike Deb's mom who loved to brag about her daughters to everyone who would listen. That had been clue number one. Clue number two had been even bigger. When Deb had asked her sister about her plans for the holiday, Nora had given her some story about winning a cruise, an easy lie to see. One, Nora was as unlucky as they came—her inability to find a man of any decent caliber was a testament to that, and two, if Nora had won anything, she would've called Deb, screaming and hollering up a storm. She would never have waited and then just casually brought it up when Deb asked what she was doing for the holiday. So Deb knew then and there that Nora was surprising her by coming to visit for Christmas. What she didn't know was that Luke had orchestrated the whole thing. At least not until she'd told Luke that she knew Nora was coming. When Luke's face had fallen, it had taken Deb two seconds to realize the truth. Luke vowed to never try surprising Deb again. The words had been said jokingly, and obviously he wasn't keeping to them, but it looked like he *was* going to take every precaution to make sure Deb didn't ruin her own surprise.

There were three little words you were determined not to say first. And yet you did.

Deb laughed even harder as she recalled the memory—so hard that she now had a tear rolling down her cheek. She took the lovely bouquet and walked back to her car.

The memory replayed in Deb's mind as she got into her car and drove toward where she knew Luke's clue was guiding her. A few months back, Luke and Deb had gone to the grocery store together because Luke had been determined to cook for her on one of their dates. They had probably been about two months into dating at this point, and Deb had been feeling the blossoming of love in her heart for long enough that she felt ready to say something. But she wasn't sure Luke felt the same way yet. Things had been going so well between just the two of them, but they had pushed back the meeting of one another's kids due to various circumstances. Even though the reasons for the delay had been legitimate, a small part of Deb wondered if Luke was hesitant to move things forward. So, naturally, Deb was feeling a little cautious about saying the L word. It didn't help that the previous man in her life, Rich, had taken her trust for granted and then decimated it, causing Deb to really hope that Luke would say the words first.

While grocery shopping, they'd pointed out foods that they liked and disliked. They were in the aisle with olives, salad dressings, and pickles. Luke stopped in front of the sweet pickles and gave Deb a smile that made her insides absolutely melt. Then he proceeded to tell her that he hated sweet pickles. Deb was churning with feelings of love for Luke along with a very strong reaction to his dislike of sweet pickles. How could he not like them? They were literally one of Deb's favorite foods. With those feelings so close to the surface, Deb declared, "I love ..." Sweet pickles was what she'd meant to say, but she looked at Luke and said, "You!"

Luke's eyes went wide, and Deb clamped a hand over her mouth. It took Luke hardly any time to recover, and he pulled a very red, blushing Deb into his arms.

"I love you," he said in his husky voice, kissing her deeply. Suddenly Deb was hot and bothered for a completely different reason, and they only stopped kissing when the voice of a little girl asking her mom why the man and woman were kissing in front of the pickles somehow wormed its way into Deb's consciousness.

So, obviously, the pickle aisle Deb now stood in held a very significant place in her and Luke's hearts. She looked up and down the aisle, peering behind the sweet pickles, when a woman wearing a shirt with the grocery store's logo came up to her. In the woman's arms were the loveliest pink peonies Deb had ever seen. Okay, *this* was now her favorite bouquet.

"I think these are for you," the grocery employee said, and Deb caught a glimpse of her nametag.

"Thank you, Sandy," she said as she took the flowers and then a white envelope from the woman.

Sandy smiled as she hurried back to her duties, and Deb beamed as she gazed down at the lovely flowers. The flowers alone were surprise enough for the day, but Deb felt a small, growing hope for where this scavenger hunt could eventually lead. However, she and Luke had been dating for such a short time. He couldn't be ... could he? Deb had to admit she really hoped he was.

Deb tore open the envelope.

I'm still not convinced you meant to say sweet pickles.

"I did," Deb argued aloud with the card but stopped when an older man came into the aisle and gave her a strange look.

Deb looked back down at the card.

But either way, I'm glad you said it. I should've gotten up the nerve to do it long before because, Deb, I think I loved you the first time I laid eyes on you. You were vivacious, strong, and gorgeous to boot. I knew I needed you in my life. But call me a coward, it took you saying the words for me to do so as well. And for that I should be ashamed, but I'm not. Because being with a powerful woman means that sometimes I'll be the one leading us but sometimes you'll be the one taking charge. And have I told you how sexy that is?

Deb blushed, looking up to see the older man was now gone. Thank goodness.

We've had so many significant moments together, so many blessings. Meeting your kids, you meeting mine. Our first "I love you," our first date. Meeting your friends, you meeting mine. But this was my very favorite first. Can you guess what it is?

Deb took her flowers back into her car and had a very strong feeling she knew just where Luke wanted her to go. After their second first date—their first first date had ended in disaster, so they'd decided to redo their first date—Luke had led Deb from the restaurant where they'd shared a lovely meal to the boardwalk that overlooked the water right next to it.

The main part of town on Whisling was full of restaurants, hotels, and other places of business. They all sat on a beautiful stretch along the Pacific Ocean, but there was nearly no sand between the water and said places of business. The buildings were literally right next to the water. It was nice for the restaurants in town because it gave them the feeling of basically floating on the water. But it wasn't so great when you wanted to walk along the beach after a great second first date. So she and Luke had ended up on the wooden walkway that lay just next to the ocean and connected the open space between the restaurants. It would have still been highly romantic if it weren't for the dozens of tourists who were also trying to squeeze into the same space. But Luke had taken charge of the moment and somehow created a good amount of space for them within the throng of people. Then he gave Deb a kiss that made her heart tumble and definitely left her wanting more. Deb had had quite a few first kisses in her day, but none came close to the one she shared with Luke. She was almost positive this was the "first" Luke was referring to in his latest clue.

Deb parked in an open space along Elliot Drive, the main street on the island that traversed right through the busiest part of town, and then walked the rest of the way to the boardwalk, which was already teeming with tourists at nine am.

She looked down Elliot Drive, affectionately referred to as The Drive by locals, toward The Winder, the restaurant where she and Luke had had their second first date. There were no flowers to be seen. Deb wondered if she'd gotten the wrong spot when she looked over the ledge of the walkway and saw a single purple rose floating in the water.

She grinned as she looked down at the rose. Luke had always said the purple rose should be their flower since he'd fallen in love with Deb at first sight, and the lovely flower represented that very phenomena. She knew the purple rose was for her. But where was the note? The walkway was too crowded to investigate well, but Deb realized she had to try. She was in the right place, so a note had to be around.

She looked around the wooden railing that divided the walkway from the ocean and then on the ground. Luke wouldn't have brought her this far to not have another clue readily available.

Deb glanced down the street toward Gen's, Bess's sister's, salon and then back toward The Winder. She startled when she realized this time there *were* flowers—an enormous bouquet of purple roses just in front of The Winder. She knew those hadn't been there minutes before, so she jogged down the wooden walkway toward The Winder. Luke had to be waiting there, and Deb felt butterflies in her stomach as she anticipated seeing him.

She stopped by the lovely bouquet and, sure enough, there was an envelope. She tore open the envelope and read, *Did I get you this time? You thought you came to the wrong place, huh?*

Deb laughed. That she had.

But I'm here.

Deb looked up from the envelope and grinned when she saw that Luke had magically joined her in front of The Winder. Of course his appearance would be magical, just like the rest of this beautiful scavenger hunt.

It took everything in Deb not to fling the vase of flowers and jump into Luke's arms. Instead, she gently put the roses down and then flung herself into Luke's waiting arms.

Luke chuckled as he held Deb and pressed his lips to the top of her hair.

"That was so fun. Thank you," Deb said as she felt Luke pull away.

"I'm pretty sure the fun is just beginning," Luke said, a twinkle in his gray eyes as he dropped to one knee.

"Oh my gosh," Deb gasped, her heart flipping in anticipation as she brought her hands over her mouth. He was going to do this.

"Deb, I knew from the moment you told me 'my dad jokes

were an okay attempt at being funny' that you were the woman for me."

Deb giggled, not even remembering the moment. But it sounded very much like something she'd say.

"You were kind but honest in your assessment, which told me I could trust you. So I did. I trusted you with meeting my girls and with my heart. Now I'm telling you I trust you with my future, and I ask for you to do the same. Deb, will you marry me?"

Deb was pretty sure the gigantic, goofy smile that had to be covering her face was now going to be a permanent fixture. She was so absolutely happy, she felt like she could practically float away.

But her happiness was only compounded when Luke brought a blue box out from his pocket. Deb felt her eyes go wide. He opened the box to reveal a gold band holding a rainbow of small stones. Exactly the ring of Deb's artist heart but not what most men would give a woman. The ring alone told Deb how much Luke truly knew her.

"Of course I'll marry you," she said as she pulled Luke to a standing position and wrapped her arms around him.

"She said 'yes'!" Deb heard her daughter, Bailee, call out, and then there was a chorus of cheers from within the restaurant.

Deb looked around Luke to see her kids and his, along with Bess, Gen, and Gen's husband, Levi. Otis, the owner of The Winder, grinned from the side of the group, and Deb could see there were quite a few more bodies behind the ones she could see.

"You are incredible," Deb whispered for Luke's ears alone, and he grinned as she gazed up at him.

"I know not every day with me will be perfect, but I really wanted this one to be," Luke said.

Deb smiled. "Well, it's almost perfect," she said, and Luke's mouth dipped into a frown.

"Because we haven't done this yet," she said as she pulled Luke's head forward and pressed her lips against his.

"Oh, Mom!" Deb heard Bailee groan, but Deb didn't care. She had to celebrate. Because she was going to become Mrs. Luke Jordan.

CHAPTER TWO

GEN HELD a hand under her ever-growing belly, thinking it felt especially heavy and tight today. She beamed at Deb and Luke as they kissed for much longer than any of their children would've liked.

Wes had resorted to throwing a balled up napkin at the back of Luke's head while Bailee took Deb's roses captive, but the couple continued to kiss.

The rest of the group gave up on the lovebirds and decided to go back to the room Luke had reserved for a breakfast engagement party.

Gen smiled at her friend, Lily, who sat next to her holding Gen's daughter, Maddie, in her arms. Lily was technically Maddie's babysitter, but Gen had begun to think of the woman more like family. Lily's husband, Allen, who sat on the other side of Lily, looked adorable with the baby carrier strapped on his chest that held their own daughter, Amelia. Gen wasn't sure how many men would proudly sport the pink and white carrier, but Allen was one of them.

"If she gets to be too much—" Gen offered, but Lily shook her head.

"I've missed her," Lily said as she nuzzled her nose into Maddie's hair.

Lily had babysat Maddie every day up until the new year when Gen had finally been able to cut her hours down at her salon to three days a week. Gen's eventual goal was to get down to two days, but since she'd have to be taking maternity leave soon, she'd decided to keep as many clients on her books as she could for now. She would cut back the additional hours when she could.

But that meant Lily only saw Maddie three days a week instead of the five or six she'd been used to. Gen knew Maddie missed Lily as much as Lily missed Maddie. They'd formed a special bond, and for that, Gen couldn't pay the woman enough. So even though Lily now worked less, Gen was determined to pay her the same amount, especially because Lily had told Gen she'd be happy to still care for Maddie some days during Gen's maternity leave. Lily felt the time Maddie spent with her would give Gen and her new baby daughter more bonding time. Gen hoped it might also give her extra chances to catch up on missed sleep. She'd heard the horror stories about being a walking zombie during the first few months of having a newborn.

"Can I grab you a few pieces of fruit?" Levi, Gen's husband, questioned, pulling her out of her thoughts.

Gen looked around the room to notice that everyone else at the party was munching on the delicious breakfast fare. Between Otis insisting that The Winder provide its Sunday brunch for the event and Bess wanting to bring a few creations of her own to her best friend's engagement breakfast, the food table was a sight to behold. Just looking at it made Gen feel full.

Gen knew Levi worried because she wasn't eating the same amount as she had in months' past, but in the last month or so of pregnancy, the baby had started to take up so much space that it felt like there was little room for food.

"Sure," Gen acquiesced because she knew it would help Levi feel better if she ate something. The poor guy wished he could do more since Gen was the one bearing the brunt of bringing their child into the world. And pregnancy had been a rough ride for Gen. But she was too grateful to finally be pregnant to complain very much about anything. She'd been waiting for this day for so long, she wondered if the actual experience of giving birth—which she'd been warned would be the worst pain of her life— would even feel like a burden.

With Gen's approval, Levi hurried to the buffet table. Gen was going to bet that he'd come back with a plate loaded down with a whole lot more than fruit.

"How is my Cute Belly Mama doing?" Bess asked, calling Gen by the nickname she'd penned as she took the seat Levi had just vacated and pulled her sister into a side hug.

"Wonderfully," Gen said, even though that wasn't quite the truth. Every part of her body hurt, and she felt heavy. And honestly, right at that very moment she was experiencing some tightening and pain in her belly. She also really, really wanted to enjoy a meal. But she figured those were some of the costs of having a baby, and she knew whatever the cost, in the end it would all be worth it. So she wasn't going to waste her time dwelling on the negative. She was going to enjoy the kicks that always made her smile and the swooshing feeling she got any time baby girl moved. These had been sensations Gen wasn't sure she'd ever experience. Now that she got to, she was going to savor them.

"You're a beautiful liar," Bess said.

Lily laughed, acknowledging that she was also aware that Gen was lying through her teeth.

"It's not lying, per se," Gen said. "I think of it as focusing on the positive."

"You do that," Lily said with a smile as Bess let go of her

sister. "But just don't tell any of the men that you're doing wonderfully at nine months pregnant. They'll expect that of all of us."

Bess and Gen laughed as Allen looked over at the women, knowing he'd missed something.

"Do I want to know?" Allen asked an innocent-looking Lily.

Lily shook her head as Allen took her hand and pressed a kiss to it. Gen smiled at the gesture. Allen wasn't going to let a little thing like the fact that he and his wife were both holding children or that they were in a room full of people keep him from showing her just what he felt for her.

"I am so happy for Deb," Gen said, turning her attention to the couple of the hour who had apparently stopped kissing long enough to begin greeting their guests.

"Oh, I am too," Bess said with a huge grin and a sigh of relief that her best friend had found a really great man.

Lily didn't say anything, probably because she didn't know Deb as well as Bess and Gen. She and Deb had only recently become friendly acquaintances, thanks to their interactions with the sisters. But it was easy to see from the smile on Lily's face she was happy for Deb as well.

"After a guy like Rich—" Bess said and then snapped her mouth shut.

Gen knew her sister didn't like to speak ill of others, but if anyone deserved Bess's ire, it was Rich. He had hurt Bess's best friend in a way only a person who was truly loved could. He'd taken Deb's love and thrown it right back at her by not only cheating on her but lying about it for months and then marrying his mistress once he'd realized his ruse was up. The man was a snake. And Gen, for one, wasn't afraid to say so but only kept her mouth shut for the sake of her angelic sister.

"Deb won the fiancé lottery this time," Bess added, looking much more in her element complimenting someone.

"That she did," Gen agreed as they all looked over at the newly engaged pair who were laughing with the people they stood conversing with.

Deb and Luke were slowly making their way around the room, greeting their many family members, friends, and colleagues. Luke had somehow gotten the entire group together without Deb knowing, which Gen knew was a feat considering the woman could sniff out a secret like a greyhound. Gen noticed that Deb's face still held a look of astonishment as she glanced around the room full of guests.

Her perusal of Deb and Luke was cut short when Levi rejoined their small group, holding a plate out for Gen to inspect. "I got you a couple of other things as well," Levi admitted as he handed Gen the overflowing plate that was so full of food, it looked like it might break in the middle.

"Levi," Gen said, and Levi shrugged sheepishly. Gen had been expecting more than just fruit, but this plate was piled high with bacon, waffles, eggs, and sausage. Gen spied a few pieces of fruit somewhere under the waffles.

"Just in case," Levi said, and he looked so concerned, Gen decided to refrain from teasing him.

Gen broke off a piece of the waffle with her fork and put it into her mouth. By the grin Levi was giving her, you'd think he'd won some great battle, not simply gotten his wife to take a bite of food.

"Thank you," Levi said, leaning down to whisper into Gen's ear before placing a kiss on her cheek.

Gen opened her mouth to respond when she felt the strangest sensation. Had she just peed her pants?

She had lost a bit of control of her bladder in the last few months, but this? It felt like ...

"Oh, my gosh. My water broke," Gen tried to say quietly because the last thing she wanted to do was disrupt Deb's party.

"Your what?!" Levi exclaimed too loudly as Gen hushed him.

"Did you just say—" he began again when Gen pinned him with a look that was as effective as a hand over his mouth.

Levi clamped his mouth closed and then looked at Gen's feet.

Sure enough, all around the feet of the chair on the wood floor of The Winder was a clear puddle of liquid. And Gen really, really hoped it wasn't pee.

Bess had been speaking to Alexis, Bess's cook on her food truck who was helping to cater the event, but her attention had been pulled by Levi's outburst. One look at the ground and Bess was out of her chair and onto her feet.

"I'm going to go find Otis and ask him for some towels," Bess said.

"How are you feeling? Have you had any contractions?" Lily asked as she still held Maddie. Even Allen hovered nearby.

Had she had contractions? Maybe? She had assumed they were Braxton Hicks, but now that her water had broken ...? Gen nodded her head in the affirmative, answering Lily's question as she tried to wrap her mind around what was happening. This wasn't the way it was supposed to go. She still had two weeks before her due date. Fortunately, she was a person who liked to be over-prepared and had packed her hospital bag the night before. But she guessed, in this instance, she hadn't been over-prepared. She'd barely even been prepared. Because she was having a baby. Right now.

"Tell Deb I'm so sorry," Gen said when Bess came back with the towels.

"She will tell Deb no such thing." Deb's voice came from behind Bess, and the woman joined their ever-growing circle of bystanders.

"Gen, you're having a baby. A baby!" Deb squealed loudly,

showing Gen Deb's priority was clearly the baby and not her party.

Gen felt tears fill her eyes. "I am," she said before being overcome with fear. She had been so focused at looking on the bright side of things when it came to pregnancy that she'd pushed every fear out of her mind. She had wanted to enjoy every minute of this miracle, but what if childbirth really was as bad as everyone said it was? Gen did not do well with pain. Maybe that was another reason why she'd shoved thoughts of the actual birth away. But now that the moment was here ...

Gen was going to have a baby. Her eyes went wide with panic.

"I know that face," Bess said as she helped her sister to stand, and Levi hurried to her other side. "You will be fine. And at the end of this, you'll have a baby girl. Focus on that."

Gen drew in a deep breath. Bess was right ... as always.

"We've got Maddie. You two just worry about baby girl," Lily called out as Bess and Levi led Gen out of the restaurant. Gen didn't know what she would do without her village. She also realized she and Levi needed to come up with a name for this little one asap. They hadn't been able to agree on a name, but now the time had come. Gen couldn't very well put "baby girl" on a birth certificate.

They were almost to the door of the restaurant when Gen doubled over, causing Bess and Levi to stumble with her. The pain was overwhelming, a tightening of her stomach that made her want to screech out in pain.

"Contraction?" Bess asked, and Gen raised her eyebrows once the pain had gone.

Was that what that was? Gen had been having scattered, bad period-like cramps throughout the day, even while they'd been enjoying Deb's party, and assumed contractions would be along those lines. But what she'd just experienced was—

Gen doubled over again.

"These seem really strong," Bess said as Gen tried to breathe through the pain. That was what she was supposed to do, right?

"Have you been feeling contractions all day?" Bess asked, and Gen nodded. Although they'd hurt, nothing had stopped her in her tracks. Nothing had been consistent. And nothing had felt like this.

"I'm guessing your water breaking has jump-started this labor. Do you need an ambulance?" Bess asked.

Gen shook her head. That was the last thing she wanted. Besides, she could make it to the hospital. This was her first child. People had warned her first children took a very long time to deliver.

"Otis gave me these towels for your car," Bess said as Gen doubled over in pain again. Was this just the beginning of labor? She tried not to freak out, but how did women survive this? Had it really just been half an hour before that she'd wondered if giving birth would even be a burden because of the gratitude she felt for this baby? Gen quickly realized that she could feel gratitude and still think labor was a very heavy burden to bear as she slid into the seat Bess prepared for her, hoping she could get all the way seated before the next contraction came.

Gen held on to her sister's hand as another contraction hit her hard. This was a lot of them in a short amount of time. Didn't that mean the baby was coming soon? Gen knew she was supposed to be timing these, but how was she supposed to do that with liquid flowing out of her. And, oh my goodness, the pain. No one had prepared her for how bad it would truly be. Those screaming women in the movies definitely underacted.

Bess began getting into the backseat of Gen's car as Gen shook her head. "Stay here for Deb," she instructed.

Bess scoffed. "This is Deb's second engagement but my first niece. If I went back into that party, she'd shove me out the door.

You're stuck with me, sister," Bess said in a tone that Gen wasn't sure she'd ever heard her sister use. Bess was not going to back down. And since another contraction was coming, there was no way Gen was going to argue with her.

"The contractions are only three minutes apart," Bess said to a white-faced Levi as he got into the driver's seat. Maybe it was a good thing that Bess was coming with them. Gen and Levi had no idea what was coming. Thankfully, Bess did.

"You might want to put that pedal to the metal," Bess suggested, and they shot out of their parking spot and peeled onto The Drive.

"Okay, maybe not that fast," Gen said as she held her ever-tightening belly.

Levi eased off the gas slightly, and Gen breathed a sigh of relief. Her husband wasn't really the speed racing type. He was more the relaxed, meandering along the road after a long day type. Seeing her husband behind the wheel at twenty miles above the speed limit was giving Gen heart palpitations along with her labor pains.

"Ohhh," Gen groaned as another contraction hit, and her body tensed so tightly that she wondered if she might pop.

"Gen, I know this is the last thing you want to hear, but try to relax through the contractions," Bess said.

Fifty seconds later Gen turned to glare at her sister.

"I know it seems impossible. But it helps. I promise," Bess said, sincerity written all over her face. Gen faced forward before another pain hit. Bess had always given Gen the best advice. Maybe this piece of advice wasn't as terrible as it sounded. Gen leaned back in her seat, determined to try to stay relaxed for this next contraction.

"Breathe in deeply as the pain hits and then exhale to release," Bess said, and Gen felt her body begin to tense.

Relax, she tried to command herself, but her body seemed to have a mind of its own. The pain was just so bad.

Gen heard Bess tell her to breathe, but there was no way Gen could. Survival was all she could manage.

Thankfully the hospital came into view right after that contraction, and Gen breathed a sigh of relief that she wouldn't be having this baby in her car.

She'd abandoned all thought that this could possibly be early labor. If by some chance Gen was wrong, she just wouldn't survive childbirth. She thought about Levi needing to raise their two girls on his own and really hoped, for both of their sakes, that they were close to the end. Three minutes apart was active labor. It had to be.

Bess jumped out of the car as soon as it pulled to a stop and somehow appeared back beside the car with an attendant and a wheelchair before Gen could even think about opening her door.

Gen felt the pain begin again, and she fought the desire to scream. Each time was getting worse. This baby had to come out now!

As the pain subsided, Gen felt cool air, telling her her door had been opened. As soon as she was ready to move, Bess and Levi helped her into the wheelchair.

The next moments were filled with Bess and Levi talking to personnel and filling out forms, but all Gen could concentrate on was getting through the pain.

Gen heard a nurse tell Levi they had to assure Gen was really in active labor before giving her a bed, and Gen finally gave in to the impulse to scream through a contraction. The sound startled everyone around her, but the next thing she knew, she was finally in a bed.

"Drugs, please. I just need something," Gen begged a nurse as she hooked Gen up to all kinds of monitors. Gen was reminded of the time they'd come to this very area of the hospital a few months before, thinking they'd lost their sweet baby girl. Gen suddenly remembered what this pain meant, and although her hazy mind had a hard time registering anything, she tried to remember that she was grateful. This pain would bring her a baby.

"We've got to check a few things before we can get there, but I'll try to help you through this as much as I can," the nurse said.

Gen nodded before she was hit again with a contraction. The nurse never left her, holding her hand through the worst of it.

"This is a first baby?" Gen heard someone, not the nurse, ask, and Gen heard Levi respond in the affirmative.

"But the contractions are already two to three minutes apart and last about a minute," Gen heard Bess say as the last contraction finally subsided.

"I need drugs," Gen finally managed as a doctor came into view.

Gen watched the doctor exchange a look with the nurse, and Gen realized she was not going to get her drugs. She fought back tears as another contraction moved in. She was hardly even getting a chance to breathe between them. It felt like they were coming right on top of each other. How was she supposed to live through this? What if she didn't?

"Let's check how things are going," the doctor said to Gen as she barely registered she was being spoken to. She was pretty sure the man had told her his name during her last contraction, but Gen couldn't muster the will to care. She just wanted drugs or this baby out of her.

The doctor shifted Gen as she felt a little less pain, and she realized she was between contractions. At this point there was always pain, but sometimes it was a little less than at others. She had to be near the end, right?

"She's one hundred percent effaced and at a nine, pretty close to a ten," the doctor said.

Gen wanted to shout *hallelujah*. That was close to the end, right?

"But the anesthesiologist is busy in a surgery right now. By the time he gets out, you'll have a baby. That's the good news. But the bad news is that means no drugs," the doctor said with what sounded like a smile as Gen was pulled back into the worst pain she'd ever felt. She wished she could pass a little of the pain on to her doctor.

"Where is Dr. Fern?" Gen asked when the pain had gone through its terrifying loop again. She was able to breathe and didn't feel like she was being torn to pieces, so she could try to speak.

The nurse by Gen's head stroked her hair softly, and Gen realized this was as close to heaven as she was going to get during this experience. It was the only relief she'd experienced in what already felt like days.

"I'm afraid you're too far along for Dr. Fern to make it here in time. But Dr. Johnson is one of the best. I've delivered many babies with him and will personally vouch for his abilities," the nurse said, before whispering, "Although his bedside manner could use a little work."

Gen agreed wholeheartedly as she was pulled back into the throes of pain. She tried to breathe, relax—she was willing to try anything—but nothing registered through this immense pain.

"We really can't give her anything?" Levi asked, his voice bordering on angry. Levi didn't do angry often, so Gen knew things must be pretty bad if Levi was upset.

Why was the room so loud? Couldn't they have put her in a more private area? It was only when the contraction ended that Gen realized the loud screaming in the room had been her. She wanted to roll her eyes at pre-labor-Gen who was sure she'd never be one of those women.

"I can't ..." Gen tried to explain the incredible pressure that she was suddenly feeling on top of the pain.

"Doctor," the nurse called out to the man who'd had the audacity to leave the room. He was the one who'd said Gen was at a nine, maybe ten. Baby came next, right?

It was only after the height of her next contraction that Gen felt a little ashamed by her thoughts. She wasn't the only woman in the hospital, and she had to—her thoughts were interrupted by pain. So much pain.

Gen felt herself being jostled as someone asked her to move with them. Gen was in no shape to do anything other than just lay there. If they wanted Gen to move, they could sure as heck do it themselves.

"It's time to push," the doctor said, and Gen could've kissed the man. Pushing meant baby. Gen knew that much about labor.

"So Gen, you are going to feel the urge to get this baby out fast. But I promise, the best way is to listen to what doc tells you to do. You need the breaks between pushes, even if it feels like you don't," the nurse said softly from her place beside Gen.

Gen knew Bess and Levi were somewhere around, but it seemed they both knew this nurse was who she needed right now. She was like a heaven-sent angel, doing the perfect thing at the perfect time.

Gen felt her legs being moved as many hands around her moved her closer to the bottom of the bed.

"Our hope is that we can get this baby out in just a few pushes, Gen. You with me on this goal?" Dr. Johnson asked, and Gen felt herself nod. She could do this. She would do this. Good pushes meant baby would be out sooner. She needed good pushes.

"This can be our practice push," the doctor said, and Gen wanted to shake her head but another contraction hit. She didn't want to practice. She wanted the real thing. She wanted the thing that would get this baby out of her.

"Push now," Dr. Johnson said as the nurse said, "Press down, Gen. Your body knows what to do. If you feel the urge to push hard, do it. If you don't, don't."

Gen felt her contraction, but now that she had a new goal, she swore she experienced a brand new burst of energy. Her mind relaxed as her body took over, pressing and pushing the baby. She imagined the birth canal and getting the baby to move down and out of her. She could do this.

"You're doing great, Gen," the nurse said as she continued to stroke Gen's hair.

"I am so proud of you, Gen," Levi said, his voice coming out of seemingly nowhere. She didn't realize that he'd been standing on the other side of her, and as he stroked her hair, she felt like maybe she could endure this.

Gen felt the next contraction gather, and she knew it was time to push before Dr. Johnson or the nurse said anything.

"That's it, Gen," the doctor said, and Gen knew it was. She could feel it. Just like the nurse had said she would.

"You are a pro, Gen," the nurse encouraged as Gen pushed through her third contraction. Her baby was coming.

Suddenly Gen was hit with a whole new pain, and she screamed in shock.

"I can see her head, Gen," Dr. Johnson said, and it was literally only those words that kept Gen pushing. Every part of her ached and stung at the same time.

Gen pushed through the following contraction, and by the end of it she knew she had so little left in her. She had given all of her strength. This baby had to get out of her with this next push. Gen had to do it now.

As she heard people telling her what to do, she ignored it all and tried to concentrate on what her body was saying. She could do this. She felt her last reserve of energy course through her, and she pushed with all of her might, suddenly feeling relief.

"She's here," Dr. Johnson announced as Gen's head fell back against her bed. *She's here.* Were there ever more blessed words in the English language?

Dr. Johnson lay an extremely upset bundle right against Gen's bare chest, causing Gen to hold her breath. Immediate love welled within her for this wrinkly, screaming baby girl. Gen's arms tightened around her baby as she squirmed, and suddenly her baby seemed to find a spot that felt just right because the crying stopped as she curled into a ball on Gen's chest. Her baby had found her place. Gen was her home and this was her baby girl. She had never felt more needed.

Gen looked up to see tears streaming down Levi's face. It was only after seeing him that Gen realized she had her own falling down her cheeks.

A nurse urged Gen to try to get her baby to latch and begin to nurse, but Gen's baby girl seemed just as stubborn as she was because all she seemed to want to do was stay curled up right against Gen and sleep.

"We'll try again soon," the nurse said with a smile, helping Gen to feel at ease. She hadn't wanted to fail with her first attempt at breastfeeding, and the nurse's smile told her this wasn't anything to panic about. "But for now, we'd better get her cleaned up and checked out for you."

The nurse took the baby off of Gen's chest, and Gen urged her husband to move from beside her and go where ever their baby went.

Levi nodded, understanding what Gen was thinking without any words exchanged. He followed their baby as she screamed her way over to a well-lit setup where the nurses took over with caring for their sweet little bundle.

Gen craned her neck to see where they'd taken her baby, but there were too many nurses around the station for Gen to see much of anything, so she lay back in her bed, taking a moment to relax.

"You were a trooper, Gen. She came hard and fast, but you were tough enough to match it," the nurse who had been Gen's angel of mercy for the entire labor said.

Gen smiled. "I guess I had to be," she said, and the nurse laughed.

"That you did," the nurse responded.

Gen realized she'd never gotten this nurse's name. The woman who had been her salvation. The least Gen could do was know her name.

"I'm afraid I didn't catch your name," Gen said.

The nurse laughed. "I'm Cami. You were a little busy, so I'll forgive you," she said.

"Are you new to the island?" Gen asked.

Cami nodded. "I moved here a few months ago," she said. "I'm guessing this is the kind of place where everyone knows everyone else?"

"Not everyone, but a good part. There's usually only a degree or two of separation between us," Gen said.

"So you're a lifer?" Cami asked, and Gen nodded.

Cami smiled. "And I guess baby girl will be one as well," she said.

This time it was Gen's turn to smile. For as long as she could remember, she'd hoped to raise her own children on the island. Whisling was the best place to grow up, and Gen had hoped to give that gift to her kids.

"I can't imagine a more perfect place to live. We came to visit three years ago, and my husband knew we had to live here one day. It took a couple of years, but here we are," Cami said proudly.

"Did you move from Seattle?" Gen asked since that's where Whisling got most of its transplants.

"The Bay Area," Cami corrected. But she turned her attention as another nurse approached them, holding the most beautiful tiny bundle Gen had ever seen.

"Are you ready to get your baby back?" the new nurse asked, and Cami stepped away, knowing this was a moment just for mother and daughter.

Gen nodded, the smile on her face growing by the second.

The nurse placed Gen's baby on her chest. How was it possible to go from the worst, most excruciating pain to this pure, sweet joy? It seemed impossible, and yet here it was.

"She's perfect," Gen said, and she heard Levi murmur in agreement as he took his spot by her head again.

Levi kissed Gen's forehead and then bent down to do the same to their precious new bundle.

"You did good, Gen," Levi said, and Gen beamed up at her husband. She did, didn't she.

"Maddie is going to love her," Gen said.

Levi laughed. "We'll have to remind her this is a real baby, not a doll," he said, and Gen nodded. That was the truth.

Their room was still a flurry of activity. Gen had barely delivered her placenta, and the doctor and nurses were still hard at work. But somehow she, Levi, and baby girl were in their own bubble of peace.

"We have two kids," Gen said as she kissed her perfect baby's head. Her baby. Gen was in the hospital. She had carried and birthed a baby. What had seemed impossible just a year before was now her reality.

"Congratulations, Mom," Levi said as he kissed Gen again.

"Same to you, Dad," Gen responded, still loving the way the

word sounded when directed at Levi. He deserved this role so much.

"Is it weird that I miss Maddie?" Levi asked, and Gen chuckled. She'd literally just thought the same thing. As much as they loved this new baby girl, without Maddie, they weren't a family.

"I guess you don't have to worry about your love for this baby competing with your love for Maddie?" Gen teased Levi about the concern he'd had when they'd first learned the gender of their second baby.

"I guess I don't. But I was already pretty sure I'd be fine. Thanks to the advice of a very wise woman," Levi said as he kissed Gen again, this time on the lips.

"You're lucky to have her," Gen said, remembering the way she'd practically smacked him over the head with the "advice" she'd given him. She'd basically told him he was an idiot and of course he'd have enough love for both of his daughters.

"Yes, I am." Levi leveled his stare at Gen, making her feel treasured and wanted all at once.

"I guess I'm pretty lucky too," Gen said as she gazed from her husband to her daughter and thought about their other sweet daughter. Boy did Gen have her hands full. But she didn't want it any other way.

CHAPTER THREE

"CALL me back when you have a chance." Bess had to nearly yell into the phone for Gen to hear her above the crying of sweet little Cami and the tantrum Maddie seemed to be throwing. Gen had taken to motherhood like a champ, but that didn't shield her from having bad days ... or weeks.

"Wait, wait," Gen instructed Bess as she called to Levi to help Maddie with whatever it seemed she needed, and then Cami finally calmed.

It had taken Levi two seconds to jump on board with the name Gen had felt was perfect for their baby. Gen had always liked the name, but after hearing it was the name of the nurse who'd "saved" her during labor, Gen felt no other name would suffice. Fortunately, Levi had been easy to win over, and Bess also agreed the name was perfect.

"Maddie *needed* a granola bar, and Cami was insistent on nursing. What am I going to do when Levi goes back to work full-time?" Gen lamented over the phone, and Bess smiled. Levi had taken a paternity leave longer than most, thanks to him running his own business. He still worked a bit from home but didn't visit job sites the way he had before Cami had come. But

Gen and Bess knew that couldn't last forever. Levi had warned Gen he would need to go back full-time in the next week or so. And now Gen was sure she'd never make it on her own.

Bess remembered thinking the same thing about Jon after they'd had James. One kid had been difficult, but Bess had managed pretty well on her own, even though Jon had had to go back to work the day after Bess had given birth. Two kids had been a little harder, but Lindsey had been an angel baby, and Stephen had been a fairly easy two-year-old.

But with baby number three, Bess had been terrified to let Jon go to work every morning, unsure of what he would come home to nine or ten hours later. James wasn't colicky, but he cried nonstop, while Lindsey had made up for her angelic baby nature by being a terror in her terrible twos. At four, Stephen was just old enough to want to be independent but too young to be of any help. However, Bess had survived. In part because she had to, but also because Jon had done everything in his power to make things easier for her. The same way Bess was sure Levi was going to for Gen.

Although Jon had had to go back to work just days after James was born, the same way he'd had to with each of their kids, he had called the older two during every one of his lunch hours in order to give Bess a break, entertaining them with silly jokes and stories. He also often prepared pb&j sandwiches for all of them the evening before and never made Bess feel badly when she needed to have him grab take out for dinner as well. He hadn't minded as their beautiful home became a crazy mess, and he even spent most of his Saturdays cleaning because he knew it meant a lot to Bess.

Bess sighed.

"I know that sigh," Gen said, and Bess wished the insanity at Gen's home had been loud enough to cover it.

"I was just thinking you'll do wonderfully, Gen. Levi will

continue to help in every way he can, but you'll still do amaz-
ingly while he's gone. You've excelled at everything in life, and
this is what matters to you most. How can you do anything but
succeed?" Bess said, wanting to focus on her sister's problem
until it was solved before moving on to her own. The reason for
her sigh was also the reason she'd called Gen in the first place.
But she wasn't sure how Gen was going to take her news. So she
was being a coward and hiding for as long as she could behind
her sister's challenges.

Gen giggled. "Nice try, Bess. Although I thank you for the
kind words, I'm pretty sure that sigh had much more to do with
your reason for calling me than with worrying about me."

"I am worried about you," Bess said.

"I know. And again, thank you. But quit changing the
subject, Bess. Why did you call?"

Bess sighed once again, unsure of how to tell Gen what
she'd decided to do. But the island was too small to keep secrets
from her sister. People were bound to see Jon arrive on the
island or, worse, drive right up to Bess's house. And that kind of
gossip would spread like wildfire.

"I've decided to go on a date with Jon." Bess said the words
quickly, hoping they would have less of a shocking effect if she
said them fast.

"Uh-huh," Gen said as if she expected more.

How could she expect more? This was groundbreaking
news. Bess was going to go on a date with her ex-husband who
had cheated on her. She was giving the man a second chance
that no one felt he deserved.

"That's it," Bess said.

Gen was quiet, and Bess wasn't sure if it was because of
their conversation or because of Cami. She heard the adorable
baby snort.

"Bess, I knew this was coming. You two have been texting

and calling for months now. If you were going to give this a real second chance, which I could see you were determined to do, of course you'd need to go out," Gen said matter-of-factly about a situation that, in Bess's mind, felt anything but matter-of-fact.

"I just didn't expect you to be so calm. I thought you wanted me to move on," Bess said as she tucked her phone under her chin and readjusted her white blanket that matched the new couch cover she'd just gotten.

Once Bess's home had become her own after the divorce, she'd felt the need to give it a face lift. She'd remodeled her entire kitchen but couldn't afford to do the whole house. So she'd sought out cheaper alternatives in the other rooms, like couch covers instead of new couches and flowery curtains that went well with the brown shutters that she'd had for the last twenty-plus years. The changes were minor, but they made all the difference to Bess. Besides, all she really cared about was that her living room was inviting and that the view from the huge picture windows which overlooked the cove she lived on was never too covered up.

"I'm not sure what I want, Bess. Jon was like a big brother to me, and his betrayal hit me hard. But I am forever grateful that I didn't give up on Levi after his indiscretion. I would never tell you that you have to give up on Jon."

"But Jon's and Levi's situations were very different," Bess said, and she could imagine Gen nodding as she nursed her baby. "Levi was heartbroken because you'd kicked him out and hadn't let him come home for weeks ... and he hadn't done anything to deserve that in the first place. Whereas Jon knew I was sitting at home waiting for him. As far as I was concerned, our marriage was strong and beautiful."

"That's a very basic explanation to a very complicated situation, but yeah, I guess you're right. And a big part of me wants you to move on with a guy who doesn't carry the kind of baggage that you and Jon have between you."

"Like Dax," Bess said quietly as she thought about the man who would have stolen her heart had she not already given it to her husband of thirty years. She had tried to date Dax late last year, but she wasn't ready for him, no matter how incredible he was.

"Like Dax," Gen parroted. "If anyone knows how hard it is to wade through that baggage, it's me. Dax is an easier road. But it doesn't mean he's the right one. Only you can decide that."

"Tell that to Deb," Bess muttered, remembering the freak out Deb had had when Bess had told her best friend she was going on a date with her ex.

"I can imagine she didn't take the news well," Gen chuckled.

"Not at first, but she came around," Bess said.

"Because she loves you."

Bess nodded.

"But she did threaten to castrate Jon should things go south again."

Gen burst out laughing. "That sounds like our Deb. Speaking of which, is she loving engaged life?"

Bess grimaced. "Not exactly. She is ready to skip the stage altogether."

"She's ready to be married?" Gen asked, her voice going high.

It was a surprise to Bess as well, considering Deb had only dated Luke for six months. She was sure her friend would want to take her time with the engagement since dating had been a very quick phase for them, especially after the way her first marriage had ended. Bess had thought Deb would be gun shy about committing again.

But Deb had told Bess her first experience with marriage was why she wanted to hurry through the parts of the process that didn't matter. Because of Rich, she now knew what a good catch she had in Luke. She didn't ever want to let him go, so why not be married today?

"She says she is," Bess answered, and Gen let out a whoosh of a breath.

"Well, good for her then," Gen said, and Bess could hear the smile in her words.

"Now back to you. When's the big date with Jon?" Gen asked, sounding genuinely curious and maybe even happy for Bess. She seemed like she was cautiously optimistic about Bess and Jon's second chance, the same way Bess felt.

"Tomorrow," Bess said, and Gen gasped, causing Cami to cry.

It took a few moments for Gen to calm her baby but she came back with, "That's Valentine's Day, Bess."

"Mmm hmm," Bess responded because she knew exactly what day it was.

Gen laughed. "I guess Jon did always like to go big for his holidays," she said.

"He did and still does, apparently. He said he's already missed so many days with me because of his stupidity, but he can't miss another Valentine's Day. It's too special," Bess said, feeling herself blush when sharing her ex's sweet words. She didn't tell Gen the last part of what Jon had said for just her ears. He'd finished with telling Bess that he also couldn't miss Valentine's together again because *she* was too special.

"Sounds like he's saying all the right things," Gen said.

"Yup," Bess said.

Gen was quiet.

"I'm going in with eyes wide open, Gen," Bess promised, understanding her sister's fears. Bess had many of the same ones.

"I trust you, Bess. But if the man hurts you again, Deb won't be the only woman he has to worry about," Gen said.

Bess laughed. She really did have the best people in her life.

BESS STOOD in front of the full-length mirror in her bedroom. She'd taken the day off from working at her food truck because she didn't want to be in a hurry before her date and have enough leisure time to do just this. Alternate between looking at herself, wondering what the heck she was supposed to do, and then falling back into memories of past dates. With thirty years of memories to wade through, Bess knew the time she'd need to be ready for tonight would be significant. And the few hours between when she usually finished with work and when Jon was supposed to come over just weren't enough.

Besides, she had to get ready for this date all alone. Make decisions like what top to wear and what color of lipstick to put on, all by her lonesome. That would also take time.

She would be getting ready alone because it would be inappropriate to call the same person she'd called up for her last fashion emergency, since this time she'd be going out with said helper's father. It would put her daughter in an awkward position.

Bess really shouldn't be thinking about when she'd last gotten fashion advice from her daughter, Lindsey, because that was when Bess had been preparing for her incredible date with Dax. But she wasn't going to dwell on that ... or on Dax. Although she and Dax still texted as friends, Bess had made her choice to give Jon a real second chance. She couldn't do that if she was constantly comparing him to the younger and oh-so-very handsome Dax.

So back to her helper dilemma. She also knew Deb was out of the question. There was no way her best friend would want to help Bess get ready for a date with Jon. Deb was still on the side of the fence that was anti-Jon, even if she was closer to coming to terms with Bess's decision. And although Bess knew her friend loved her enough to help her despite Deb's personal feelings about Jon, Bess wasn't going to put her in that position. Not when Bess was a grown up and could very well dress herself.

Except maybe she couldn't?

Bess contemplated calling the very busy Gen, but she'd already talked to Gen for over half an hour the night before. Bess felt that was more than her fair share of sister time considering all of the demands on Gen these days.

Bess's chef at the food truck, Alexis, would've been more than happy to help as well. If she weren't stuck on the truck taking Bess's shift so that Bess could stand here in front of the mirror.

So there she stood. For the better part of an hour.

This was ridiculous. Bess hadn't been anywhere near this concerned the first time she'd gone out with Jon back in college. They'd begun as friends and then had grown into the best of friends. So when Jon had finally gotten the nerve to ask her out, Bess had been so comfortable with him that she'd known he'd find her attractive in anything she wore. She knew his likes and dislikes, she knew his jokes, she practically knew the innermost workings of his mind by that point.

And maybe there was the rub. Bess no longer knew Jon like that. She knew Jon from a year ago, but thenthought about how much she'd changed in the time since she'd lived with him. She knew if his change was only half as much as hers, he'd practically be a new man. Bess didn't know that man.

Bess sighed as she sat on her bed. She'd gotten an entirely new bed set after Jon had left. Their mattress was still the same, but other than that, she had completely changed things. She'd found a relatively cheap headboard on sale and then snagged the matching nightstands when they'd gone on sale as well. She'd repainted the dresser, which had always been a dark wood, with a blush pink color that matched her new bedspread. It was easy to see this room was the room of a single woman, not a married couple. And that was what Bess had wanted.

As she looked around at how hard she'd worked to remove Jon's presence, she had to wonder if she was being naive in giving him another chance.

Bess made her way out of her bedroom and into the kitchen. She needed to relax and maybe think. And the best time for Bess to do both of those was while she cooked. She realized she could've very well stayed at work if what she needed to calm herself before the date was to cook, and maybe she shouldn't have taken the day off. But it was too late to change anything now.

So Bess got out her mixing bowl and the ingredients for her world famous brownies. Her secret was that she used five kinds of chocolate, making them all kinds of decadent.

No matter how much Jon had changed, Bess doubted that he no longer liked these brownies because they'd always been one of his favorites. Jon was a sucker for chocolate.

She had thought about making a number of different things but had decided to keep it simple. Besides, dessert was all Bess felt she could make since she'd promised Jon that she'd let him cook their complete Valentine's dinner. She'd been shocked by the suggestion since Jon had never once cooked a whole meal for her in their entire thirty years of marriage, but Jon had insisted. However, Bess figured dessert was not dinner. Bess could help with that course.

Her thoughts stayed pretty focused as she mixed up the brownies and then put them in the oven. The rhythmic mixing put Bess a little more at ease, and she calmed herself to the point where she felt ready for this date. She could do this. It was Jon. Maybe not *her* Jon anymore, but he was still a man who wanted to date her and, if he was to be believed, was willing to fight for her. So Bess would go on this date and enjoy it. She could do this.

Bess hurried into the shower after the brownies were in the oven so that she could beat their timer. She barely did so, rushing into her kitchen in just her towel. But she made it in the nick of time.

It was only after she was back in her bedroom that she looked at the large Tuscan clock on her wall and realized she only had an hour left before Jon was supposed to show up. Had she really lollygagged for so long?

But under pressure, Bess worked a lot better, choosing a white sweater that made her feel beautiful and comfortable along with a pair of blue slacks that were dressy enough for a dinner but stretchy enough to make a night at home comfy. She put a few loose curls through her naturally wavy, shoulder-length brown hair, adding some of the product that Gen had insisted would give Bess the best styled hair for the longest amount of time. A face of makeup and a couple of tiny, gold hoops later, Bess was ready. At least physically. Was she emotionally as well?

Her doorbell rang.

She guessed she was ready to find out.

"Jon," Bess said as she opened her door and saw her ex-husband standing and waiting for her.

He wore a green polo that offset his olive skin well. His dark hair was still full and a little unruly. Bess had always been the one to try to tame his wavy hair into submission, and it was weird for her not to step forward and brush his disobedient hairs into place. But then again, after all that had happened, it was weird that Bess wanted to touch Jon in such an intimate way.

She drew in a deep breath as she stepped to the side so that Jon could come in. Things were bound to be a little awkward. They were trying to start from the beginning after they'd already had an end. Bess was sure this wasn't a typical dating situation.

Oh ... my ... gosh. Everything about what was happening hit her like a bolt. Bess was dating her husband. Nope, her ex-husband. The fact that she had slipped while trying to figure out Jon's role in her life didn't bode well for this new start. She needed clear definitions and boundaries if she was ever going to make anything beyond this date work.

Nope. If she was going to make this date work, she needed to calm the heck down. She could set the definitions and boundaries for their dating life later. Right now she needed to focus on the here and now: Jon at her front door. She could do this.

"It's good to see you, Bess," Jon said as he stepped inside and placed a kiss on her cheek. "You look great."

Jon's mellow presence was like a calming balm to Bess, and she bit back the sigh that threatened after Jon's touch. He may not be the same man and she may not be the same woman, but she knew his touch. And it felt like home.

Feeling those same feelings from before wasn't setting clear boundaries, was it? Bess wasn't sure. Did everything need to be new if it was a fresh start? How could she pretend none of their past had happened? This was a whole lot messier than she'd been anticipating. But she decided her mind running away with her thoughts was helping nothing. She decided, once again, that all she needed to do was get through this night, hopefully enjoying herself while she was at it, and then regroup. Figuring out their entire future here and now was helping no one, most of all Bess. She drew in another deep breath, fortified and ready for her date.

"Thank you," Bess said with a smile as she took one of the

bags of groceries Jon had in his hands. Judging by the amount of food he'd brought, she and Jon would be able to feed the whole neighborhood after he finished cooking.

Jon cooking. That was something else Bess was going to have to get used to. She guessed he would've had to learn a few things after living on his own, but her Jon could hardly make a bowl of canned soup. He'd actually burned that when he'd left it on the stove for too long. Bess realized she had to give Jon a little more credit than that. He *had* made sandwiches for Bess and the kids nearly every day in that first year after James was born, but her Jon just didn't seem to have the patience to actually cook anything. Bess figured the burning of the soup was more a case of neglect than Jon not being able to cook.

But this man wasn't *her* Jon. He was just Jon. She was going to have to divide the memories she had with the man from the man who stood here presently. Even after telling herself to just enjoy the evening, it was proving harder than Bess had anticipated.

"I think you forgot the kitchen sink," Bess joked as they walked into her kitchen and placed the groceries on the island. Joking was good. Joking was enjoying herself and not analyzing things too much.

"I figured you could provide that," Jon joked right back as he pointed to the large farmhouse sink in Bess's kitchen. Then his eyes roved over the remainder of the kitchen.

Bess noticed that, once again, Jon's eyes lingered on the space above their dining table that used to house their wedding portrait, the same way his eyes had done when he'd come to Sunday dinner with the rest of the family a few months back. Bess had replaced that photo right after her divorce with an abstract painting Deb had made. It was gray and white to match the rest of Bess's kitchen and absolutely beautiful.

"What made you decide to go so trendy with the kitchen

remodel?" Jon asked as he moved on from the painting and looked around at the grays and whites that were similar to all of the kitchens Bess had seen in the interior design magazines she loved to read. "I always thought you liked more of a traditional look."

Her cabinets, which used to be a dark wood color, were now painted white, all of her appliances were stainless steel, and her counters were a white and gray marbled top.

"After we outfitted Scratch Made by Bess with stainless steel, I knew I had to have it my kitchen at home as well," Bess said, remembering how in love she fell with her food truck's appliances. Was that a weird thing to fall in love with? Probably. But Bess did love them. "The rest of the kitchen just kind of fell into place."

Jon paused as he turned his attention to really look at Bess, and she wondered what he was looking for. She met his gaze, and he held her eyes for a few seconds before turning to the groceries.

Had Jon found what he was looking for?

"Well, it's nice," Jon said, and his generic answer did little to answer Bess's question. But she figured it wasn't something she needed to worry about, so she began to help Jon unload the rice and many packages of seafood onto her counter.

"Are you going to make sushi?" Bess asked, causing Jon to grin.

"I thought you'd like it. You always did love Japanese food, but you didn't make it all that often," Jon said, his grin lighting up his eyes.

Bess nodded, trying to return his smile but feeling a little wary. She'd never made Japanese food because it was out of her wheelhouse. Sure, maybe she could learn how to cook a few dishes. But didn't sushi chefs train their whole lives to create a perfect nigiri? And Jon was going to make that for her tonight?

"One of the professors had a party, and it was a make-your-own-sushi night. This stuff I make won't compare to Maguro," Jon mentioned the Japanese restaurant in Seattle he and Bess used to go to, "but it's decent. If I do say so myself."

Bess raised a skeptical brow, and Jon laughed.

"Hey, you built a business and food truck from scratch in our time apart. Is it that hard to believe that I may have learned something as well? Granted, it's just making a sushi roll, but I promise I've changed in other ways too. I'm hoping for the better," Jon said, and Bess smiled. Bess hoped that was the case for her as well.

"Great," Bess said as she rolled up the sleeves of her white sweater. There was no way she was letting Jon do this all alone.

"You're supposed to sit there and watch a guru at work," Jon said when he realized Bess's intention.

Bess laughed. "Guru?"

"Okay, that's a stretch. But I can at least make the rice on my own," Jon said, and Bess nodded reluctantly. She really did have a hard time letting anyone take over in her kitchen.

Jon took the bag of rice and began to wash the amount they would use that evening before putting it in the rice cooker Bess had bought many years before.

"I thought we'd make some California rolls and Ahi rolls," Jon said as he laid the ingredients he'd brought on the counter.

"The chef taught us how to make a sauce to go on the ahi that was excellent," Jon added as he found soy sauce, Sriracha, mayo, and sesame oil at the bottom of his grocery bag.

"Those look like good ingredients," Bess said as she watched Jon turn to the plethora of fixings in front of him, looking a tad bit overwhelmed.

"I'm going to admit this was easier with Chef Kenji talking me through each step," Jon said.

Bess fought her urge to grin. "What do you do with the

cucumbers?" she asked as she pointed to the vegetable that seemed to be one of the easiest ingredients to start with.

"They need to be sliced for the California roll," Jon said.

"Then maybe start there?" Bess asked.

Jon grinned. "You always did know how to best direct me," he said as he looked again at Bess, this time the longing in his eyes more than evident.

But Bess wasn't sure she was ready for longing.

"And I'll slice up the avocado," Bess said, finding a cutting board for each of them along with a sharp knife. There was only so long that she could sit there and direct. Fortunately, Jon seemed just overwhelmed enough to let Bess back into her own kitchen since he nodded at both of her directives.

As Bess cut, she realized cooking side by side with Jon was a change she was prepared to deal with. But she wasn't sure she was ready for more than that yet. Her heart was still healing. She wondered if it would ever be able to completely trust Jon again.

Jon was deep in concentration as he cut the cucumber and then placed it on a plate. He added the already shelled crab to the plate while Bess cut the ahi fillet into slices that would fit perfectly in the seaweed and rice wrapper.

"Chef Kenji said it should be to taste," Jon said as he put a finger in the bowl where he'd been mixing the spicy mayo concoction that would go on the ahi.

"How does it taste?" Bess asked after Jon licked his finger.

"Good, I think? Here." Jon offered Bess the bowl, and she used the spoon instead of her finger.

Bess nodded. "It should work. It's a little strong, but we want it to be so that when we taste it with all the sushi ingredients, it will be just right."

"That's exactly what I was thinking," Jon said. Then he added with a grin, "See Bess, we work well together."

Bess thought that maybe they did.

She and Jon laughed and joked, mainly about memories, as they rolled out a few sushi rolls and filled them with the prepared ingredients.

"These actually look delicious," Bess said as she cut into the first roll.

"Better than my attempt at waffles," Jon said, and Bess burst out laughing.

"I forgot about that," she said between her bouts of laughing. "You just added water to the flour and tried to cook it."

"You told me that was all I had to do," Jon said, trying to stick up for himself.

"To the mix." Bess was now holding on to the counter to keep herself up because she was laughing so hard.

"How was I supposed to know the mix isn't just flour?" Jon asked.

"Because how is flour a mix? And there was a clearly marked bag that said waffle mix," Bess said as she shook her head. She and Jon had made so many messes over the years, but they'd always been with each other to clean them up. Could they clean up this most recent mess? Could they find every piece of Bess's broken heart?

Jon plated up the rolls, and Bess's stomach growled as he brought the plates to the table.

"Thank you for doing this, Jon. I know it's outside of your comfort zone," Bess said as she and Jon got seated at the table.

Jon smiled. "But outside of our comfort zone is the place we grow."

Bess nodded. Boy had she learned that the hard way this last year.

"Happy Valentine's Day," Jon said as they bowed their heads over their food to say a prayer of gratitude.

Bess nodded again, unsure if she was able to return the

sentiment quite yet. The words might not be a big deal to most. In fact, Bess had said them to many people other than Jon. But when the words were exchanged between the two of them, they carried a different weight. They were a message of love. And she had love for Jon, but was she in love with him anymore? Maybe she could fall in love with him again.

Bess put her first bite of sushi into her mouth.

"Wow, this is really good, Jon," Bess said, feeling like she was eating a bit of crow along with the delicious sushi. It was much better than she'd been anticipating, almost on par with Maguro.

"I told you I've learned a little something," Jon said with a smirk, and Bess shook her head as she chuckled. Jon did love being right.

Bess was about to take a second bite when she heard a knock at the door that she jumped up to answer. It wasn't often that she got visitors, but when she did, it was usually for an important reason.

"Do you have to get that?" Jon asked, his tone bordering on annoyed.

Bess paused in the space between her kitchen and foyer. Why wouldn't she answer it?

Her face must've asked as much because Jon went on, "It's just, we're on a date and ..." Jon let his words trail off.

"If you don't want me to answer, I won't," Bess said as she crossed her arms across her chest, feeling a bit on the defensive that she had to explain answering her own door to Jon. It wasn't a big deal, at least it shouldn't be, but Bess kind of felt like it was. Why was Jon second-guessing her decision?

"Do you want to answer?" Jon asked, and Bess shrugged, unsure of what to say because of her warring emotions.

But as she thought about it, she guessed she did want to answer the door. That was why she'd stood to answer it.

Because if someone was at her door, it was probably a person significant to her. She didn't want to put that person off.

She realized that was why she was upset. She had shown her intent by going toward the door. Jon knew answering the door was what she wanted to do, and yet, he'd tried to stop her. She was about to explain what she felt when another knock sounded.

"Just get it," Jon said.

Bess may not've been married to Jon anymore, but she knew that tone. Bess had already made her mistake, and there was no coming back from it. Jon was annoyed, so she might as well do what she wanted.

Bess felt frustrated that Jon thought that it was okay for him to be annoyed. This was her home and her door. Where did he get off telling her what to do? So, it may have been a bit petty, but Bess did exactly what she knew Jon hoped she wouldn't.

She went to the door and opened it.

If Bess had known who was on the other side, she probably wouldn't have opened it. No, she definitely wouldn't have. Or maybe she would have? Especially after the way Dax's face lit up when his gaze landed on Bess.

"Bess," Dax said, and Bess felt her heart flip flop.

Dax was here. He was back on the island. The man who had made it clear that he was interested in Bess and was willing to wait for her, even while she figured things out with Jon.

Jon. Right. Jon was on the island as well. At her table. On a date.

Bess swallowed.

"This doesn't mean anything, Bess," Dax said as he handed her a beautiful bouquet of white roses, lilies, and daisies. "I'm just home for the weekend and ... okay, it means a little something. I wanted to see you today."

Dax smiled, and Bess couldn't help but return his smile. His presence was like sunshine for her, warming and sometimes a bit overwhelming. But in the best way.

Bess felt the door torn from her grasp as it opened further, and Jon now stood beside her.

Bess swallowed, feeling shocked at the turn of events her evening had taken. She looked from Dax to a very angry Jon and then back to a surprised Dax.

But Dax seemed to recover from his emotions first.

"I'm Dax Penn," he said as he offered an outstretched hand to Jon.

Jon looked down at Dax's hand, and Bess swore she would tell Jon off if he didn't respond. Fortunately, he did, albeit slowly and carefully.

"I'm Jon Wilder. Bess's husband," Jon said.

Dax's smile only grew wider. "Ex-husband, right?" he said.

Jon glared at Dax who continued to smile in return.

"So you're the Penn boy?" Jon asked. No one could miss the way he emphasized *boy*, as if Dax were still twelve instead of the forty-something man he was.

"That I am. Although no one's called me a boy in about twenty years. Thanks for that," Dax said, his smile never slipping.

"Bess, I thought you don't like flowers," Jon said, making the meaning of his words clear to Dax before he turned to Bess, who still held the lovely bouquet to her chest.

Bess met Jon's intense gaze with a stare. The banter the men had been sharing was now bordering on rude, at least on Jon's side and she hoped her look would tell Jon as much.

"When we were young and poor, I told you that flowers weren't worth the money," Bess said honestly. "But in recent years I've grown to love them, especially the sentiment behind them."

Bess smiled kindly at Dax who had turned all of his attention to her. He had to know she appreciated his gesture, even if Jon didn't. He gave Bess a devastating smile of his own before breaking their eye contact.

"Well, have a nice evening," Dax said as he walked a few steps back toward the front of Bess's porch. "I'll see you soon, Bess." And then he turned and walked assuredly back to his parent's home next door.

Jon cleared his throat, and Bess realized she was still watching Dax as he walked away.

"I guess I'd better get these in water," Bess said as she turned to go back into the kitchen.

Jon stepped in front of her, stopping her. "Did you want flowers tonight, Bess?" he asked, causing Bess to look down at the bouquet in her arms. She knew Jon well enough to know that he wasn't just asking about the flowers.

"I appreciate them," Bess said, unsure of how to answer Jon. He was wondering if he should be worried about Dax. If the man was his competition.

Bess didn't want Jon to have competition. She'd never dreamed of juggling two men at the same time. But she also really appreciated having Dax to talk to and text. He'd been exactly who she'd needed when reeling from her divorce, and he'd become a really good friend. One she wasn't sure she ever wanted to give up.

But that was what Jon was asking. He wanted Bess to give Dax up and put everything into what they were starting. Bess didn't feel she had to do one in order to follow through with the other. She could give her all to Jon and still be friends with Dax. He'd been so good to her. She wouldn't just drop him now.

"What if I had brought you flowers?" Jon asked.

"I would like them too," Bess said.

"But you would still want his flowers?" Jon asked.

"Jon, I am in this one hundred percent. I am trying with you.

But a lot has happened in the past year. I can't change that. This," Bess waved her free hand in front of her and her flowers, "is me now. So I guess the real question isn't whether I would still want these flowers. It's if you can accept me, flowers and all."

Jon took a step back. Bess was sure he'd been expecting a more complacent woman. But Bess wasn't the woman Jon had left.

"Okay," Jon said as he moved to the side so that Bess could go to her kitchen.

"Okay?" Bess asked, unmoving.

Jon nodded. "You did change, Bess. But that won't stop me from loving you."

Bess walked into her kitchen and looked for a vase, needing a few moments before responding to Jon's words.

Won't stop him? So were her changes a bad thing in his book? Because they were amazing to her. She guessed they didn't have to agree, but ...

"Do you wish I was still the woman you left?" Bess asked as she filled a vase with water and then turned to look at Jon who had gone back to sit at the table.

Jon pursed his lips. "I don't know, Bess. Because I loved that woman with all of my heart. She was my other half. It's hard to see she's gone now."

"She isn't gone. She's just improved," Bess said.

Jon gave her a small smile. "I can see that. What matters, what's at your core, is the same. I'm just working on getting used to this new and improved Bess," Jon said.

Now it was Bess's turn to smile. She guessed that was what they were both trying to do. And if they could make it work, she had a feeling she and Jon would also be better than ever. That was why she had to give this her all.

CHAPTER FOUR

LILY SAT at her dining room table, watching her dinner get cold. She had somehow managed to put together a gorgeous, if she did say so herself, three-course meal, tripping over Amelia the entire time. A near impossible feat. She'd made a shrimp cocktail sauce from scratch while Amelia had played with her teddy bear, literally at Lily's feet. She'd cooked a steak while Amelia crawled between her legs, and then she'd baked a chocolate soufflé with the soundtrack of Amelia crying in the background.

She had now finally gotten Amelia down for her second nap of the day. Allen had promised to be home in time for the early dinner Lily had prepared. The only way they were going to be able to celebrate Valentine's Day together in peace was if Amelia was sleeping. Although Lily's parents and sister had volunteered to watch Amelia that evening, Lily didn't want to rob any of them of their chances for a dreamy evening of their own. Her mom and dad had always celebrated the holiday in a romantic fashion, and Kate was dating a guy she actually liked. Lily wasn't about to ruin their first Valentine's Day together.

So Lily had planned it perfectly. Allen could get out of work by 4:20. She could have dinner on the table by 4:30, the same time Amelia went down for her second nap. Lily could've waited to cook until Allen came home, but she'd wanted what she was making for dinner to be a surprise. It was the only gift she was getting Allen this year since finances were tight, so she'd wanted it to be done while he wasn't there. She wanted to be able to give him that perfect moment when he walked through the door to a perfectly romantic meal.

But now that Allen was twenty-five minutes late, all Lily felt like giving him was a good piece of her mind. He'd known how important it was that he get home on time.

She looked at the time again. It was still 4:45. The clock read the same time it had when she'd last checked. But she was done waiting.

Lily found her phone on the table next to the couch and dialed Allen's number.

"I'm so sorry," Allen answered, sounding out of breath.

"4:30, Allen. That's what you promised," Lily reprimanded. "Now it's almost five. Where are you?"

"Lenora held us up at the faculty meeting—" Allen began.

"On Valentine's Day?" Lily asked, feeling a bit skeptical. She understood late faculty meetings on most days, but this one?

"We've been having issues with the new language program," Allen said, and Lily nodded. She knew that program was Allen's baby. He felt strongly that his kindergarteners could do more than was presently expected of them. He continually bragged about how they were such a clever bunch. So Allen had talked their administration into creating an afterschool language program where kids from kindergarten to sixth grade could learn a second language. The program had taken so much of Allen's time already, but he really hoped that he could head it when it was put into place. And that would mean a little more income for their family.

"So did everything work out?" Lily asked.

"Just about," Allen said, and Lily heard the smile in his voice.

"Well, hurry home then. I have cold steak and warm shrimp cocktail to serve you."

"I'm so sorry, Lily," Allen said.

"Yeah, yeah," Lily muttered.

"I'm about to run out into this rain so I should put my phone away. I love you, Lily," Allen said.

Lily grunted, letting Allen know she'd heard him. She knew his tardiness wasn't his fault, but it stunk that her whole dinner was ruined. What could she give Allen now?

Lily set her phone on the kitchen counter as she sat back down at her seat at the table. The house rumbled with the noise of the wind and rainstorm outside, making Lily grateful that she was nice and warm inside. Whisling got its fair share of rain, but this kind of torrential storm was always a little terrifying.

Lily regretted not telling Allen to drive safely, but then again, didn't she say that to him nearly every day? She was sure she'd told him to do so this morning. But Allen never seemed to listen to her admonitions when it came to driving.

The rain began to come down even harder, and it was only when Lily heard the pinging against her windows that she realized it wasn't just raining out there. It was hailing.

She stood and walked to the window of her kitchen that looked out at the driveway in front of their home. Sure enough, little balls of ice were falling from the sky. Thankfully the school was only a ten-minute drive away or Lily would be worried about Allen driving home in these conditions. If hail was falling, didn't that mean the roads could very well be icy?

Lily heard a cry come from their bedroom and groaned. The hail must've awakened Amelia. She hurried back to the room, hoping that with a little bit of rocking her baby would get back to sleep and at least a portion of their evening could be salvaged.

But as she ran into the room, she saw that Amelia was on all fours, a sure sign she was good and awake. Lily groaned. Well, there went their dinner. Lily would now be spending the entire time trying to keep Amelia occupied as she shoved a few bites of her once-delicious dinner in here and there. Then she'd eat the majority of her meal as she cleaned the kitchen. Why did Allen have to be late today of all days?

Lily got Amelia settled with a cracker treat at her high chair when she looked up at the clock and saw that it read 5:15.

That was strange. Allen never took more than ten minutes to get home. With the way he sped, it was usually more like seven minutes. But it was now officially over twenty minutes since Allen had gotten off their call. A pit formed in her stomach, but Lily told herself she was overreacting. Allen must've just had to stop for something on his way home.

Amelia cried out for another cracker, so Lily went to grab it as her thoughts went wild.

Allen knew Lily wanted him home. He wouldn't have stopped today. Unless he saw an accident or someone in need. And in a hail storm, that was a likely possibility. Lily focused on that thought, unwilling to let her mind go other places. Scary places.

Amelia finished her second cracker, so Lily cleaned her up and got her down from her high chair, knowing it was getting to be really late now.

Lily looked at the clock that read 5:30. Forty minutes since his call. The pit grew.

She could call Allen. He must've stopped to help someone and had gotten so involved that he'd forgotten that Lily was home waiting for him. She'd call him, and her name on his caller

ID would help him to recall what day it was. He'd answer, apologize profusely, and hurry home safely.

A small part of Lily's mind told her that if Allen was going to be this late for any reason, he'd call if he could. But he hadn't called. So what did that mean?

She needed to call Allen. Just to put her mind at ease.

Lily listened to too many rings followed by the sound of Allen's voicemail. She closed her eyes, willing away the tears that threatened.

Maybe Allen lost his phone?

But she knew that wasn't likely considering Allen had just been talking to her on said phone.

The clock now read 5:40, officially fifty minutes since Allen should've left the school.

Something was wrong. Very wrong.

Lily looked from Amelia to the rain that was now falling again. The hail had only lasted a few minutes, but Lily was willing to bet the roads were probably very unforgiving.

She had to get out there though. What if Allen was hurt?

Lily's phone rang, and her heart jumped. That had to be Allen.

But as Lily hurried to grab her phone, she saw that the person calling her wasn't Allen. It was Kate. Lily felt her chest balloon with dread, somehow knowing there was awful news on the other end of that call.

"Lily," Kate said as soon as Lily picked up. Kate sounded terrified. Lily lost control of her tenuous hold on her emotions and started crying.

"I'm coming right now," Kate promised. "Stay right there."

"Is it Allen?" Lily asked through her sobs, even though the question seemed unnecessary at this point.

"I'm coming," was all Kate said, telling Lily all she needed to know.

Practicality took over as Lily dried her eyes and prepared for Kate to come and get them. Lily was sure she would continue to fall apart at some future moment, but right now she needed to get herself and Amelia ready to go with Kate. Lily dressed Amelia in a warmer outfit and then tugged her coat on over it. Lily found her own coat and then waited, holding her baby girl until Kate pulled into the driveway.

It looked like Kate was about to get out of her car, but Lily was ready. So she ran out of her home, barely registering that she needed to lock the door behind her.

"Where is he, Kate?" Lily asked after she'd secured Amelia in the car seat Kate kept in the back of her car just for her niece. Kate really was the best aunt in the world.

"They took him to Whisling Memorial for now," Kate said quietly as she drove toward the hospital on the island.

"Kate," Lily said, tears flowing down her cheeks.

"You'll be okay, Lily," Kate said.

Lily noted that her sister had said she would be okay, not that Allen would be okay.

"How did you know?" Lily asked.

"Kevin was the first on the scene," Kate said about her police officer boyfriend.

"I thought you and Kevin were going out tonight." Lily wasn't sure why she was asking such an unnecessary question, but no question seemed right at the moment.

"We are. I mean we were. Kevin was about to finish his shift when the call came in. He recognized the make and model of Allen's car. He was worried ..." Kate glanced to look at her sister, and Lily wondered how dreadful she must look for that kind of concern to be etched on Kate's face.

But Lily fought to be strong. For her sake and Amelia's. She refused to go to the worse-case scenario. She'd always been a glass half-full kind of girl, and she wasn't going to change that now. Even if she was more scared than she'd ever been in her entire life.

"So Kevin called you?" Lily asked, trying to find some semblance of peace in her turmoil-ridden soul.

"He wanted to make sure you had someone with you when you came to the hospital," Kate said as she cautiously drove them toward their destination.

"He's a good guy," Lily managed before she was consumed by her own thoughts.

Allen had to be okay. Lily couldn't continue her life without him. So he had to be okay. She knew her logic was flawed, but for now, it was all that was keeping her sane.

Kate's phone suddenly rang, and a minute after she said hello, she pulled a U-turn and headed away from the hospital.

"Yes, go with him. Thank you, Kevin," Kate said before hanging up.

Lily swallowed. She didn't have to ask Kate where they were going. Whisling Memorial was a good hospital for most of the needs of the island. But for life or death situations, patients usually had to be sent to Seattle.

Lily looked at her sister who glanced from the clock on her dash to the road.

"If we can make the 6:30 ferry, we can bring the car with us," Kate said.

Lily nodded. It was good that Kate was in task-completion mode. It helped Lily to feel the same way. They just needed to get to the hospital as fast as they could. Lily could focus on the why of their visit later. Right now she had to deal with the how. She couldn't break down.

Kate pulled up to the ferry just as they were allowing the last cars on, and Lily breathed a sigh of relief. Something about this detail working out for them in the midst of this horrific situation made Lily feel like the rest of their evening could go in the same way. Allen would be fine. He had to be.

"Did Kevin fly with Allen?" Lily asked as they began to travel across the water to Seattle.

Kate nodded.

Lily blinked back tears, wishing she could've been the one to go with Allen but grateful to know that someone was there with her husband.

"Did he say why they had to leave Whisling?" Lily asked, and Kate shook her head.

"Is he that bad off?" Lily asked, knowing her thoughts were spiraling to a dark place and wanting to have a reason to climb out of them.

"I hope not," Kate whispered as Amelia clamored for attention. So Kate turned in her seat to play with her niece.

Injuries from a regular accident would've been taken care of at Whisling. Leaving meant ... Lily's throat went dry at the implication.

But maybe they just needed a specific kind of specialist that Whisling couldn't provide. Going to Seattle didn't mean Allen was on the brink of death. Lily forced those negative thoughts away. Allen would live. He would be by Lily's side to raise Amelia. He would pull through. He had to.

The ferry came to a stop, and Kate plugged the coordinates for the hospital into her GPS. Amelia was an angel. The only noises out of her for the entire trip were her sweet talking and babbling.

Twenty long minutes later, Kate pulled into the parking lot of the hospital and drove Lily straight to the doors of the emergency room.

"I'll take care of Amelia. Kevin should be in there. I'll come as soon as I've parked," Kate instructed.

Lily nodded woodenly before she got out of the car.

Allen was alive. He had survived the accident. And now he had made it to a very good hospital, so that was a great sign. As long as Allen lived, everything would be okay. Lily could manage every alternative except for the one without Allen in it.

"Lily," Kevin said as he greeted her just inside the hospital doors. The giant of a police officer with a big, sweet heart had hardly let her take a step into the emergency waiting area before coming to her side.

"Is he okay?" Lily asked.

"He's in surgery," Kevin said softly. But Lily didn't miss the way he evaded the question.

"This hospital has some of the best surgeons in the state," Kevin tried to assure Lily, but she felt her knees go weak.

Kevin caught her before she fell and took her to a row of unoccupied chairs.

As Kevin helped her take a seat, Lily drew in a deep breath. Allen was alive; he was in surgery. She could manage this. Fainting and losing her head would help nothing.

"What was he like when you found him at the scene?" Lily asked Kevin, and she looked up to see his face crumble.

"Um," Kevin said as he wiped his hands against the legs of his uniform. "Lily ..."

"Tell me the truth please, Kevin. I have to know what to prepare for," she said, and Kevin nodded with a sigh.

"He was unconscious. And there was a lot of blood, Lily," Kevin said.

Lily felt her eyes close, trying not to imagine the scene Kevin must've encountered. But images of movies and TV shows she had watched with mangled bodies at car wreck scenes came to Lily's mind, and she could easily see Allen in any of those actors' places. Her Allen. Crushed within his car. Her heart dropped.

"The paramedics were so quick to get on the scene," Kevin

continued.

Lily nodded. She imagined Allen got the best care. The island was great about that.

"Kevin," Kate called out as she hurried across the waiting room with Amelia in her arms.

Kevin stood to give Kate the seat next to her sister and moved to stand in front of the two women.

Lily took Amelia from Kate's arms, needing the comfort of her sweet baby girl.

"Dada?" Amelia asked Lily, and the tears could not be stopped.

"Do you want me to take her to get a treat?" Kate asked.

Lily shook her head. She needed Amelia, and Amelia needed her.

"Dada is here," Lily said through her tears. Amelia seemed satisfied with that answer. Amelia had finally begun to understand what Dada meant in the past couple of weeks, and she liked to ask about the man whenever she could. She sure loved her Dada.

"Momma?" Amelia asked as she swiped at a tear falling down Lily's cheek.

"Momma is crying," Lily said as she held her daughter closer, and Amelia snuggled into the hug.

Lily tried to get ahold of her emotions for her daughter's sake, knowing her tears were worrying Amelia.

"The surgery is going to take a while," Kevin said to both women as he looked back and forth between them, obviously offering them to go somewhere more comfortable for the duration.

"She's not going anywhere," Kate answered for Lily, knowing her sister almost better than Lily knew her own emotions at that point.

It was only after Kevin subtly suggested maybe there was

somewhere else they wanted to go that Lily remembered what day it was and that her sister and her boyfriend definitely had plans for the night. Even though it felt like days since that last phone call Lily had had with Allen, it was still Valentine's Day.

"You two go on your date, please. I know you had something planned," Lily said, feeling the need to let her sister off the hook but also feeling just selfish enough that she hoped her offer wouldn't be taken.

Kate scoffed.

"Lily Anderson, if you think I am going anywhere ..." Kate said, putting an arm around Lily's shoulders.

Lily almost felt the urge to smile at her sister's sweet and sassy retort. Almost.

"Lily! Kate!" Lily looked up to see her mom dashing across the waiting area with her dad a few feet behind, an amazing sight for her sore eyes.

Lily allowed Kate to take Amelia from her arms seconds before Lily's mom crushed her in a hug.

"Mom," Lily moaned, really allowing all of her fears to surface now that her mother was there.

"I know," Marian, Lily's mother, said as she held on tight.

Lily cried in her mother's arms until she felt like a wrung out sponge, Marian never pausing in the cradling of her daughter, rubbing her arms and back.

"I'm scared, Mom," Lily finally croaked as she looked up at her mom.

Marian nodded. "I am too, Lily."

Lily's dad, Paul, handed Lily a bottle of water that she immediately opened and drank from until it was nearly empty.

"Can I get you some dinner?" her father offered from his seat across the aisle, but Lily shook her head. There was no way she could stomach anything more than water.

"You need to eat, Sweetheart," Paul added when Lily refused.

Lily knew what her father said was the truth, so she nodded toward her dad and then began to reevaluate the rest of her situation. What else did she need to do?

Lily lifted her head so that she was no longer being held by her mom and sat up in her own seat. As much as Lily wished her parents could continue to coddle her and then go on to solve this terrible situation, the way they'd been able to do for most of her life, she knew that couldn't be the case this time. The consequences were out of all of their hands. And Lily needed to remember she was a grown woman with responsibilities of her own. Lily's sorrow would have to come second to what Amelia would need from her mother.

"Where's Amelia?" Lily asked, looking around and seeing that Kate, Amelia, and Kevin were all missing.

"Kate took her to grab some dinner," her mother answered. Lily felt guilt for a second that she hadn't considered her daughter's need for food, but she realized she'd needed that time to cry with her mom. And, thankfully, there had been others around to care for Amelia.

But as soon as Amelia got back, Lily would now be able to be a better mother because she'd dealt with some of her emotion. Lily said a quick prayer of gratitude that she wasn't enduring this night alone.

With nothing left to do but wait for Amelia to return, Lily looked at her watch to see how late it had gotten. It was now almost nine o'clock, meaning they'd already been at the hospital for nearly two hours. Oh how their lives had changed in so short a time.

Lily thought back to four hours before and how angry she'd been with Allen for being late for their stupid dinner. Lily blinked back more tears. Would that angry phone call be the last conversation she ever got to have with her husband? No, she couldn't think like that.

But it was hard not to.

"Mom, I was mad at Allen for being late. I bet he was speeding home because of me...." Lily said, turning to look at her mother as she broke into more tears.

"Lily, you can't think that Allen's speeding was your fault. If Allen was driving, Allen was speeding," Marian said, and Lily felt the strange urge to laugh. All of her emotions were piled on one another, and she never knew which one would appear next.

"But I don't think I told him I love him," Lily said as Marian took Lily's arm and rested Lily's hand between her own.

"That man adores you. And if he knows one thing, he knows how very much you love him, Lily. So don't go saying things like that. There is a lot about this situation that we can't control, but Allen knowing how much you love him is not one of them."

Lily nodded. Her mom was right. As always.

Lily turned so that she was once again sitting forward in her seat to see that her dad was no longer sitting across from them. How had she missed him going somewhere, and how long had he been gone? Lily was amazed by how little she was able to notice outside of her little bubble of grief.

"Where's dad?" Lily asked as she leaned her head on her mother's shoulder again. Even sitting up felt like too much of a chore.

"We need to eat, and your dad likes to be useful," Marian said.

Typically, Lily would've laughed at that. Her dad was a doer. Relaxing was the bane of his existence. He was always fixing something, cleaning something, making something. Marian never needed to make a honey-do list because Paul was on top of anything that needed to be done. But that made Paul nearly useless in times like this where there was nothing to do but sit and wait.

"I'm still not hungry," Lily said as she tried to appraise her body. But she felt weirdly disconnected from every part of her physical being. It was almost as if her mind was racing too fast for her body to keep up with it. She wasn't sure quite how to describe it.

"I know," Marian said as she put her head on top of Lily's. "But that doesn't change that you need to eat."

Lily wasn't sure how long they sat like that, but before she knew it, Kate, Amelia, Kevin and Paul were back. The latter two were laden down with way too many bags of food.

"Paul," Lily's mother admonished when she saw the amount of food they were carrying in.

"You never know what we'll need, Marian," Paul replied, and Lily could imagine her mother rolling her eyes.

"Momma," Amelia called out as she squirmed in Kate's arms.

Lily sat up, no longer able to revel in her mother's comfort. It was time she stepped up to do the same for her own daughter. Lily held out her arms for her baby who smiled as she nuzzled into Lily's embrace.

The nuzzle told Lily that Amelia was ready to sleep, and there were only three places she could fall asleep. In Lily's arms, in her bed, and in Allen's arms. Since the last two weren't available, it was up to Lily to take care of her baby girl on her own. Was this how things were going to be from here on out?

As Lily put Amelia to sleep, Kevin pulled a coffee table from the other side of the room to the aisle between where her dad and she and her mom were sitting. Paul began to unpack the bags of food onto the table, and Lily felt her eyes go wide. There was enough food to feed the entire waiting room, not that the amount of food surprised her. It was just like her dad to buy out an entire fast food place if he could do it in the name of being useful.

It only took moments for Amelia to fall asleep, and Kate was ready with Amelia's stroller that Lily's mom and dad kept in their trunk for times like this. Lily had never been more grateful for her incredible family who were all helping to raise her daughter.

Lily put Amelia in the stroller, wrapping a blanket tightly around her, and then sat back in her seat. Those few moments of holding Amelia until she slept had been the best ones since she'd gotten to the hospital. She'd had a purpose for those minutes, and something had felt like it was in her control. Now, with Amelia asleep, everything felt up in the air again. Lily breathed deeply, trying to calm her racing heart.

"I got chicken, fried and grilled. I got a salad, some french fries, onion rings, burgers. Burgers with bacon, burgers with cheese. Or if you want some pasta, I have that too," Lily's dad offered.

Lily couldn't help the smile she gave her dad. "Thank you, Dad. Maybe the grilled chicken?" she said because the idea of stomaching anything heavier than that seemed impossible. But her parents were right. She needed to eat.

Paul handed Lily the container with the grilled chicken, his smile so wide Lily worried his face might break.

Her father placed a kiss on top of her head before going back to his seat and claiming some of the food for himself.

Lily opened her container and was about to take her first bite when she was hit with a thought that made her drop her chicken.

"Kevin, was anyone else hurt in the accident?" Lily asked. How had she only thought to ask this question now? Granted, she had a lot on her mind, but still.

"No. It was a single car accident," Kevin said as Lily

breathed out a sigh of relief. But since she was getting details of the accident, Lily figured she might as well continue. She'd need to know all of this information sooner or later.

"What happened?" Lily asked, and Kevin sent the briefest glance in Kate's direction before turning his full attention to Lily.

"Are you sure you want to know, Lily?" Kevin asked as Lily nodded. Maybe she didn't want to know, but she needed to know.

"We aren't sure yet because our people haven't had time to recreate the accident, but to me, it looked pretty straightforward. Allen took the turn on Mulholland a little too fast," Kevin said, and the huge curve in the road that led up to Lily's home on the island easily came to mind. It was one she'd warned Allen about time and time again.

"Between his likely speed and the slick road conditions, we think he lost control of the car and spun into that big oak tree," Kevin finished.

Lily nodded as her throat got tight. She wanted to rail at Allen. What was he thinking, speeding on that turn when it had been hailing? But she was as much to blame. She'd urged him to hurry when she knew what the conditions outside were like. Her stupid dinner had taken precedence.

Suddenly Kate was beside Lily, holding her fork. "You need to eat, Sis. So either you feed yourself or I feed you," Kate said.

Lily nodded. She was beginning to feel lightheaded, and she had a feeling her bouts of crying along with too little food and water were to blame. Somehow a new bottle of water had appeared on the floor next to her feet, so she made it her mission to finish the container of chicken and that bottle of water. She could do this. This was another purpose. She would move herself from purpose to purpose until she got news of Allen. And then ... what would she do then?

Lily focused on her food. She would cross the next bridge when the time came.

The food that Lily normally loved tasted dry in her mouth, and it took the entire water bottle just for her to down enough food to satisfy her family. She was glad they'd all fallen into conversation while she was eating, relieved to not be their focus for even a few minutes.

Lily glanced over at Amelia who was sleeping peacefully. There was one blessing in all of this. Amelia seemed untouched by the terror that threatened them. One day she would know about this moment, but it would all be words and a story, hopefully a time she and Allen could look back on as something they'd overcome together. No, there was no hopefully about it. She and Allen would look back on this time together. They had to.

Lily set her empty container on the table and then curled up in her chair. It was now past ten, about the time she typically went to sleep. She knew that blissful state would elude her tonight. But pretending to sleep was better than having her family worry over her. As much as she loved them for being there, she was starting to wilt under their concern and pity. She needed some time to breathe, and feigning sleep would give her that.

As Lily sat with her eyes closed, she heard less and less talking around her until only the hum of the television in the corner accompanied her sleep-deprived mind.

"Lily Anderson," a voice said quietly, and all four of the adults waiting with Lily hopped to their feet.

"I'm Lily," Lily answered, her voice sounding strained as the doctor approached their group. As Lily took a few steps toward the doctor, she could feel Kate's shoulder against her own. She knew her sister was with her every literal step of the way.

"Hi, Mrs. Anderson. I'm Dr. Warren." The doctor gave Lily

his hand, which Lily shook, but she really wished he'd get past the niceties and tell her how Allen was doing.

"Is he okay?" Lily had to ask the question that had been plaguing her for hours.

"He's still under anesthesia. We'll know much more after Allen wakes up," Dr. Warren said.

Lily held tightly to Kate's arm. "He's going to wake up?" she asked, and she watched as Dr. Warren swallowed.

"We expect him to. He was unconscious when he was brought in, but he regained consciousness for a few minutes before he received anesthesia," Dr. Warren said as Lily nodded. This all sounded like great news.

"He has no head injuries. He did break his leg, but most of his injuries were spinal related," Dr. Warren recounted, and Lily felt a sudden lump in her throat.

Spinal related? Did that mean ...?

"The injuries are quite severe," Dr. Warren said, and Lily felt more tears pool up in her eyes.

No crying, she demanded. Allen was alive. That was all she needed.

"We did everything we could during surgery, but we can't make a prognosis until he wakes. We are hopeful that the repercussions of the spinal injuries won't be extensive," the doctor said candidly.

Lily felt the words swimming around in her mind. Spinal injuries. Extensive.

"What is the worst-case scenario, doctor?" Paul asked.

"I can't say," Dr. Warren replied. "For now we have to hope for the best. We'll do everything in our power to make that come to pass."

Lily nodded, more than grateful for Dr. Warren. He'd been operating on her husband for hours, and now he was out here speaking to her and her family.

And Allen was going to live. Lily knew it in her heart and soul. He was just under anesthesia. He would wake up. Everything else could be dealt with. Lily wasn't going to lose her Allen.

"Thank you, Dr. Warren," Lily said as she extended her hand again. The man had given Allen, and therefore Lily, a new lease on life. Lily was going to take it.

"The nurses will be out to see you soon. As soon as Mr. Anderson awakes, you should be able to go back and visit him. One at a time," Dr. Warren said as he looked at the waiting group.

Lily nodded as she relayed her thanks again, and the doctor headed back behind the doors into another area of the hospital.

"He's okay," Lily breathed as she fell into her dad's waiting arms.

"He's okay," Paul said.

Lily felt more tears spill over, but these were tears of relief and gratitude. She knew how close she had been to losing Allen, and although they weren't out of the woods yet, Lily had so much reason to hope. So she was going to hope.

CHAPTER FIVE

"MADDIE, don't dump the box of ..." Gen reprimanded her older daughter while Maddie proceeded to dump said box as Gen's younger daughter screamed from where she lay on the ground on a blanket.

"Tummy time," Gen said to explain Cami's screaming to Olivia who had brought over a box full of little girls' clothing. Olivia was working hard to keep her face neutral as she and Gen stood next to one another in the entryway of Gen's living room. Olivia could remember the crazy chaos of two baby girls like it was yesterday. Hearing Cami scream didn't make Olivia miss it too much.

Olivia had offered the clothing she'd once used for her own girls to Gen, who had accepted in a heartbeat. All of the pieces were in pristine shape—Olivia had made sure her daughters were the best dressed little girls around—but what was Olivia going to do with them now? She figured sharing them with Maddie and Gen was better than having them take space in her own tiny closet. She'd one day get them back and give them to Rachel and Pearl as they grew up and had daughters of their own. But it didn't make sense for the clothes to be unused for so long when she knew Gen could definitely use them. Gen had the money to get new clothes for her girls, but she lacked the time to actually go shopping. She'd called Olivia a godsend when Olivia had offered.

"Pearl hated tummy time as well," Olivia said as she watched Cami wriggle on her blanket. The girl was strong; Olivia would give her that.

"And we have to do tummy time not only for Cami but also because it's one of the few times we get Maddie time, huh?" Gen said as she lifted her two-year-old in her arms, who instantly rubbed her face against Gen's shoulder, showing Olivia how much the little girl was enjoying being held by her mom.

But then Maddie must've remembered the upended box of girls' clothes, and she wriggled out of her mom's arms in order to continue making her mess.

"Even with Lily taking Maddie for a couple hours a week, I still feel guilty about how little one-on-one time I spend with her. Cami just needs so much attention, and I don't know how to balance it all." Gen scrubbed her hands over her face. "Does it stay this hard forever?" Gen whispered as she looked from one daughter to the other.

"In some ways, no," Olivia said honestly. Her own girls were almost exactly two and a half years apart, the same as Gen's daughters.

"But in some ways, yes?" Gen asked.

Olivia shrugged. She didn't want to lie, but she also didn't want to overwhelm Gen any more than she already was.

Poor Gen was still in her pajamas at noon, and Olivia had definitely seen Gen's place look a lot cleaner. But these first months with a newborn were hard. Gen would master this stage, and then just as she was getting her bearings, the next stage would pull the rug out from under her. But Olivia was definitely keeping that little parenting tidbit to herself. No one needed to know that was coming.

"Can you thank Bess for the food?" Gen said as she pointed to the bag of takeout Olivia had brought from the food truck. When Bess had heard Olivia was taking clothes over to Gen, she'd sent Olivia with a big bag of food as well.

"Will do," Olivia said.

"You know, if it weren't for her, I would probably only manage one meal a day," Gen said. Then she added, "But I am so dang hungry all the time. Why did no one warn me that breastfeeding would make me want to eat like the very hungry caterpillar?"

Olivia laughed at that comparison, but it was the truth. At least it had been for her.

"I kind of forgot about that," Olivia said, and Gen pinned her with a glare.

"Really. You'll forget about lots of this stuff. So much of the time gets swallowed up in lack of sleep, and the only memories I was able to keep were the good ones," Olivia added.

"Lucky you," Gen muttered.

Olivia fought a chuckle. She didn't doubt this time was hard for Gen. Olivia knew she had been more than grateful to be beyond that stage, but Olivia also knew that time was fleeting. Even if it felt like forever as Gen lived it.

"Bess gave me the lowdown, but I haven't had a chance to ask you about the conversation you two had about her love life. I take it you guys had a good talk?" Gen asked abruptly, changing the subject as she went to the blanket to pick up Cami.

"Yeah. We really did. It wasn't necessary, but I was grateful to Bess for filling me in. She has to do what's best for her, and I respect her for that. And personally, I think Dax could use a little competition. He's had women falling all over him for years, and he's never taken any of them seriously. Now here's our Bess telling him she's going to date her ex instead of him, and this is when Dax decides to stick around. Whatever Bess is doing, apparently she's doing something right," Olivia said with a grin.

Olivia had had a long conversation with Bess about her and Dax a few days before. Bess had been honest about her feelings for Olivia's brother—maybe a bit too honest—and Olivia had been thankful for it. Evidently, she liked Dax a lot. But then Bess had also told Olivia that she felt she needed to give Jon another chance. After speaking to Bess, Olivia understood why. She'd also told Olivia she'd been just as honest with Dax. But Bess had wanted to be sure that what happened between her and Dax didn't affect her relationship with Olivia. Olivia had assured her that wouldn't be the case. Olivia loved her brother with her whole heart, but getting involved with his relationships wasn't her style. A few of the women in his past had tried to create a relationship with Olivia, especially when they'd felt they were losing Dax. So Olivia had decided to stay out of things until Dax found the right one. She figured once Dax finally settled down, she would get to know the woman who ultimately stole his heart. But until then, Olivia wasn't going to get attached. After the trail of broken hearts in Dax's wake, this situation with Bess was actually kind of amusing.

Since that conversation, Olivia had begun to lightheartedly joke with Bess about her real life love triangle. According to Bess, Olivia wasn't the only one loving Bess's unlikely situation. Gen and Deb were also very much enjoying teasing Bess about her fun little mess.

"And then when I talked to Dax, he told me that he went over to Bess's again after the whole Valentine's Day fiasco. He wanted to apologize if he'd done anything to put Bess in a tough position with Jon," Olivia said as Gen laughed.

"Don't you wish you could've seen that *manly* showdown?" Gen asked. She didn't even try to hold back her laughter as she spoke, and Olivia responded with a chuckle. It would've been pretty funny to be a fly on the wall in that situation.

She could just imagine her brother's grin in light of Jon's annoyance at his appearance. She knew the exact grin Jon must've seen because Olivia was very familiar with it. If there was anyone in life Dax enjoyed annoying, it was his little sister.

"Wait, so did Dax say anything else when he went back to Bess's the next day?" Gen asked when her laughter had died down.

"He laid it all on the line," Olivia said with her eyebrows raised.

Gen's eyes went wide, obviously impressed with Dax's bravery.

"He reiterated that he would be whatever Bess needed. And that until she told Dax she was choosing Jon and didn't want Dax in her life, he was going to stick around as whatever she wanted. If that was a friend, he'd be a friend. And then he emphasized *for now*." Olivia told Gen what her brother had relayed to her with a huge grin, and Gen returned the grin happily.

"After being stuck in the house for so long, that is the best news I've had in weeks. Thank you," Gen said. Then after a moment of thought she added, "Dang it. I didn't mean to sound so depressed about having to be home. I'm trying to be more positive about all of this. Staying at home with my two little girls is literally my dream come true. I need to be more grateful."

Oliva shrugged. "You know just because you're living your dream doesn't mean the reality of that dream isn't hard work. Your feelings are legitimate, Gen. Don't let the guilt make this any harder on you."

Gen nodded as she held her baby girl a little closer to her chest. "You're right," she said, although she still didn't sound a hundred percent convinced. Olivia understood that. Mom guilt was a force all of its own. "Thanks, Olivia," Gen added. "I don't know what I would do without you."

"You'd be fine," Olivia assured.

Gen shrugged. "I'm glad I don't have to find out. And thank you again for the clothes," she said, nodding her head in the direction of the tipped over box. "Contrary to what you've just seen, I promise we'll take good care of them."

Olivia smiled. She knew Gen would.

"Well, I'd better get out of here. I'm meeting with Dr. Bella in ten minutes," Olivia said as she walked over to give Maddie, who was still investigating all of the clothing, a hug. Maddie must've realized right at that same moment that she was done playing with the clothes because she reached up her arms to Olivia, silently asking to be held. But Olivia really had to leave if she was going to make her appointment on time, so she decided that making Maddie's play kitchen seem appealing would help her cause. Olivia pretended to stir something in a little fake pot on the cute fake stove, and the action had its desired effect. Maddie immediately copied Olivia's action and then proceeded to continue playing.

"How did you do that?" Gen asked as Olivia walked toward the door.

Olivia knew the feeling of awe Gen was experiencing. Olivia's mom had been able to redirect the attention of her girls all the time when they were little, and Olivia had never understood why she couldn't do the same.

"Because I'm not her mom. Not being held by me is a lot easier on her than not being held by her mommy." Olivia said the same thing her mother had told her, but Gen shook her head as if she didn't accept Olivia's explanation.

"It's still a miracle. And you are a miracle worker. She's had no interest in that kitchen since this one came along," Gen said, holding up the bundle in her arms.

"Love you, Gen," Olivia said as she pulled Gen into a hug that Gen returned. Olivia wasn't sure what more to say or do to help Gen because, although she knew what Gen was feeling, she had no idea how to make it better. Life just had to be lived, sometimes purely endured, during the hard stages of raising children.

"Call me if you need me," Olivia said as she opened the front door.

Gen nodded. "And you call me if you hear any good gossip. I know I'm only on maternity leave for three months, but I'm dying to go back to the salon just for the news. I am so busy and so bored all at once. Is that crazy?" Gen asked.

"Nope. Not at all. I'll keep an ear out for anything good," Olivia said, and Gen smiled as Olivia hurried out the door. She was going to be late if she didn't get a move on.

The five-minute drive to Dr. Bella's went quickly, and as Olivia walked briskly from her car to Dr. Bella's office, she thought about the many times she'd taken this trek, both by herself and with her daughters.

Olivia had been meeting with Dr. Bella since her separation from Bart, her ex-husband. So when Olivia's daughters had begun to have issues with their father that she didn't know how to fix, they'd all come to Dr. Bella. Pearl had wanted to see her dad, but Bart wouldn't see Pearl unless both girls visited him. Rachel had no desire to see her father, so therein lay the conundrum. Olivia wouldn't force Rachel to see Bart—their custody arrangement gave Olivia all the power when it came to parenting their daughters—but she felt badly for Pearl. She wished Bart would grow up and just see the one daughter who wanted to see him. But so far, he'd been a stubborn mule. The girls had gone to see Dr. Bella a handful of times now, and although they were no closer to visiting Bart, both girls now felt comfortable sharing their feelings with the doctor. She'd helped them to work through a number of their insecurities. Because of that, Olivia had hope that one day the situation with Bart would work out as well.

"Hi, Shannon," Olivia said, greeting the receptionist as she came into Dr. Bella's offices.

"Hey, Olivia," Shannon said as she stood so that she could see over the high counter that divided the waiting area from her work space. "Did you want something to drink?"

Olivia shook her head.

"Alrighty then. The doctor should be with you in a moment," Shannon said.

"Thank you," Olivia said as she pulled out her phone to check her messages. Bess was the best sort of boss and allowed Olivia to work whenever she could, as long as the work got done. Olivia never took that for granted and made sure she not only had the work done and done well, but she tried to go above and beyond.

Olivia had one unread work email from a business on the island who wanted to hire Scratch Made by Bess to cater an event for them. Olivia wasn't sure how to respond until after she spoke to Bess. Moving into catering would be huge for them, but it would also mean a whole lot more work. Olivia wasn't sure the risk was worth the reward—the business was doing exceptionally as it was—but Bess would be the one to make that decision, not Olivia.

Olivia shot back a quick response to the business, telling them that she would get back to them soon, just as the door to Dr. Bella's main office opened and Mrs. Edmunds emerged.

"Olivia," Mrs. Edmunds greeted with a smile. Olivia had known Mrs. Edmunds ever since she was a little girl. Mrs. Edmunds used to be the only ballet teacher on the island during the time Olivia dipped her toe into dancing for a few years back in elementary school. Olivia quickly found out ballet wasn't for her, but she'd created a lasting relationship with her kind teacher.

"Hi, Mrs. Edmunds," Olivia said, realizing it might be strange for her, a grown woman, to greet another grown woman by her title and last name instead of by her first name. But it was hard to change what you called someone just because you got older. To Olivia, Mrs. Edmunds would always be Mrs. Edmunds.

"How are your girls?" Mrs. Edmunds asked, and Olivia smiled, grateful to only be asked about her daughters. There were still times, nearly a year after her divorce, that a nosy neighbor or island gossip would ask Olivia about Bart. But she was glad that most people she knew on the island had moved on.

"They're doing so well. Pearl is playing soccer, and Rachel has decided she wants to play the piano," Olivia replied.

"Do either of them want to follow in their mom's footsteps?" Mrs. Edmunds asked.

Olivia shook her head. "We both know their mom doesn't have a single dancing bone in her body. If they take after her, neither should dance," Olivia said.

Mrs. Edmunds laughed. "You always were too hard on yourself. I think you could have excelled."

"That's because you're too nice," Olivia said, and Mrs. Edmunds moved to the side so that Olivia could enter Dr. Bella's office.

"We'll agree to disagree on that one. Dr. Bella said you could head right in," Mrs. Edmunds replied as she walked toward Shannon's desk. "It was nice to see you, Olivia."

"Same to you, Mrs. Edmunds," Olivia said as she walked into Dr. Bella's office and then closed the door behind her.

"Hi, Olivia," Dr. Bella greeted from her desk as Olivia took a seat on the main couch in the office. There were many places to sit, but Olivia tended to take the same seat on the couch each time she came in. Dr. Bella usually took one of the chairs that sat on either side of the couch, facing each other. There were a few times Dr. Bella had chosen to sit at her desk chair, which faced the couch, but that wasn't often.

"Hello, Doctor," Olivia said as she watched Dr. Bella move from her desk to take a seat in her typical chair.

"How has your week been?" Dr. Bella asked, and Olivia smiled as she thought about the visit she'd just had with Gen. Olivia relayed the experience, causing both women to laugh.

"It is nice to no longer have a newborn, huh?" Dr. Bella asked.

"And yet, like a crazy woman, I miss it," Olivia said with a grimace.

Dr. Bella laughed again. "I sometimes feel the same way," she agreed. "Until I remember the sleepless nights."

Olivia nodded. "That's true. But the smell—"

"There is nothing better than a baby's smell," Dr. Bella quickly agreed.

Their conversation moved to Olivia's daughters.

"How have you been dealing with Pearl's coach?" Dr. Bella asked.

Olivia felt herself curl up. She didn't want to talk about Pearl's coach, but she knew that probably meant she needed to.

Olivia shrugged. "After we cleared up the mix-up with her teammates and explained that Dean is not Pearl's dad, I think things have been going well," Olivia said, trying not to cringe as she remembered the way Dean's face had gone red when Pearl's teammates had started calling him Pearl's dad. They now all called him Coach Dean, but Olivia could see why there had been a mix-up. What other man would step up to coach the daughter of the woman renting his backyard cottage?

Okay, maybe that wasn't fair to the relationship she and Dean had. They were friends. Good friends. Olivia's heart had blurred the line between friendship and something more, but it was now clearly drawn again. Dean had a serious girlfriend, Charlotte, and Olivia really liked Charlotte.

"How do you feel about Dean?" Dr. Bella asked.

Olivia shrugged again. "He's the best man I know."

"But ..."

"But he's dating Charlotte, and I'm no good for anyone," Olivia said honestly.

"Why do you say that?" Dr. Bella asked quietly.

"Because it's a fact?" Olivia responded.

"The first part of your statement is a fact, but not the second."

"It sure feels like it," Olivia said as she shifted so that she could lean on the arm of the couch.

"What makes you no good for anyone?" Dr. Bella asked as she jotted down a few notes.

When Olivia had first started therapy, she'd hated how whiny she sounded. She thought it sounded like she was either complaining or fishing for compliments. But Dr. Bella had taught her that voicing her inner feelings was neither of those things. It had taken a few visits, but she'd eventually come to terms with the fact that that was how therapy went ... at least for her. She worked hard not to whine in any other part of her life, but Dr. Bella didn't seem to mind her complaining. And so far, it had worked.

"My baggage. It's too much," Olivia said with a shrug of her shoulders.

"I thought that Gen pointed out to you that Dean knows your baggage. And he still cares about you."

"She did. And I kind of believed it, for a bit. But I guess I don't really know. Why would anyone choose me when they can have someone who doesn't come with such a heavy load? The years of abuse Bart put me through, I'm still working to break down my perfectionist façade. And even though I love them with every fiber of my being, I know my girls are also part of my baggage. How can all of that fit into anyone else's life?"

Dr. Bella met Olivia's eyes as Olivia finally landed her gaze back on the doctor. Olivia tended to look everywhere other than at the doctor when she spoke, but when Dr. Bella spoke, Olivia was sure to try to make eye contact. It felt like the right thing to do.

"Don't you think most people dating at your age have their own fair share of baggage?"

Olivia nodded. She knew that for a fact. Dean was divorced. He had trust issues because of his first wife. Charlotte had been left by her son's father when she was pregnant. They did have their issues. But they had a carry-on's worth whereas Olivia came with two full-sized suitcases and a backpack to boot. Olivia would keep whoever traveled with her waiting at the baggage claim for a long time.

"I think you're avoiding dating because you are scared," Dr. Bella said, still keeping Olivia's eye contact.

Olivia wouldn't disagree with that.

"And that's not a good reason. If you didn't *want* to date or if you weren't ready, those are reasons I would support. But I think you want to meet someone, right?"

Olivia nodded. She did. Even though Bart had hurt her in ways no human should hurt another human, Olivia had also seen beautiful examples of love and marriage. She had to admit she would love to have that one day.

"So we need to overcome that fear, Olivia." Dr. Bella said the words Olivia had been dreading, but she also knew she needed to hear them. Olivia knew she would never date without a push. And now she was being pushed.

"You're saying I should date?" Olivia asked, needing clarification. She wasn't about to jump off the dating cliff without knowing it was Dr. Bella's idea. If the doctor thought she was ready, maybe she was. It was only the doctor's confidence in her that would move Olivia along.

Dr. Bella nodded.

"Okay," Olivia said thoughtfully because she really wanted to do as the doctor asked; Dr. Bella had yet to steer her wrong. But because it was a brand new idea, she needed step-by-step instructions. "How do I do that? I haven't dated anyone besides Bart since high school. And the world is a little different now."

Olivia cringed, thinking about how hard it had been to date back when she was fifteen. How much harder would it be now ... as an adult ... with kids?

"That it is." Dr. Bella paused, and Olivia knew it was because she was getting ready to gauge Olivia's response for whatever she was about to say next. "You could join an online dating site?"

Olivia started shaking her head before Dr. Bella had even finished speaking. She knew online dating worked for many, including her friend Deb, but it was not for Olivia. How she could say she knew that without trying? She didn't know. But she did know online dating and Olivia would not mix.

"Okay. No online dating. My next suggestion would be the singles scene, but I'm guessing hanging out in bars isn't what you'd like to do either," Dr. Bella said.

"Nope. That sounds terrible as well. Besides, is there a singles scene here?"

"I would've suggested going to Seattle."

"Yeah, that's not happening."

"Well, you probably won't like this one either, but it's kind of my final suggestion."

Olivia braced herself for what was coming next.

"Let your friends and family know you're ready to date."

It only took two seconds for Olivia to catch on to what Dr. Bella was telling her.

"Ask to be set up?" Olivia asked, trying to think of anything that would be less mortifying.

Dr. Bella nodded.

"I can't."

"You can. It really won't be that bad. I bet most are chomping at the bit for the chance to do so. And it's better than going to a bar, right?"

Olivia nodded slowly. That was true. But ...

"It will come up in conversation, I promise. You don't have to be awkward about it and send a mass evite."

Olivia giggled as she imagined that email. *To all the dear family and friends of Olivia Penn. You are hereby invited to set Olivia up with any and all eligible males, beginning immediately.* Yeah, Gen would never let her live that down.

"At least try?" Dr. Bella asked. "I think even going on a few dates will help you to understand your baggage isn't so much. And you need to know that for your own growth."

Olivia nodded. All of what Dr. Bella said made sense. And as scary as this next stage of therapy was, she knew it was the right thing since Dr. Bella had suggested it. Olivia trusted her doctor. But oh my goodness, was she really going to solicit date options from her family and friends?

CHAPTER SIX

"IT'S COMPLETE PARAPLEGIA," Dr. Warren said, and Lily felt like she was under water.

It had been two days since Allen had awakened, and he'd undergone numerous tests. They'd had to wait for the swelling around his spine to go down before they could do a complete neurological test. Lily knew this had been Allen's greatest fear after waking up ... but to hear it aloud?

Lily drew in a deep breath, chancing a glance at Allen who looked pale. He looked crushed. She had to make things better.

"There's always physical therapy though, right?" Lily asked. She'd taken time during all of Allen's testing to find everything the internet had to say about this worst-case scenario. She'd read many stories about the marvelous new technology and intense physical therapy that could result in restored mobility.

The doctor nodded.

"It's always a possibility, and we won't close that door. But for now, Allen is fully paralyzed from the waist down," Dr. Warren said.

Lily fought the urge to cry as she watched Allen crumble against his pillows.

"But people defy the odds all the time, don't they?" Lily asked, making sure to allow all of the hope she still felt about the situation to infuse her voice. Allen was alive. It was a miracle and a blessing. Whatever else came their way, they could handle it.

Dr. Warren fixed his gaze on Allen and then moved to Lily. "When they defy the odds, that's exactly what they're doing. *Can* you defy those odds? Yes. You absolutely can, Allen. Will you? I've given my honest prognosis."

Lily blinked back the tears that threatened. Part of her wanted to be angry with Dr. Warren for killing her hope along with Allen's, but that wasn't right. The man was doing his job. He had to tell Allen and Lily what he saw as the truth. If he raised hope in each of his patients only to let them fall, what kind of doctor would he be?

But seeing Allen's head lying dejectedly on his pillows, Lily kind of wished for false hope at this point. Anything besides the utter sorrow that must be filling her husband now.

"Thank you, Doctor," Lily said.

Dr. Warren nodded once before making his way out of the hospital room.

Lily swallowed before turning to Allen.

"But he doesn't know you, Allen. Of course you'll defy the odds. Do you remember that silly car we had back in Alabama? Your dad laughed when you said you were going to get it running. That poor piece of junk didn't even believe you could do it. But you did it, Allen."

Lily watched as Allen swallowed. His Adam's apple bobbed in his throat.

It was almost in slow motion that his mouth opened, and he said, "Lily, I'm not a car."

"I know, Allen. I get it. I really do."

"That's the thing, Lily. You don't get it."

Lily stopped to think about what she'd said and how insen-
sitive it had been. Allen was right. She couldn't understand
what he was feeling. She knew what she felt being his spouse,
but enduring the trial before them as a partner was so different
from going through it personally. Just because she was devastated for him didn't mean she was devastated in the same way
Allen was.

"I'm sorry. You're right," Lily responded, but that just
seemed to make Allen's face pinch in more frustration. What
had she done wrong?

"Complete paralysis. Do you understand what that means,
Lily?" Allen asked, his voice sounding angry. Allen hardly ever
raised his voice at Lily. Surprise at his vehemence made her take
a step back.

"I do," Lily said softly.

"What does it mean?" Allen demanded.

Lily swallowed. She knew Allen felt out of control of his life
and maybe his emotions right now. Lily didn't blame him. He
had to be terrified, angry, and heart-broken all at once. She
needed to say the right thing. She had to help him. She was
his wife.

"You may never regain mobility. But it's just from the waist
down, and *may* is a very powerful word." Lily said the first
sentence slowly but then rushed over the second. She wanted to
get every word out so that Allen could hear there really was still
reason to hope. There was always reason to hope, especially
now that he was alive.

Lily couldn't forget the dark hours while Allen had been in
surgery—waiting, unknowing. She knew paralysis was terrible,
but she would take it over death any day of the week. They were
the lucky ones. But she refrained from saying those words to
Allen yet. She knew he didn't feel lucky right about now.

"Just from the waist down." Allen spat out the words and let out a laugh that sounded nothing like the man she loved. "The ... waist ... down."

Allen began nodding, and Lily had no idea what he was doing.

"Do you know what I wanted to do just then?" Allen asked.

Lily sat ramrod straight, afraid for the first time in her marriage that she might do the wrong thing. Allen had always been so forgiving of her. Even when Lily said or did the wrong thing, he often laughed it off. But now ...

"I wanted to move so that I could sit up straight. You know, what you're doing right now. But being paralyzed from the waist down keeps me from doing that."

Lily nodded, trying to put herself in Allen's shoes. To feel his frustration with him.

"Do you want to know what else it will keep me from doing?"

Lily felt tears prick at her eyes and willed them to go away. This wasn't about her.

"Peeing on my own. This lovely bag of pee will now be with me anywhere I go. What do you think about that?" Allen said as he pointed to the bag attached to his catheter.

Lily understood that. She'd done quite an impressive amount of research in the last couple of days, as soon as the doctor had said this could be a possibility. She knew all that Allen was losing. But she also knew what he had gained by living through that surgery. He and Lily would get to be side by side for the rest of their lives. Lily didn't care if Allen would take that journey in a wheelchair or if he wouldn't be able to run with Amelia when the time came. He would be there to see it all, and he would be able to participate in their lives. Maybe things would look different from here on out, but he was here. Didn't he get that that was all Lily cared about?

"We'll make it work, Allen," she said softly.

Allen reared back as if Lily had hit him. What had she done now?

"You've always been so willing to make things work, Lily. When my income wasn't enough to take care of our family, you were willing to make things work. When my mom wanted our wedding colors to be cream and blush instead of the white and purple you wanted, you made things work. But this isn't that, Lily. We can't just make it work." Allen was now shouting, and Lily really wanted to cry but she wouldn't. She couldn't. She longed to shout right back that of course they would make it work. What other option did they have?

But would that help Allen? She doubted it. So Lily kept stoic and silent, doing her best to be everything Allen needed.

"I just can't, Lily," Allen said as he looked down at the blankets around his waist.

"That's okay, Allen. I can do the heavy lifting. I can only imagine how tough this is for you."

Allen spat out that angry laughter again, and Lily stopped.

"No. I know I have to do *this*," Allen said, waving a hand over his body. He stopped and looked Lily right in the eye. "But I can't do this." He pointed a finger to his chest and then toward her.

Lily felt her heart drop. What?

"I don't understand," Lily said, her voice sounding smaller than ever before.

"You need to go," Allen said.

This time Lily could not hold back the tears. She wiped them away quickly, hoping Allen hadn't noticed. But by the way his gaze dipped down to her cheeks and then went back to her eyes, she knew he had.

"Allen ..." Lily began, and she watched as his face hardened. She hadn't understood that phrase until now, but she literally watched as Allen's mouth, cheeks, and even eyes turned to stone.

"Go," Allen said.

Lily shook her head. She'd just gotten him back. She wasn't going to lose him again.

Lily suddenly realized what Allen was doing. He'd always tried to shield and protect her from the terrible parts of life. Is this what he thought this was? Something he could protect her from? She didn't need protecting. She wanted to journey this trial together, and in order to do that, she had to know the pain he was experiencing. Together they could do this.

"No," Lily said, her tears drying.

"What?" Allen asked.

"I see what you're doing, Allen, and it won't work. I love you. I won't stand by and let you do this on your own just because this will be hard for me. I know it's going to be hard. Heck, it will probably be harder than I'm imagining. But I love you. I. Will. Help. You." Lily said the words forcefully, hoping her husband would hear her.

Allen closed his eyes and then opened them again, almost looking through Lily.

"You don't get it, do you? My dad always said the pretty ones are harder to talk to because they just don't get things." Allen said the cruelest words he'd ever uttered to Lily, but she forgave them immediately. He was hurting, and he was lashing out.

"I'm not hiding from your insults, Allen."

Allen shook his head. "This is not about *you*," he said, each word piercing Lily like a dagger's point.

"I know," Lily said.

Allen's eyes narrowed. "And yet you don't. I am *not* protecting you. I am not telling you I can do this on my own for *your* sake. *I* want you gone. I have cared for you and protected you for years.

But I can't do that anymore, Lily. I need to focus on me. Take care of me. And if you're around, guess what will happen? You will make this all about you, the way you have for our entire marriage. This can't be about you, Lily. This is me telling you I need to be alone. Because you take too much from me," Allen said calmly, the tone of cruelty from his earlier words gone, making them easier for Lily to hear. But at the same time so much harder.

He couldn't mean that, could he? Lily thought about the times Allen had told her he loved loving her and caring for her. Those two had always been intertwined. With one came the other. But had he found it a burden?

No. Lily wouldn't believe that. But was loving her a burden for him now?

"I'll help you," Lily said. and Allen closed his eyes again.

"Help me how, Lil?" Allen asked honestly, as if he couldn't possibly understand what Lily could do for him.

"We can learn how to navigate this new life. We can find the best physical therapists."

"And there it is. You only want me if I'm working to become whole again."

"No," Lily gasped. "Not at all. I don't care if you stay in that bed for the rest of your life, Allen."

Allen shook his head. "You say that now. But when the doctor was here, all you could talk about was the possibility that this wasn't forever. What if this is forever, Lily?"

"Then we'll be fine. It will be fine."

There was that angry laugh again. "None of this is fine, Lily. It's my new normal, but it isn't fine."

Why did she keep saying the wrong thing?

"I only asked the doctor about the possibilities because I wanted you to have hope," Lily said, trying to defend her actions.

"Hope for what, Lily? The slimmest possibility of a normal future? I need to see my reality for what it is."

"Okay. I get that. I'm on board, Allen. However you want to do this, I'm with you." Lily could feel the desperation in her voice, but she needed Allen to understand her.

Allen shook his head. "I don't need you, Lily. I don't want you."

And it was with those words that the very thing Lily had been fighting against, ever since the moment Kate called, happened. Her heart simply shattered.

"You don't mean that."

"Why can't I mean that? Because I'm in a hospital bed, and you are whole?"

"That has nothing to do with it. You've always wanted me. Why would that change now?"

"Don't you get it, Lily? The moment my car hit that tree, everything changed."

"I won't believe it changed the way you feel for me."

Allen looked Lily from head to toe, his eyes lacking the emotion and love they'd always held for Lily.

"It did."

How? Lily wanted to scream, but that would do nothing. She needed to stay rational. To show Allen she wasn't afraid. She was brave and strong enough to go through this with him.

"I need more in my life, Lily. I am a changed man. You are the most beautiful woman I have ever laid eyes on. And that one trait has always been enough to overshadow your faults. But now it's not enough. I need more, Lily. More than you."

Allen somehow further obliterated the shards that had been Lily's heart.

Lily swallowed back her own pain. Allen couldn't mean this. Any of it.

The door to the hospital room opened, and the last person Lily had been expecting came walking in.

"Allen," Gretchen, Allen's mother, gushed as she rushed to his bedside and pulled her son into her arms.

Lily and Allen had lived in Washington for over a year now, and this was the first time they'd seen his mother. Allen had had no desire to go home, and his mother had had no desire to see their new home in the Pacific Northwest. However, because she was here now, Lily guessed this tragedy took precedence over Gretchen being upset that Lily and Allen had left Alabama. But it made sense. Even though Allen's mother was lacking a few maternal bones, what kind of mother would not rush to her son's side after a near-death experience?

"It's the worst case," Allen uttered, and his mother began to cry.

This desperate reaction seemed like it was anything but helpful for Allen's condition—it was everything Lily had fought against doing herself—but what could Lily do? This was his mom.

Gretchen continued crying on Allen's chest for a few minutes before abruptly sitting up and drying her eyes.

"I'm here now, baby boy. It will all be okay," she said as she took in the room, pausing when she came face to face with Lily.

"Oh, Lily," Gretchen said as she turned to face Lily where she sat. Gretchen acted as if this was the first time she'd seen Lily, but she'd literally had to walk right past her to get to Allen's bedside.

"Hi, Gretchen," Lily said as she stood to give her mother-in-law a hug, but Gretchen stuck her hand out so that Lily had to shake her hand instead.

Lily fought her urge to frown and, instead, gave her mother-in-law a smile.

Lily had always felt less than adequate when it came to

Allen's family. They hadn't appreciated that he'd found love during the demise of his parents' marriage. How that had been Lily's or Allen's fault, Lily didn't see, but they'd always held that against Lily.

They also didn't like that Lily hadn't pushed Allen to be more than a kindergarten teacher and that Lily was just a nanny. They told Allen that they'd hoped his wife would see more in him than just a teacher, but Lily couldn't understand that. Allen was made to be an example to young children, and he loved it with every fiber of his being. How could any woman who loved Allen not want him to do what he was meant to do?

These reasons and many more had made relations between all of them tense. Lily felt ultra-grateful when they left Alabama.

But now Gretchen was here. Standing between Lily and Allen and the conversation they needed to continue having. It had been cut off before Lily could convince Allen that she should stay.

Gretchen turned her back on Lily and spoke to Allen. "Your father may be a good-for-nothing SOB, but he's agreed to pay for your long-term care. We can get a nurse lined up in no time."

"That won't be necessary, Gretchen," Lily said firmly as she sat back down in her seat. She knew Allen had no desire to be financially dependent on his parents. He didn't want to rely on them in any way since they'd shunned his career choice and other life decisions time and time again.

"I can care for Allen," Lily added, shooting a smile at Allen and finally feeling like she was doing the right thing. Maybe Gretchen showing up had been a good thing. Because if there was one thing Lily knew about her husband, she knew he would do anything to not have to rely on his parents. Lily could help him with this. He would see that she was on his side. She would do anything for him.

"A nurse sounds good, Mom," Allen said.

Lily would've stumbled if she weren't seated. She felt her mouth drop open and saw the look of satisfaction on Gretchen's face before she turned to look at her son.

"Mom, do you mind going out to the nurse's station and seeing if you can get ahold of Dr. Warren? I think he probably has a few good suggestions for at-home nurses," Allen said, sounding way more upbeat than he had with Lily moments before. What was going on? Why did Lily feel like she was living in some alternate universe?

"Of course. And I'll see if I can find a decent coffee machine while I'm out there. I have a feeling I'm going to need it," Gretchen said as she looked between Lily and Allen. She had to be sensing the turmoil between them. And judging by the look of satisfaction on her face, she wasn't torn up about it.

As soon as Gretchen closed the door behind her, Lily knew she had to beg her case. This was all too strange, but she could deal with it. She could do anything Allen asked of her as long as he didn't shut her out.

"I've asked for so little of you during our marriage, Lily," Allen said before Lily could speak.

"I know," Lily said. He'd always spoiled Lily in every way that he could.

"I am asking you this one thing," Allen said.

Lily shook her head. "I can't leave you," she said.

Allen pursed his lips, seemingly only annoyed at Lily's reluctance to leave him. He didn't seem to feel any of Lily's terror at leaving the man she loved.

"Think about me, for once," Allen said, and although that wasn't fair, Lily wasn't going to let his words affect her. Let him hit below the belt. Lily wouldn't budge.

"I am, Allen. You don't want to take your parents' charity."

"It's not charity when it's family," Allen said, starting to sound angry again.

"Fine, take the nurse. But I'll be there too," Lily said.

"No!" Allen shouted.

"Yes. I won't leave you, Allen. You are hurt, angry, I'm sure scared, and so many other things. I can't help any of that. But the one thing I can do ... you won't be alone, Allen."

"That's what I want!" Some of the anger had leaked from Allen's argument, and he now sounded exasperated.

"Go to that drawer," Allen demanded as he pointed to a drawer in the nightstand next to his hospital bed.

Lily did as she was directed. She opened the drawer to see a small, black, velvet box.

"What is this?" Lily asked.

"The reason I was late," Allen said. "The reason I was racing home to the Valentine's dinner you made."

Lily didn't understand how she still had a heart after what Allen had said, but it somehow flipped as her stomach dropped. Why was Allen showing this to her now?

"Open it," Allen demanded when Lily just stood there staring at it.

"What is it?" Lily whispered.

"Open it," Allen said again, and Lily opened the box to see a beautiful diamond ring. The kind that had never graced her finger. The kind that Allen had promised he would one day get for her. The diamond center was small, but it gleamed gorgeously, and Lily would've loved it if it weren't for the circumstances. She didn't think Allen was giving her a ring. It felt like he was proving a point.

"I was meeting the guy I bought that from at the school when you called. So I was late because of you," Allen said as Lily stared at the ring.

"That's why I need you to go," he added.

Lily shook her head. She felt like there was information just beyond her grasp, but it didn't matter. She was staying right there.

"Leave. Please, Lily. Don't make me say the words," Allen said.

Lily shook her head. He didn't mean it. He couldn't mean it. And she felt her spirit buoy. She wouldn't leave him.

Lily finally looked at Allen, all of the resolve she felt to stay shining in her eyes.

Allen drew in a deep breath. "Like I've been saying, this isn't about you. I can't stand to look at you, Lily. Every time I do, this inexplicable anger overcomes me. *You* did this to me," Allen said.

And suddenly Lily was hit with a ray of clarity. Those thoughts just beyond her grasp came rushing at her.

This was her fault. She had been the reason he was late, and she had also been the reason he'd rushed home, taking that turn too fast. She'd been angry at him, demanding him home immediately. He wasn't protecting her by telling her to leave. He was protecting himself. From the woman who'd paralyzed him.

"I need you gone, Lily," Allen said, and she finally heard him. Finally understood him. He'd said everything had changed when he hit that tree. Because she had been the one to cause all of this. He would never walk again because of Lily. And he couldn't bear to see the person who'd caused him to lose his ability to walk.

She *had* been making this about her. About the fact that she couldn't lose Allen. And the truth was, she still couldn't. But her eyes were finally open, and she could see what Allen saw when he looked at her: the reason for the most terrible moment of his life.

Lily nodded as she gripped the arms of the chair she sat in.

She wasn't sure where she would get the strength to stand up and walk away, but she had to. For Allen.

Was this their end? No, Lily couldn't think like that. Lily wouldn't ever give up on what she and Allen had. They would get through this, just like anything else. One day he would forgive her. He had to. But Allen was asking for space and time, and Lily had to give him that. At least while he was at the hospital. There he had nurses and doctors to care for him, and he'd be okay. But as soon as it was time for him to go home, she would be there again. In whatever capacity Allen needed. Even if Allen wasn't ready to forgive his wife, he would need her help as a caretaker, and Lily was willing to be whatever Allen wanted her to be.

Lily shook her head as she realized she had misunderstood the entirety of their conversation. Allen hadn't been shielding her; he'd been guarding himself. Something he had every right to do. Something Lily had to support him in.

Lily somehow made it to the door and paused. The, "I love you," she whispered was said much too quietly for Allen to be able to hear, and then she left. Because she had to.

CHAPTER SEVEN

"MADDIE, STOP," Gen called out from where she sat in her rocker, nursing Cami. Gen loved being able to breastfeed her daughter, but she also never felt more helpless than when she was confined to her seat with her baby while Maddie ran amuck.

It was a skill that Maddie had perfected in the month since Levi had gone back to work. Little baby Cami was two months old now, and friends and acquaintances alike kept telling Gen that by the time three months came around, everything would be a bit smoother. But in moments like this one, Gen really wondered if she could make it a whole other month.

Gen watched as Maddie, undeterred, continued to push one of the barstools from the kitchen island toward the stove.

"Maddie Mae, put the stool back," Gen demanded from her seat in the living room.

"I'm going to cook," Maddie explained to Gen.

Gen shook her head. "Maddie, what is the rule about cooking?" she asked, hoping to talk some sense into her daughter without having to get up and physically move her.

"I cook with Momma," Maddie said, and Gen nodded.

Maddie paused pushing the stool, and Gen felt like she was getting somewhere.

"That's right. Is Momma there?" she asked.

Maddie looked from left to right.

"Nope," Maddie said before pushing the stool the final couple of inches to the stove.

"So no cooking," Gen shouted, alarming Cami who pulled off from her breast.

But the shout did nothing to deter Maddie. She began to climb the stool, and Gen ran across the living room, Cami now screaming that her nursing session had been cut short, and pulled Maddie off of the stool as she reached toward the nobs on the stove.

"Maddie Redding!" Gen reprimanded as she tried to cradle a still screaming Cami.

"I want noodles," Maddie said matter-of-factly, seemingly unrepentant considering the damage she could've just done.

"Maddie, no! That is hot and dangerous. Momma cooks. Got it?" Gen yelled at Maddie.

Maddie suddenly went from being intent on cooking noodles to joining her sister in screaming, all in the blink of an eye.

As both of her girls screamed their discontent at the situation, Gen honestly considered joining. If you can't beat them, join them, right?

Thankfully the sound of the garage door opening warned all three girls that Levi was home, and it was only that glimpse of salvation that kept Gen from screaming along with her daughters.

Levi opened the door to see the stool still by the stove, Maddie screaming on the tiled floor of the kitchen, Cami screaming in Gen's arms, Gen's shirt still up from attempting to nurse so that her very flabby and still stretched out stomach was on full display, and the complete mess in the rest of their home. The sink was piled full of dishes, but the dishes from lunch hadn't even made it to the sink, still littering the kitchen table. The living room carpet was barely distinguishable under every toy that Maddie owned, and Gen was sure they all had a pretty ripe smell. She hadn't showered since the morning before, and Maddie was only given a quick wipe down after she'd spilled an entire glass of milk on herself at breakfast and now hours later the lingering smell of milk had turned sour.

"Oh," Levi said as he took in the situation.

Levi appraised for another few seconds before lifting Maddie into his arms, the little girl comforted in seconds.

"The stool is from Maddie. She tried to cook noodles by herself while I was nursing," Gen explained as Levi looked around the kitchen.

Levi walked Maddie over to the stool and set her on the ground before kneeling in front of her.

"Maddie. Do you touch the stove?"

Maddie shook her head.

"Do you cook without Momma or me?"

Maddie shook her head.

"Are you going to do this again?"

"No, Daddy," Maddie muttered, and Levi pulled her into a hug.

"But Momma yelled," Maddie tattled, and Gen figured she deserved it.

"If she did, she only did it because she loves you. The stove is very hot and can hurt you. Do you understand?" Levi asked, and Maddie nodded.

"Sorry, Momma," Maddie said before taking a step forward to walk into her dad's arms.

"That's okay, Maddie," Gen said, feeling gratitude that her

oldest had stopped crying, even though Levi had been the one to make it happen. Gen remembered the days she had wanted to be the one to stop her children's tears. Now all that mattered was finding that blessed peace when they stopped.

Even Cami had stopped screaming for a few seconds since she'd found her thumb, but she suddenly began again when her thumb escaped.

"I need to feed her," Gen said, and Levi nodded.

"I'll get this one some dinner." Levi pointed to Maddie, and Gen nodded, feeling too tired to feel badly that she hadn't made dinner herself. She'd hoped that she could be in a routine by now, but that hadn't been possible.

Gen sat back down to feed Cami, the poor baby finally calm, and watched as Levi prepared the noodles Maddie had wanted. Then he sat her at her seat before pulling up his sleeves and diving into the mess that was their kitchen.

Gen marveled that her husband had yet to do anything but solve problems since he'd come home, and yet when he glanced Gen's way, he gave her a huge smile. The man was a saint.

While Gen nursed, the kitchen became spotless, and then Levi started a bath for Maddie, which filled while he cleaned cheese and noodles off of her.

"We'll get this one in the bath, and then maybe you can follow?" Levi asked, and Gen finally felt like she could breathe.

She nodded.

Levi bathed Maddie, set her up with a coloring book, and then came to get Cami.

"How do you do that?" Gen asked, marveling at the way things had come together with Levi at home.

"I get to step away from it, Gen. I miss it when I'm gone. You don't get that luxury," he said.

Gen was about to kiss her husband when she realized she

also hadn't brushed her teeth. "Remind me I owe you a kiss," she said, and Levi grinned.

"Happily."

Gen took a quick shower—it felt wrong to leave Levi for too long, even if the hot water hitting her head felt better than any luxury spa she'd been to—and then wrapped her body in a robe and her head in a towel. She would check on Levi, and if he was okay, she'd take time to actually put clothes on and brush her hair.

Gen came out of the shower to see that Cami sat pleasantly in the baby bouncer that she'd tried to put her in nearly a dozen times that day. Levi knelt on the floor beside Maddie, coloring with her, and the living room floor was spotless.

"How?" Gen asked, suddenly feeling incredibly inadequate. Tears pressed at her eyes. She'd had a whole day to get this stuff done, and Levi had done it all in less than an hour.

"Hey, hey," Levi said as he jumped up and dried Gen's tears.

"Cami was sick of being held by me. She doesn't get sick of her momma," Levi said.

Gen looked over at the happy baby who hadn't been content out of her arms all day. "It's not fair," Gen gushed as Levi held her.

"I know. It isn't," Levi said supportively.

"This is what I want to do," Gen said between her tears. She felt guilty for crying. This was her dream come true, but sometimes it felt like a nightmare. Then she'd think, who was she to look this miracle she'd been gifted in the face and do anything but adore every minute?

"I know. And you do," Levi said, causing Gen to laugh through her tears because his statement couldn't have been more false.

"I don't do this." Gen continued to laugh as she let her eyes rove over her now tidy home.

Gen felt so up and down and sideways. She couldn't seem to get a grip on what she was thinking, much less what she was feeling. She hadn't slept more than three hours at a time in two months now, and it was getting to her.

"That's why we're a team. I'm here to sub in," Levi said, and Gen nodded against his shoulder before pulling away. What would she do without Levi?

"You'll never have to know," Levi said, answering Gen's unspoken question. But it wasn't a surprise that he knew exactly what she'd been thinking considering she'd vocalized this very question at least a dozen times since Cami had been born.

"You know, even while living our dreams, we're allowed to have bad days," Levi said against her hair as Gen heard Cami begin to fuss. She was going to have to walk away from Levi's arms soon, but she just wanted another few seconds of being the one who got to be comforted instead of doing all the comforting.

"What about bad months?" Gen asked, causing Levi to chuckle. His body shook, and since he was wrapped around Gen, she also shook.

"Those are okay too."

"Daddy, I need you help," Maddie whined as Cami's fussing turned into all out cries.

"Divide and conquer?" Gen asked as Levi nodded.

"And Gen?" Levi said before letting go of her. "You are an excellent mom. The girls are blessed to have you. But even more so, I am blessed to have you."

Levi let go of Gen only after she nodded in agreement. But as she pulled away, she felt tears, this time happy tears, prick her eyes again. Was breaking down at any kind word her new normal? Post pregnancy hormones were a beast.

Gen moved to pick up Cami and Levi bent down to help Maddie. Now cradling her baby, she paused a moment to look around the room at her little family. Maybe Gen didn't have it all together, and maybe she cried at the drop of a hat. Maybe life felt hectic and even a little hellish at times, but Gen *was* really, truly happy. She didn't agree that she was the excellent mom Levi had praised, but she was trying. And for now, that was enough.

CHAPTER EIGHT

BESS LOOKED down at the workout leggings and zip up jacket she wore. This wasn't typical Bess attire, but since she and Jon had decided that they were going to date as if they were at the beginning, Bess was try making an effort to go on the types of dates that old Bess wouldn't have tried.

Valentine's Day had been a bit of a bust, at least in Jon's eyes, due to Dax's appearance. So Jon had asked for a redo of their first date, taking himself and Bess to a cooking class in Seattle a week after that all too eventful Valentine's Day. They'd gone to a movie of Jon's choice the next week and then to an art show Deb had suggested the week after that.

So now they were officially on date four, and Jon had suggested a day date doing his new favorite daytime activity: bike riding.

The last time Bess had ridden a bike was probably when she was about twelve, but people said this was a skill that couldn't be forgotten, right? She was holding on to that little bit of trivia as she went into this date. Because it was definitely out of her comfort zone. But "out of her comfort zone" was what they were supposed to be doing. Trying one another's hobbies and finding new common ground. So, to that end, Bess was even willing to give bike riding around the streets of Whisling a try.

Beep, beeeep.

Bess startled at the sound of a honking horn as she saw Jon pull up into her driveway in a truck she'd never seen before. Bess came out of her home at the same time Jon hopped out of the truck, and then he began to unload the bikes from the back of the it.

Out of the corner of her eye, Bess noticed Olivia, who was out by her mailbox with her younger daughter, Pearl. So Bess turned and waved at the girls. Olivia responded in kind while Pearl jumped up and down as she waved. The little girl was a sweetheart. Her mother, not so much. At least not right at that moment. Even from four houses away, Bess didn't miss the teasing gleam in Olivia's eye as she took in Bess's attire and the bikes Jon was unloading. Both women knew Bess wasn't exactly athletic.

"Good luck," Olivia mouthed at Bess, and then both women began to laugh.

With that, Olivia turned to go back toward her cottage. Bess knew that wouldn't be the last she'd see of Olivia today. Olivia would hound her for the details of this date as soon as she got home.

"Thanks for finding me a bike," Bess said as Jon finished taking the second bike out of the truck's bed and set it on the concrete.

"No problem," he said, moving from the bike to Bess and pulling her into his arms. He gave her a sweet peck on the lips, and Bess swore she heard a wolf whistle coming from Olivia's direction.

"It was easy to get. One of my coworkers went through a

biking phase, and now she's over it. She may have told me not to bring the bike back," Jon said.

Bess chuckled, but she stopped when she began to wonder if she was going to feel the same way about the bike in a few hours. Yes, Jon wanted to bike for a few *hours*.

"Where's the truck from?" Bess asked as she looked over the black monstrosity in her driveway.

"Do you like it?" Jon asked, and Bess wasn't sure how to respond. She wasn't a big truck girl, but she didn't dislike it. So she nodded.

"Good. Because I bought it."

Bess's eyes went wide. Jon had driven a Subaru Outback for the entirety of their marriage, and he'd kept the same one since their divorce. When had he become a truck guy?

"So no more Outback?" Bess asked, trying not to sound as shocked as she felt. Honestly, it wasn't a big deal. Just because Jon had only had one type of car for the last thirty years and now had a different one didn't mean that Bess should be freaking out ... right?

Jon shook his head. "No more Outback. Alice, she's a woman ... well," Jon paused as his face went red and he rubbed the back of his neck.

"I know you've dated women since our separation," Bess said, urging Jon to go on. But then her cheeks went pink as well. Maybe Jon wasn't embarrassed because Alice was a woman from his past. Was Jon having a hard time speaking about this woman because he was still dating her? Bess had assumed she was the only woman Jon was dating right now because he was the only man she was dating, but they hadn't expressly told one another they were exclusive. But they were ... weren't they?

Bess realized she had to ask her unspoken question immediately or she'd drive herself crazy. And if she couldn't be honest with Jon, who could she be honest with?

"You're not still dating other women, are you?" Bess asked, and Jon's face went even redder as he sputtered.

That wasn't good.

"No, no," Jon finally said, and Bess breathed a sigh of relief. But why had it taken so long for him to say so?

"When did you date Alice?" Bess asked, needing clarification.

"We went on *a* date. Singular. And realized we didn't suit. But she works at a car dealership and told me she could get me a great deal on a truck," Jon said.

Bess realized that was why Jon was acting so strangely. He wasn't still dating other women, but he had seen Alice, a woman he'd gone on a date with, recently.

"Jon, I'm not dating anyone else. Are we on the same page here?" Bess asked the question it felt so weird to say aloud. Especially considering this was a man she'd been completely loyal to for thirty years.

"Yes, of course," Jon said. But it seemed like he was going to say more, so Bess stayed quiet as she leaned against his new black truck.

"Well, now I'm not dating anyone else. But in the name of transparency, I should probably tell you that I did go on the date with Alice the day after our Valentine's date," Jon said as he moved his attention to the tailgate, pushing it up and back into place.

Bess swallowed. Okay. She was glad Jon was being honest, but it did sting that he'd been on another date so recently.

"But I talked about you the whole time, and that's why it was just the one date," Jon said.

His explanation made sense. It really did. But Bess couldn't help the knot in her stomach that made her feel like she'd been betrayed. She and Jon hadn't talked about being exclusive at that time, and they'd only been on that one date so it shouldn't be a big deal. But then why did it feel like it was?

Bess blew up her bangs in frustration as she waited for the right thing to say to hit her. Her thoughts were going a mile a minute, but none of it felt right to say out loud.

"I'm sorry, Bess. I just ... I didn't know where we stood because of Dax, and I figured I should keep my options open. But after going out with Alice, even though she was amazing, all I could think about was you. I knew I was all in on this," Jon said, and Bess nodded.

Jon had said all the right words. She understood his point of view. She really did. But she just wished Jon could've known he was all in with Bess without going on his date with the amazing Alice.

"So that's why you count cooking as our real first date?" Bess asked, and Jon nodded.

"Well that and because Dax showed up during our Valentine's dinner with flowers for you," Jon said.

Bess couldn't help her smile. Those flowers had really bugged Jon. And knowing he went out on a date the next night, Bess figured he deserved to be a bit bugged.

Jon noticed Bess's smile and returned it with a sweet one of his own.

"Are we good?" he asked.

Bess nodded. Things weren't perfect between herself and Jon. But that couldn't be expected in any real relationship, especially one as complicated as her and Jon's. Bess knew things were going to be tough when making a second go at a relationship. But that didn't mean it wasn't worth it.

"We're good," Bess said as she plopped the helmet Jon had offered her onto her head and then walked over to the shorter of the two bikes, which was clearly for her, and threw a leg over it. "Race you down the street?"

Jon chuckled. "You're on."

Bess fumbled her way onto the bike and steadied herself before even attempting to begin riding.

She noticed that Jon waited by her side and watched her carefully, making sure she was alright.

She finally put a foot to a pedal and pushed it forward. Ready or not, she was riding, albeit very slowly. And her hands were tight on the brakes since she was going mostly downhill.

Thankfully the skills *did* come back. Bess was able to balance and circle the pedals, but she was feeling a wariness that had never accompanied her as a child. Every bump in the sidewalk made her wobble. Every road crossed made her nervous. But she continued to take deep breaths and press forward. What was the worst that could happen?

Well, she could fall and break something, for starters. She wasn't as durable as she'd been at twelve years old.

But Bess could endure that, right?

She could. But did she want to?

One date. She was going to give bike riding a chance. Jon was right there with her. She would be fine. The odds of falling were ... well, she had no idea. But she wasn't going to fall. She would be fine. She could enjoy this.

Jon overtook Bess as they came to The Drive, the main thoroughfare on Whisling. Thankfully, The Drive was bordered by a bike lane on either side of the road, and she was able to follow Jon along that lane.

After going through the main part of town, narrowly avoiding a few cars that were going too fast, she and Jon came to the portion of The Drive that was less traveled because it was out of town—the gorgeous section that went right along the Pacific Ocean. This stretch of road was mostly taken by tourists because, for most of the island's residents, it was too round about a way to get downtown. It was usually only enjoyed for its scenery, not its practicality. But since tourists were fewer during the month of March, the road was pretty clear of traffic. Between the lack of cars and the beautiful, dark blue ocean view, Bess actually began to enjoy herself, rather than just enduring the ride.

"This is gorgeous," Bess shouted up to Jon over the wind and sound of the rolling waves.

"Isn't it?" Jon yelled as he turned back to look at Bess.

"I ride in Seattle every day, but I've dreamed of coming home and getting to take this bike ride," Jon continued.

Bess felt her heart warm. Jon's dream was coming home. He hadn't said it was coming home to her, and for that Bess was grateful because she wasn't sure she was ready for Jon to admit that. But she did like that Jon still thought of Whisling as where he wanted home to be.

If, it was still an *if* in Bess's mind, she and Jon were to end up together, it would have to be on Whisling. Because Whisling was the place Bess would always call home.

"We're going to go left here," Jon called back, and Bess followed as Jon crossed the street and went up a road that Bess knew would take them back into the island's residential areas.

They passed some of the mansions on the island—this was where Olivia had lived before divorcing Bart—and Bess admired the architecture and landscaping of the beautiful, big homes.

Suddenly they hit an incline, and Bess realized they were going uphill. What had just been a leisurely and fun ride was now beginning to gnaw at Bess's poor thighs. They hadn't had a workout like this in ... well, in a very long time.

"You doing okay?" Jon asked as he looked back at Bess.

She knew she must look a mess—the exertion was sure to be making her face red and blotchy—but she was working too hard to care.

Bess gave Jon a single nod because that was all she could manage under the circumstances, and Jon looked forward again.

Bess gave the bike another few pushes, but she realized her legs needed a break. She stopped suddenly and hopped off the bike, next to a wall that separated the yard of one of the mansions from the sidewalk.

Bess spent a good few minutes working on regaining her breath, doubled over in pain.

She suddenly felt a hand rubbing her back.

"The hills were a bit too much, huh?" Jon asked, but Bess was still missing her breath.

"I'm sorry. I shouldn't have taken on such a challenge. You just seemed like you were thriving back by the beach."

She had been. But she still couldn't say anything to Jon. Why was breathing so hard?

Bess finally took in a breath that felt like it had worked, and her heart stopped beating at such a rapid rate, no longer thudding in her ears.

"Yeah, the hills were a mistake." Bess stated the obvious, causing Jon to laugh.

"Good news is we can always go back down to the drive and take that for a while longer. But the bad news? We have to take hills to get back home," Jon said.

Bess cringed as she glared at the offending bike. She didn't even want to ride along the water anymore. She had seen too much, gone too far, to ever get back on that thing.

"Or I could take the short way home and come back with the truck for you?" Jon asked, and Bess nodded enthusiastically at that idea.

Jon chuckled again. "Plan B it is," he said.

"I'm sorry, Jon," Bess said, knowing she'd ruined his date idea.

"Don't be sorry, Bess. You tried. I can't ask for more than

that. Thank you for trying. But maybe we'll stick to walking along the beach as our favorite outdoor pastime?"

Bess nodded. That sounded splendid.

Jon hopped back onto his bike, and Bess knew she was in for a bit of a wait. She found a good spot to stand her bike, took off her now very sweaty helmet, and then went to sit on the curb. Fortunately, she'd brought her phone, so she'd be able to keep herself entertained while she waited for Jon.

Bess heard a car drive and then slow as it approached her.

"Hey, Bess," Susan, an acquaintance and regular at the food truck, called out from her Mercedes SUV.

"Hi, Susan," Bess said as she watched Susan take in the bike and Bess on the curb.

"Do you need a ride?" Susan asked.

Bess shook her head. "I have someone coming. Thank you though," she said, keeping Jon's name out of her explanation. Susan was nice enough, but Bess knew she and Jon were already being gossiped about plenty. There was no need to add fuel to that fire.

"Are you sure? It's pretty chilly out," Susan said as she looked up at the gray skies above them.

It was. But Bess was still sweating profusely from riding, so the cooler air felt nice. Thankfully, even though it was Whisling in March, it wasn't raining.

"Yes. I'm fine. Thank you," Bess said, hoping Susan would move along.

And she did.

But that didn't stop at least ten others from stopping in the same way Susan had. Bess truly did love the friendliness of her island, but this was an embarrassing spot to be in. Having everyone from her kids' pediatrician to the man who'd sold Bess and Jon their home see her stranded and a hot mess wasn't fun.

Where is Jon?

Several games of Word Wipe after the last car had stopped, Bess looked up to see a black truck rumbling toward her. The thing really was huge.

Bess hopped up and went toward her bike.

"Sorry it took so long," Jon said as he got out of the truck and met Bess at her bike. He took her bike from her and lifted it into the back of his truck where his own bike sat. Bess threw her helmet onto the bikes before moving around the truck to the passenger's seat.

"These hills really are killer," Jon admitted as he followed Bess and opened her door for her.

Bess grinned, both at his admission and that he was being so chivalrous. Opening doors wasn't something her old Jon would've done, and she loved the improvement.

"They took much longer than I anticipated," Jon said as he got into his seat and began driving back toward Bess's home.

"I'm glad I stopped when I did then," Bess said, and Jon nodded in agreement.

"How are your legs feeling?" Bess asked.

Jon rubbed his hand against a bike short encased thigh. "On fire," he said with a smile that told Bess he didn't mind the fire much.

"So a typical macho Jon workout?" Bess brought her voice as low as possible to tease Jon.

"You know it, babe," Jon said, using the same deep voice Bess had used, and they dissolved into laughter. The last thing Jon had ever been accused of was an overabundance of machismo.

As they laughed, Bess remembered the many times they'd fallen into uncontrollable laughter over the years. This was the fun the end of their marriage had been missing. Today had gone astronomically wrong, yet here they were laughing about it, even in the moment. They were just enjoying that they were together. This was what Bess had missed.

They returned to Bess's home, and Bess got Jon set up in the guest bathroom to shower before she went back to her bedroom to get herself ready. It was weird for her and Jon to share what had been their space in such a way, but this was what Bess was ready for, and Jon wasn't pushing her for more. He was really letting her take the lead in that department. For their first two dates, they'd only gone as far as holding hands with a brief hug at the end of each date. At the end of date number three, Bess had allowed a really amazing but sweet kiss. The same with date number four. As their physical relationship grew, Bess found she was enjoying each step of the way. But she was glad they were going at a snail's pace.

Bess came out of her room after getting ready in a comfy but, she hoped, cute dress. Her hair had only been blow dried, not styled, since she was trying to save time, and she'd done an easy makeup look that worked for the casual vibe of the island.

"You look beautiful, Bess," Jon complimented immediately.

During some of their texting conversations, Bess had admitted that she had been sad when Jon had stopped complimenting her somewhere along the way in their marriage. Jon had been trying to make up for that lack ever since.

"Thank you. You don't look too shabby either," Bess said as she took in Jon's thick brown hair that hadn't quite been tamed, even by his shower. His black rimmed glasses were the same style he'd worn for much of their marriage, but it was comforting. They were Jon. He wore a pastel purple, button up shirt that went well with his olive coloring and a pair of black slacks.

"Did you iron your shirt?" Bess asked, and Jon grinned. Bess knew how much Jon hated ironing, but he also knew how much Bess loved a pressed shirt.

"That I did," Jon said as he took Bess's hand and led her toward her front door. "Are you ready for part two of our date? Hopefully it will go much better than part one."

Bess laughed, feeling a lightness at being able to be so honest and open about her opinions with Jon. She felt safe and secure in a way she hadn't in a long time.

Jon's big truck made quick work of the drive between Bess's home and The Winder, the restaurant Jon had chosen for dinner that evening.

As the hostess seated them, Bess noticed the indiscreet glances of a few of the restaurant's other patrons who were long-time residents of the island. This was her first public date with Jon on Whisling since everything had gone south, and she was sure people were curious. Bess didn't mind the looks too much. It was part of the price of living on an island where everyone knew everyone else's business.

"Bess, Jon, lovely to see you," Otis, the owner of The Winder, greeted after the waiter had come to take their orders.

"It's good to see you, Otis." Bess greeted the man who was practically an institution on the island.

"Jon, our Bess here has made quite a name for herself since you last lived here," Otis said, and Bess noticed the strain in Jon's eyes as he nodded in response. She was pretty sure Jon wasn't upset at Otis but annoyed with himself that he hadn't been a part of Bess's life in over a year so people felt the need to fill him in on what Bess had been up to during his absence.

"She's been giving us a run for our money," Otis added as he looked around The Winder, but Bess shook her head to disagree.

"I am no competition for you, Otis," Bess said about her food truck that was oranges to The Winder's apples.

"Only because you choose not to be. I tried to hire that Alexis of yours. She interviewed with us hours before her interview with you," Otis said about Bess's head chef at the truck. "But alas, she chose you. Not that I blame her. I'd choose you as well." Otis was a blatant flirt, but since he was nearly eighty years old, no one took offense.

Although, Jon wasn't quite smiling at the man anymore. Maybe he *had* taken offense? It was kind of cute that Jon was jealous.

"Well, you two have a beautiful evening. And Jon, don't mess things up again," Otis warned, and Bess fought against a grin.

Jon may have come a long way from the man who'd cheated on Bess, but Bess figured a little reminder that she was the best thing to happen to him could only be a good thing.

"I never really liked that guy," Jon said after Otis was out of earshot.

"That's only because he's a big flirt, and you've always hated competition," Bess teased.

Jon nodded. "Exactly," he admitted, and Bess giggled.

The waiter came over with the salmon Bess had ordered and the crab Jon had chosen, setting their plates in front of them.

Bess breathed in the smell of the butter and garlic from her dish. She liked the salmon fine, but her kryptonite was the Winder's wild rice that they served with the salmon. Bess did a fair impression of it at home, but there was something about the way the Winder did it that Bess couldn't quite exactly replicate. So she was sure to order the dish anytime she went there to eat.

"Do you think there's thyme in this rice?" Bess asked after she took her first bite, and Jon laughed.

He'd endured enough dinners with Bess here to know that she was obsessed with figuring out the rice's secret.

"You know how I am with spices, Bess," Jon said, and Bess nodded.

The man had a pretty good palate when it came to some things, but he couldn't differentiate oregano from rosemary.

"So how was work this week?" Jon asked, and Bess told him a story about a tourist who'd begged Bess for her lasagna recipe. Begging for her recipes was a common occurrence, especially from tourists who knew they couldn't come back and fill their craving whenever they wished. But this story got better.

"So when I told her the gist of the recipe but wouldn't write it down or give her my secret ingredients, she offered to buy the truck."

Jon's eyes went wide.

"Seriously?" Jon asked.

"A million dollar offer," Bess said, and Jon's mouth fell open.

"Is your truck worth that?" Jon asked.

"Definitely not the truck itself. But I guess she thought as long as the recipes came along with the truck, it was."

"What did you say?"

"I laughed. I thought she was joking."

Jon nodded as he laughed. He had to be thinking the same thing.

"But she insisted she was serious, and I had to tell her the truck wasn't for sale."

"For a million dollars, Bess?" Jon asked, his eyes going wide again.

Bess shrugged. "Maybe one day. When I'm ready. But I couldn't even fathom the idea when she mentioned it. It kind of felt like she'd made an offer to buy one of the kids. Not the exact same thing, but in that arena. It just seemed impossible for me to give it up."

Jon tilted his head, and Bess knew him well enough to know that he was digesting the information. His eyes suddenly became soft.

"I'm glad you have the truck, Bess. And I'm glad you've made it a raging success. But I do wish that I had been here for the ride," he said softly.

Bess thought about that.

"I don't know that that would've ever happened. You know how much I like my comfort zone. And starting the truck was so far out of it. I needed you to break my comfort zone into smithereens before I could be brave enough to leave it."

Jon frowned. "I broke it?"

Bess didn't want to hurt Jon, and she knew telling him the truth would hurt him. But wanting to keep Jon from getting hurt couldn't hold her back from needing to be honest about what he'd done.

And in the end, it had all worked out. But it had still been a terrible, awful time.

"You did. For a time there, I was sure you'd broken all of me for good."

Jon blinked, and Bess wondered if he was crying. She wouldn't blame him. If he'd said the same words to her, she would be crying.

"But even after I'd been broken, I rose up. And now I'm better. I really am." Bess paused before she said her next words. It was vital that Jon really hear what she had to say. "However, that's why I need you to not only accept but love this new me if we're ever going to work again," Bess said, and Jon met her gaze before nodding.

She hoped he really understood.

"I broke myself too. But you came out of the shattered state much better than I did," Jon said, trying to grin.

However, Bess could see that what she'd said had truly pained him.

"I'm so proud of you, Bess. I just wish you could've gotten here in any other way. I hate what I did to you. I don't know if I'll ever be able to fully forgive myself."

Bess didn't blame Jon. But she was proud of him as well. How much easier would it have been to leave Bess and the pain he'd caused her in his past? Instead he was trying and working for them, even though it felt nearly impossible on some days.

"We're choosing the harder path, huh?" Bess asked as she met Jon's gaze.

He held her eyes for a few seconds before nodding.

"But for me, it wasn't a choice. It was always you, Bess."

CHAPTER NINE

"I'M SUPPOSED TO START DATING," Olivia said into her phone as she finished the last of the dishes for the evening. She'd made a point to try to call Gen every few nights since her visit with her friend a few weeks before. After visiting Gen, Olivia had realized how much Gen needed adult interaction at the end of the day, and Olivia recognized she needed the same. She used to get her fix from her parents and then from Dean, but now that Dean was busy with Charlotte, Olivia needed a good friend who wasn't the man she was in love with—who happened to be dating another woman.

Gen had Levi but had told Olivia some things were easier to say to a friend than to her husband, even though Levi was incredible.

Hence, their phone calls had been born. And they'd been a godsend to both women.

"And just how long have you been holding out on this tidbit?" Gen asked, knowing Olivia much too well.

It had been just about a month since that appointment with Dr. Bella where she'd encouraged Olivia to get back into the dating scene, but Olivia was a muller. She needed to consider an idea for a while on her own before she could voice it. Maybe her desire to digest and consider her own thoughts was why Bart had pulled away from her, or maybe she'd become that way because she'd always had to say things in the right way to Bart or he'd explode. Either way, Olivia often held on to her thoughts for a time before sharing them.

"For a month," Olivia said, spilling the truth.

Gen grunted. "Olivia!" she said, but Olivia could hear the smile behind Gen's reprimand. Gen understood Olivia was a muller, even if she didn't appreciate it.

"And just when were you planning on telling me this huge news?" Gen asked.

"Um, right now," Olivia said, even though she felt like it was relatively obvious.

Gen barked out a laugh. "Yeah, I guess so. But next time you have news like this, how about you don't wait a month before telling me?"

"Gen. If I had told you this information a month ago, could you honestly say that you would've waited patiently for me to be ready to get back into dating? You would've allowed me to take the time I needed? This month?" Olivia asked.

Gen stayed quiet for what felt like an eternity. "No," Gen answered candidly.

This time Olivia laughed. "Thus my waiting," she said, and she could imagine Gen conceding on the other end of the line.

"Okay, enough of why you didn't say anything sooner. I'm missing the big picture. You're ready to date," Gen said happily.

"Woah, woah, woah," Olivia said, needing Gen to push on the brakes for a minute. "I'm supposed to start dating. That's different than being ready to date."

"But if you're supposed to start dating, don't you need to be ready to date?" Gen asked, her tone going higher as she voiced her confusion.

Olivia pursed her lips. She guessed Gen was right. Especially because Dr. Bella had given her the advice a month before. She was supposed to be ready to date back then.

But she hadn't been pressed on the subject because she'd avoided all talk about dating with Dr. Bella in her ensuing two sessions, although she was pretty sure the doctor knew exactly what Olivia was doing. Fortunately, Dr. Bella knew Olivia was a muller as well.

As Olivia's thoughts continued, she felt even more confident that some part of her must be ready to date if she was telling Gen about it. Because Olivia knew, and had always known, that Gen would push her as soon as she knew about Dr. Bella's advice. And Heaven only knew how badly Olivia needed to be pushed when it came to getting back into the dating scene.

"Yeah, I guess," Olivia pouted, sounding very much like Rachel or Pearl when they were being asked to do something they didn't want to do.

Gen laughed. "This is a good thing, Olivia."

"Is it?" Olivia asked as she was suddenly struck with the apprehensive thought that maybe she was the type of woman who always chose the wrong guy. The one in the movies that you screamed at because she couldn't make a good decision when it came to men. Was she doomed before she'd even started on this venture? Her track record wasn't great. Granted, her track record was made up of one man.

"It is," Gen reassured.

"But I chose Bart," Olivia said, voicing her fear, and she heard Gen take in a deep breath on the other end of the call.

"You did. But you were also seventeen when you started dating Bart," Gen said. "I'd hope your decision making skills have grown since then."

Gen was joking, but Olivia wasn't sure that they had. At

least in the man-picking department. Her skills would be rusty, at best, with so many years of not being used.

"This is going to be so much fun," Gen said, the glee in her voice easy to hear. Olivia would be happy to feel even a tenth of the excitement Gen seemed to feel.

"So I can set you up, right?" Gen asked, and Olivia fought the urge the groan. This was what she wanted. She needed to be set up. She didn't want to do dating sites or the bar scene. And the island was too small to hope to meet a guy in the grocery store or at the bank or in whatever other cute way women met men in Hallmark movies. She knew all of the single guys on the island; the pickings were slim.

Olivia drew in a deep breath. "Yup," she finally said, even though it pained her. Olivia didn't want to be alone. She didn't. And this was why she was putting herself out there. But that didn't make it easy to do. The idea of being back in the dating scene was scary. Really, really scary. It was partly why Olivia had avoided it for so long. She was comfortable in her little life she'd created after her divorce. But it was time for her to get out of her comfort zone. Or be kicked out of her comfort zone by Gen.

"There's this guy Levi works with—" Gen began.

"Wait, ground rules," Olivia said as she leaned back against her green kitchen counter, and Gen halted her speaking.

"Okay," Gen said slowly as Olivia thought over what she wanted to say.

"Looks aren't a big deal," Olivia began.

"Nope. Not okay with that rule. You have to be attracted to a guy," Gen said, sounding incredulous.

"I can be attracted to humor, intelligence, and kindness," Olivia said as she shifted so that her hip was against the counter instead of her butt.

"And a rocking six pack." Gen added her own requirement, and Olivia burst into laughter.

"I just don't want physical attraction to be the driving force," Oliva said, knowing that had been one of her issues with Bart. She'd been blinded by his good looks and charm. She'd been easily manipulated from that first day because what good looking man treated Olivia the way Bart had? Now Olivia was sure every attractive man had an agenda. Well, at least the ones who wanted to date her. Dean had done a good bit in restoring her faith in good looking men in general.

"I get that," Gen said. "But do you really want forever with a guy that you think is just so-so? You have to look at him every morning and every night for the rest of your life."

Olivia shrugged but then realized Gen couldn't see her. "That won't be as bad as being afraid of the man I'm sharing my bed with."

Gen went quiet. "I'm not going to even pretend that I can imagine what you've been through, Olivia. I hate Bart for what he did. And I think that's why I want to push you forward. I don't want him to color your future. He already drew too much of your past," Gen said.

Olivia felt emotion well up within her at her friend's words.

"I love you for that, Gen. But I have to learn from Bart, or what was the use of the last twenty years?"

"So wise for one so young. See, you're smart, kind, and gorgeous. You can find a guy who is all three as well," Gen said, causing Olivia to smile.

"Don't forget funny," Olivia added.

"Oh no. Sorry girl. But you really aren't very funny," Gen said.

Olivia shook her head in offense. "I'm kind of funny," she retorted.

"Okay, I'll give you *kind of funny*," Gen agreed, causing both women to giggle.

"So we don't want an attractive man. Any other rules?" Gen asked when their giggles subsided.

"Not *too* attractive," Olivia emphasized. Then she added, "At least my age or older."

Gen sighed. "But the young guys are so fun," she complained.

"I thought we just established I'm not funny."

"Yes, not funny. But you are fun. Although you could use some more fun in your life."

"I don't want fun. I want serious. I don't have time for fun."

"Okay. So you want ugly, old, and boring?" Gen asked.

Olivia rolled her eyes. "No-o." Olivia knew Gen was being obtuse on purpose but still felt the need to spell out what she wanted. "I want a guy who is not *too* attractive, older than I am, and he can *be* fun. But I don't want a guy looking to *just* have fun," Olivia said.

"I literally know no one who fits those requirements," Gen moaned, and Olivia grinned. Hopefully that meant Olivia would have another few months before her first date.

"Do you want this new man to have any good characteristics?" Gen asked.

"Kind. I really want him to be kind. And sweet. And he has to love kids. Especially my girls," Olivia said.

"Those are great qualities, Olivia. Really. But don't you think you're selling yourself short to think that you can only find a man who is kind and sweet but nothing else good?" Gen asked.

"Mom!" Rachel called out, suddenly beside Olivia in the kitchen.

When had she gotten there, and how much of the conversation had Rachel overheard? She'd told both girls to finish their homework in their room while she finished the dishes so that she'd have no little ears listening in.

"Sorry, Gen," Olivia said into the phone before turning to Rachel.

"Yes?" Olivia asked Rachel.

Rachel pointed to the bar that divided their kitchen from the living room. Olivia rounded the bar to the living room side to see Pearl huddled under it, obviously eavesdropping on what Olivia and Gen had been talking about.

Great.

Olivia tried to replay the conversation in her mind as quickly as she could, but who knew how much Pearl had heard?

"Pearl Birmingham!" Olivia reprimanded as she came out of hiding .

"I finished my homework," Pearl said as if that was a good enough defense.

"So what were you doing under the bar?" Olivia asked, hearing Gen chuckle on the other end. Olivia would deal with Gen later.

"I was bored," Pearl said with a shrug.

"What has mommy told you about eavesdropping?" Olivia asked.

"It's rude, and I shouldn't do it," Pearl said softly.

"That's right. So why were you doing it?" Olivia asked.

Pearl shrugged again.

Olivia debated asking Pearl all that she had heard but figured this might be one conversation that was better not to relive. Hopefully Pearl would soon forget anything she heard.

"Are you finished with your homework?" Olivia asked Rachel.

Rachel nodded.

"Both of you outside until it's time to shower," Olivia said as she pointed toward the door.

"Why am I being punished?" Rachel complained.

"Don't you want to go outside and play with Buster?" Olivia asked.

Rachel nodded. She loved Dean's dog more than almost anything in the world.

"So it's not a punishment."

"But Pearl needs to be punished for eavesdropping," Rachel said, and Olivia closed her eyes, praying for patience before responding.

"Go outside," Olivia said to Rachel before turning to Pearl. "You too. And I'll be thinking of a punishment for eavesdropping."

"Yes, Mom," both girls finally said before running out her front door.

"Grab your jackets," Olivia yelled after them, and they came running back in to put on their jackets and then were back out the door once again.

"So that's what I have to look forward to?" Gen asked as Olivia sank onto her couch.

"I told you it only gets harder," Olivia said, and Gen laughed.

"Honestly, I would take eavesdropping over stuffing the toilet with three tutus any day," Gen said, and Olivia gasped.

"Maddie didn't."

"Oh yes she did. Levi had quite the fun job to come home to. Speaking of which, I should get off. But I'll be sure to be on the lookout for a boring, old, kind and sweet man," Gen said. "Does he need to be balding, or is that just a plus?"

"Good night, Gen," Olivia said over Gen's cackling and hung up the phone.

Olivia sat back on her couch for a few minutes, digesting what she and Gen had spoken about. She was right in her requirements. Looks would fade. She knew that firsthand. But kindness, honesty, loyalty, respect ... those things lasted and were what Olivia truly cared about.

She heard loud laughter just outside her door and knew her girls must have found Dean, Olivia's handsome *and* kind neighbor and landlord who was very much dating a beautiful, nice woman named Charlotte.

But knowing that fact didn't stop Olivia's heart from flipping every time she heard his voice, especially when she heard him laugh. Dean was all of Olivia's list and all of Gen's. But that didn't matter. Because he was unavailable.

Olivia stood, knowing she should probably be out there with her girls so Dean wouldn't feel the need to stay out any longer than he wanted to. Dean was one of the few people in the world who felt nearly as responsible for the girls as Olivia did. The others were Olivia's parents and her brother, Dax. No, Olivia would not think too deeply about how curious that was.

"Mom!" Rachel shouted as Olivia joined her girls, Buster, and Dean.

"Mom!" Pearl mimicked.

As soon as she stepped outside, the evening air bit at Olivia's cheeks—the nights on Whisling were still having a hard time moving on to spring.

Olivia shuddered in her jacket, deciding to stay on the porch instead of joining the group who was playing fetch with Buster in her and Dean's yard. Well, technically it was just Dean's, but he was an angel and happy to share with Olivia and her girls.

Olivia tried hard to keep her eyes on her girls, but they kept straying to the attractive man who played with them. Dean must've just come back from a jog. He wore a pair of fitted sweats and a t-shirt that was molded to his chest. Olivia had asked why he didn't wear something more substantial on top as he exercised in the cold, and Dean had told her he ran hot.

"Yeah, he does," Olivia muttered under her breath as she took in Dean's incredible physique. It was unfair that someone as good and benevolent as Dean looked so amazing as well.

As if he heard her thoughts, Dean looked up and then jogged her way. Olivia was waiting for the day when seeing Dean would no longer take her breath away, but nearly a year into being his backyard renter, today was not that day.

"How was your day?" Dean asked as he joined Olivia on the porch, and they both watched her girls as they continued to play with Buster.

"Good. I got a bunch of work done, and Bess even taught me her spaghetti recipe," Olivia said, proud of the meal she'd made for her girls that evening. It wasn't up to par with Bess's cooking but miles ahead of Olivia's typical fare.

"Wait, really?" Dean asked, his eyes going wide. "Do you happen to have any leftovers?"

Olivia laughed as she went back into her home, jogged to her fridge for the container full of leftovers, and brought it out to Dean.

Dean lifted the lid, sniffing the meal, and then looked back at Olivia with a huge grin on his face.

"It smells so good," he said.

Olivia returned his grin. She'd never understood Bess when she'd told Olivia she loved cooking for others just for their reaction ... until that moment. If Olivia could bring that kind of a smile to Dean's face with some spaghetti, she would happily make it every day.

"I'm glad," Olivia said, feeling her cheeks redden as Dean continued to look at her like she was a marvel. She hoped Dean would blame the redness of her face on the chilly evening air.

"Dean?" Pearl asked as she joined the adults on the porch.

Rachel was running and laughing with Buster still, but either Pearl had gotten bored or Rachel had told her to leave.

Olivia was sure either could've happened, but since Pearl wasn't complaining, Olivia decided she wouldn't intervene this time.

"Yeah, Pearly?" Dean answered.

Olivia refused to let her heart flip flop at the sound of Dean using the nickname only the family did for Pearl.

"Are you older than Mom?" she asked.

That was a weird question, and Olivia scrunched her eyebrows as Dean answered.

"Yeah, by a few months," Dean said.

Pearl crossed her arms in front of her chest.

"And you're kind and sweet," Pearl said.

Olivia felt her eyes go wide. No, no, no.

"And you like us," Pearl added before looking up at Olivia. "Mom, what did you mean by *not too attractive?*"

"Pearl, that was a private conversation," Olivia reprimanded, but Pearl didn't even look slightly repentant.

"You asked Mrs. Gen for her help. I wanted to help too," Pearl said.

Olivia wasn't sure how to go on. One part of her was beyond embarrassed that Pearl had brought this up in front of Dean, obviously looking at the man as a possible solution for Olivia's need to date, while the other part of her thought Pearl's desire to help was absolutely adorable. But the fact remained, either way, that Pearl should not be sharing her ill-gotten information.

"'That's why you shouldn't eavesdrop, Pearl. I'm grateful you want to help, but I didn't have the conversation in front of you and your sister on purpose. This is a grown up problem," Olivia said as she knelt down so that she was level with her daughter, and Pearl nodded.

"Okay," Pearl said as she unfolded her arms. "I won't eavesdrop."

"Thank you," Olivia said as Pearl raced back into the

growing darkness of the yard. She would have to send the girls to bed pretty soon.

"Not too attractive?" Dean asked, and Olivia felt her ears go red.

Oh man, she'd hoped they could move past what Pearl had said without discussing it.

Olivia stood, taking in Dean's demeanor.

He stood with his arms folded across his broad chest, and although his facial expression was neutral, Olivia didn't miss the laughter in his eyes.

"Gen's just helping me get back out there," Olivia muttered. She wasn't comfortable having this conversation with anyone, but with Dean it was nearly unbearable.

"Get back out there? Are you dating, Olivia?" Dean asked, and Olivia felt the redness from her cheeks spread to her ears. But she knew Dean wasn't going to let this go. So better to get it over and done with.

"Yeah. It's about time," she said quietly.

"It's way beyond time," she swore she heard Dean mutter, but he said more loudly, "I'm happy for you, Olivia."

Olivia nodded, hoping that was it.

But that bubble burst quickly.

"So what did you tell Gen you're looking for? Does that mean you're open to setups?" Dean asked.

"Why? Do you have someone in mind?" Olivia asked light-heartedly as a joke, but Dean nodded in response.

"You do?" she asked.

"Yeah," Dean said, and Olivia felt her stomach drop.

The rational part of her knew Dean was dating Charlotte, and Olivia hoped for Charlotte and for Dean that he was fully invested in his relationship with her. But Olivia had to admit, a carnal and very selfish part of her wanted Dean to be unhappy that Olivia wanted to date ... anyone other than him. But that was stupid and silly, and Olivia willed her disappointment to leave.

"What are you looking for?" Dean asked, and Olivia relayed the list she'd told Gen. She tried to pretend she was talking to Bess or another girlfriend who would want to set her up, not to her all-too-attractive, very male neighbor. Dean was her friend. That was it.

"I'm with Pearl. What do you mean by *not too attractive?* I've got to say, my friend is pretty dang attractive," Dean said.

Olivia laughed. "I just ..."

"Don't want another Bart," Dean said softly.

Olivia nodded. "Looks fade."

It was Dean's turn to nod. "But good looking doesn't mean the guy is going to be Bart."

"I know. Of course I know that. But that was what I'd first looked for when it came to Bart."

"Give yourself a break, Liv. You were seventeen."

Olivia sighed. "Yeah, I know. But that's why I have to be so much smarter now."

Dean nodded. "I understand that. I swear my friend is no Bart. I've learned from my mistakes as well."

Olivia looked at Dean, and his sincerity was easy to see. If anyone knew Bart, Dean, Bart's best friend from high school, did. And if he said this guy wasn't anything like Bart, Olivia trusted him. Who better to find her a date than the guy she really wished she could date? Okay, that was messed up, but somewhere in there was a bit of logic, wasn't there?

"What do you say? Can I give him your number?" Dean asked, his eyebrows raised in hope.

"Are you sure he'd be into me?" Olivia asked, suddenly aware that she wasn't the only one to have standards.

"Um, yeah," Dean snorted. "We'll have no issues there. Olivia, I am sure you are every guy's type."

Olivia bit her lip. What did Dean mean by that?

Probably nothing. Dean was just being nice, the way he always was. She wouldn't allow herself to investigate Dean's remark anymore—for Charlotte's sake, of course—so a flippant joke seemed like the best response.

"Right. A woman with more emotional scars than she can count and two daughters is every guy's type," Olivia said, trying to keep her tone light. But what had started as a joke turned into a far too real statement.

"That's not what I see. I see a woman who walked through hell but somehow still came out a saint," Dean said softly.

Olivia was quite sure that was the sweetest thing anyone had ever said to her.

"Mom, can Buster sleep over?" Pearl asked, and Olivia was grateful for the interruption. Dean was another woman's boyfriend. She needed to step away before her not so repressed feelings came to the surface.

"Pearl, Buster lives with Dean," Olivia said as she took a literal and figurative step away from the man.

"I know, but I want him to sleep in my bed," Pearl complained.

"No, I want him to sleep in my bed," Rachel said, telling Olivia just the kind of night they'd endure if Buster did sleep over.

"Tell Buster good night, girls," Olivia said, using a tone that told her daughters there would be no room for argument.

"Good night, Buster. Good night, Dean," Rachel said as she pouted and then ran into the house.

Pearl seemed a little more willing to accept Olivia's decision as she ran with a smile toward the dog she'd hoped would sleep over. "Good night, Buster," Pearl said as she gave the dog a hug and then ran to the man beside Olivia. "Good night, Dean,"

Pearl said, hugging Buster's owner just as tightly as she had the dog.

Suddenly Olivia felt more than a slight tinge that dating might be good for her. She realized she needed a new guy in her life. Now. Seeing the way Pearl was attached to another woman's boyfriend, and maybe one day husband, wasn't good for Pearl. And it definitely wasn't good for Olivia. Olivia had assumed her feelings for Dean were harmless because they weren't reciprocated, but she was now recognizing that that didn't make what she felt for Dean okay. It wasn't fair to Charlotte, Dean, her girls, or even herself.

But Olivia knew her feelings wouldn't just disappear. She had to make them leave. And she was pretty sure a great way to do that was to make sure her affection was otherwise engaged. Maybe with the man Dean proposed.

Pearl ran into the house, and Olivia followed her, pausing at their front door.

"Yeah, you can give him my number. Thanks, Dean," Olivia said. Then she rushed to close the door behind her. She needed to shut these feelings for Dean out of her heart.

CHAPTER TEN

"HEY, ALEXIS," Bess heard Cassie call out as the door to the food truck opened, and Bess heard Alexis enter.

The lunch rush had died down a few minutes before, and Bess had been busy prepping for the dinner rush. She liked to leave things as well stocked as possible before leaving the truck to Alexis for the evening.

"Hi, Cassie, Bess," Alexis said as she washed her hands and then put on her apron.

"How was it today?" she asked, turning to Bess and then looking at Cassie.

"Busy, but not crazy," Cassie said, and Bess nodded, turning her attention back to the basil she'd been chiffonading.

"That's good," Alexis said as she joined Bess in prepping foods for the evening.

"How many lasagnas are left?" Alexis asked, taking inventory of what she could still sell that evening.

"Two whole pans and about half of this one," Bess said as she pointed with her knife to the pan of gooey, cheesy deliciousness under the heating lamp.

"Awesome. And I saw we're doing a shrimp diablo special.

How many more orders do we have of that?" Alexis asked the same questions she always did at the start of her shift.

"Probably about fifty," Bess said, and Alexis nodded.

A customer came to the truck, so Cassie's attention was turned out the window as she took his order.

"Uh, Bess. I have a question for you," Alexis said, and Bess stopped her chopping to turn her attention to Alexis.

"What's up?" Bess asked.

"Um," Alexis bit her lip nervously. "I have a date on Friday. Would you mind terribly if we traded shifts that day?" Alexis asked.

Bess shot an instant smile at her beautiful chef, thankful that Alexis was finally going on a date. Bess felt like a protective mother hen to the somewhat mysterioys woman who'd come back to the island just a year ago, after many years away. Alexis had had it tough growing up on the island. She was the daughter of one of Bess's high school acquaintances, and Bess knew the road for both women had been rough. Alexis's mom had gotten pregnant during her junior year of high school—something that was terribly looked down on during that time period—and both mother and daughter had been shunned for years because of it. Bess had done her best to stay in contact with Tracy, Alexis's mom, but it had been hard since Tracy kept to herself and Bess spent many of the years right after high school away at college. By the time Bess started having her own babies, people were beginning to be kinder to Tracy and Alexis. But Bess was sure the stigma of being the pregnant teen's daughter had followed Alexis for most, if not all, of her childhood on the island. Alexis had left Whisling right after high school and had bartended at some of the finest restaurants in Seattle, according to Tracy. She'd decided to go to culinary school in her thirties and was now one of the best chefs Bess had ever seen. Bess still wasn't sure why Alexis had come back to the island the year before, but was certainly glad she had.

And she was almost just as glad that Alexis was going to go out and enjoy herself. This date was the first mention of a social life that Alexis had told Bess about in the almost one year that they'd worked together. The curvy, raven-haired beauty probably attracted a ton of male attention, but Bess guessed Alexis was picky. Which she should be. A few of Bess's friends' choices in mates were testament to the fact that some men just weren't worth the time.

"Of course," Bess responded. Not only was she glad Alexis was going on a date, Alexis had covered for Bess quite a few times in the past few months, and Bess was glad to return the favor.

"Thanks," Alexis said as she set down her knife, seeming relieved that the conversation was over.

"You know that you can ask for whatever you need, right?" Bess asked, understanding that it was difficult for Alexis to speak up for herself. Bess had hoped Alexis felt comfortable enough with her to push past that fear, but Bess might've been mistaken.

"I know. You've been good to me, Bess. I just don't want you to think I'm taking advantage of that," Alexis said softly, all while still looking down at the tomatoes on the cutting board.

"I've never felt that, and I doubt that I ever will. You don't have a manipulative bone in your body," Bess said with a grin that Alexis looked up to return.

"Thank you," she said with a sweet smile and then went back to work.

"One lasagna," Cassie called back to the cooks, but she continued to speak with the customer at the window at the front of the truck. Bess would guess the customer was a friend to her gregarious employee since Cassie was loved by most everyone on the island.

Bess served up a piece of the delicious fare and then passed the container to Alexis who added a rustic chopped salad and a piece of garlic bread to the plate.

"Who is the lucky guy?" Bess asked, suddenly curious about the date. Then she realized that might be prying, so she added, "If you want to talk about him."

Alexis beamed at the mention of her date, so Bess figured she hadn't meddled too far.

"His name is Dalton. I knew him years ago when I was first bartending at a dive in Seattle. He was the manager of the place, and we were always friendly. But he was married then," Alexis said, her smile never fading.

Bess was busy working on cutting up some more red onions for their chopped salad but glanced over to Alexis to show that she was listening.

"How did you guys get reacquainted?" Bess asked between knife cuts.

"Social media. Lame, right?" Alexis asked.

Bess shook her head. This was the twenty-first century. She was pretty sure social media had a hand in many, if not most, of these kinds of stories nowadays.

"I guess he left Seattle a few years after I left the bar we worked at. He's been in California for the last fifteen years, but now he's back in Seattle. I wrote to him, welcoming him back to the state. Then we got to talking...." Alexis let her words trail off.

"And you like him," Bess said.

"I do. I mean, enough to go on a date with him. It's just drinks at some fancy place in the city," Alexis said, her excited tone belying the casualness of her words.

"That sounds like fun," Bess said.

Alexis nodded. "It does."

Bess grinned. She was thrilled for her adorable, quiet chef. Alexis deserved to go to some fancy place and be pampered. Bess would hold off on worrying if Dalton was good enough for Alexis until things became serious.

"Oh, hi Dax." Cassie loudly drawled out the name, and all thoughts of Alexis's date fled as Bess felt her stomach flip.

Dax was here? Her Dax? Not her Dax. Her friend, Dax, who didn't live on the island ... so of course Bess was happy that he was visiting. A friend visiting. Fun.

Okay, she was now babbling in her mind.

"One scampi, coming right up," Cassie said, and then she laughed at whatever Dax's response was.

Bess was not curious to know what had made Cassie laugh. She was fine being so far back in the truck that she couldn't hear a word Dax said.

Man, first babbling and now lying to herself? Bess needed to calm the heck down.

"I'll ask her," Cassie said, the smile in her voice easy to hear as she left the window and approached Bess who had already started on Dax's scampi.

When Bess looked up from her hot pan, she saw Cassie right in front of her and Alexis smiling widely behind Cassie.

"Our customer is hoping that you can personally deliver his meal to him?" Cassie asked, her grin growing with each word. Bess knew Cassie and Alexis were both Dax fans. Bess didn't blame them. She was a Dax fan as well.

Bess looked from Cassie and Alexis to where she could see just a bit of Dax's arm through the serving window.

"Sure," Bess said, trying to sound professional about the prospective delivery that she was feeling anything but professional about. She was thrilled Dax was here—not only back on the island but at the truck—and even more excited that he wasn't going to leave without seeing her.

Jon. The name came to Bess's mind like a figurative bucket of water over her potential enjoyment. Bess was supposed to be putting her all into her relationship with Jon. Was she doing that if she spent time with Dax?

But she *had* told Jon she was going to stay friends with Dax. And friends delivered food to friends, right? Of course they did. This was no big deal. Bess was only eager to see a friend she hadn't seen in a while.

"I'll let him know." Cassie's smile was now so wide, she looked like she'd not only caught the canary but managed to snag a whole flock of them. She turned to go back to the window.

"No need, Cassie. I heard Bess's thrilled response for myself," Dax called through the window, causing all of the women in the truck to laugh as Dax walked away.

Bess finished Dax's scampi in no time, and after boxing it up, she realized it was about time for her to leave for the day anyway. Might as well deliver Dax his meal and then head on home. Bess held on to Dax's to-go container and fork as she found her purse and made sure everything else was in order before telling Alexis and Cassie she was leaving for the afternoon.

"Have fun," Cassie teased as Bess opened the door of the truck.

Bess ignored her cute employee's admonition as she took her first step into the dreary weather. She'd only just caught a glimpse of the gray, gloomy, drizzly day when she saw Dax at the bottom of the stairs, ready with an umbrella.

Bess shook her head. Of course the man wouldn't let her take a step in the rain.

"I figured the least I could do was offer you dry transport since you're delivering my meal," Dax said with his grin that always knocked Bess a bit off-kilter.

We're just friends.

"And where did you want your meal delivery?" she asked, trying to sound as jovial as Dax had.

Dax pointed toward his waiting car. "I was hoping a little bit of conversation could come with the delivery? I've missed you, Bess," Dax said sincerely, and Bess knew she'd missed Dax too. He'd become someone she'd come to rely on after her divorce. They still texted while Dax was in LA where he lived and worked, but it wasn't the same as face to face interaction. They hadn't had a real conversation in months, when Bess had told Dax she was going to date Jon exclusively. Bess knew she should take a minute to chat with her friend.

And although Bess really wanted to return Dax's "I miss you" because it was true, it didn't seem quite right for Bess to tell another man she'd missed him. It somehow felt like a betrayal to Jon. But having a conversation with Dax? That much she could do.

So Bess nodded toward Dax and went with him to his car. She didn't miss the beaming smile on his face.

"Looks like the food truck is as popular as ever," Dax said as they settled into his rental car. He pushed the seat as far back as it would go before placing his to-go container of food on his lap.

Bess cocked her head in confusion. "There was no line when you got here. Nor is there one now. Not exactly a sign of thriving success."

"You caught me," Dax said, opening his container of shrimp scampi and taking a deep breath of the garlicy butter scent, which immediately filled the car. Bess had to admit, even though she was around the smell all day every day, it was still intoxicating. "I may not have gotten my information with my own two eyes. I might've let my curiosity about your well-being get the better of me by asking Olivia how you all are doing."

Bess smiled. She liked that Dax cared enough to check up

on her. Granted, his sister's livelihood was intertwined with Bess's, so it made sense that he cared about the truck. But Bess knew that Dax would've cared about her truck, with or without Olivia as an employee. They'd been through too much for Bess to deny that Dax cared for her.

Dax took a huge bite of his noodles and shrimp before turning to Bess with an enormous grin. He cleared his mouth of food before saying, "You are a magician."

Bess shook her head. Her food was good, but it wasn't magic.

"Or maybe a woodland fairy brought to us as a gift from another world," Dax said, and Bess giggled.

"Yeah, that was a bit over the top," Dax said, surely replaying his words in his mind.

Bess nodded. "A bit."

"But your cooking really is an incredible gift, Bess."

Bess felt her cheeks go red and shifted in her seat. She both loved and hated when Dax got like his. He was the most complimentary person she knew. His sincere and sweet compliments thrilled as well as embarrassed Bess. She wasn't sure she deserved all of his praise.

"I know what you're thinking," Dax said as Bess looked over from her seat to where Dax sat.

"Do you?" Bess asked with a skeptical raise of her eyebrow. At least Dax's bold statement helped her embarrassment to flee.

Dax nodded. "And I mean every word of what I say, Bess. I've literally eaten at some of the best restaurants around the world," he said. Then he breathed on his curled up fingers and rubbed them against his chest. It took every effort Bess possessed not to dwell on his well-formed chest. The guy had to work out a lot.

"I would guess your job demands some pretty tough things of you. Like eating at five star restaurants," Bess teased.

Dax nodded solemnly. "It's a rough life. But someone has to live it," he said.

"Poor, poor Dax," Bess said through her laughter.

Dax joined Bess, both of them laughing together, and Bess felt a warmth swell in her chest.

"But really, Bess. You have to understand the kind of talent you have. I know restaurant owners who would kill to have a chef like you," Dax said earnestly.

"Home cook. Definitely not a chef," Bess corrected.

"You say tomato, I say tomahto," Dax said with a lazy shrug.

Bess couldn't argue with that, so she just grinned. As much as she argued with Dax, she really did love the things he told her. And every time he reiterated how much he loved Bess's food, she felt her own belief in herself grow a little more.

"Speaking of your tough life, how is it going?" Bess asked just as Dax took another huge bite.

Dax nodded as he chewed and then said, "It's going really well. I've never been busier. My company is thriving, and I've got some really great agents working for me."

"You say that so matter-of-factly. As if you haven't achieved what others only dream of. A thriving business in Los Angeles and Nashville. Isn't that like catching a unicorn?" Bess asked.

Dax grinned. "Yeah, I guess it is. You're good for my ego, Bess," Dax said before digging back into his food.

"Ditto," Bess said as she waited for Dax to finish his bite.

"But my life is boring. How about you? Tell me about you and life here on Whisling while I eat?" Dax asked, his eyes shining with hope.

Bess didn't know many in Dax's position of success who didn't want to spend time boasting about themselves, instead wanting to hear about the small-town life of a middle-aged woman. But Dax wasn't most men.

"You've heard about the truck—" Bess began.

But Dax put up a finger, cleared his mouth and then said, "But I'd like to hear it from you."

Bess smiled softly. "We're serving approximately four hundred customers a day and selling an average of one thousand plates," Bess boasted in a way she only could with those she trusted.

She knew there were others who, for not so friendly reasons, wanted to know just how well Bess's truck was doing. They wanted numbers and stats, but she didn't want that kind of information spread all over the island. However, she knew what was said to Dax would go no further.

"That's amazing," Dax said.

Bess grinned. It really was. They'd hoped to be doing half of that in sales per day just a few months before. They were growing like wildfire, and Bess really felt blessed.

"And the kids are as busy as ever. Jana and Stephen are engaged again but taking it slowly. Jana won't set a date, but she did say she hoped Scratch Made by Bess would be willing to cater the event."

"Did you tell her the truth?" Dax asked with a mischievous gleam in his blue eyes.

"The truth?" Bess asked.

"That she should only be so lucky?" Dax asked.

Bess chuckled. "Of course," she said, even though she'd told her future daughter-in-law nothing of the sort.

"Lindsey is working hard and moving up the corporate ladder."

"I bet her mom is proud," Dax said.

Bess nodded. She was really proud. Lindsey had always been a go-getter, but after college, an even stronger drive had awakened in her daughter. Lindsey was a machine when it came to her career goals. But, like most women Bess's age, she hoped Lindsey would slow down in the near future and maybe take a moment to look around and find a good man worthy of her. Bess was definitely cliché when it came to grandchildren. She wanted them soon, and she wanted a whole brood of them.

"And James now officially has a job lined up after graduation. It's weird that not only have they all left the nest, even college is almost a thing of the past as well. I didn't anticipate this stage of life," Bess said as she leaned back in her seat.

"I'm guessing you also weren't planning on doing this stage alone?" Dax asked tenderly, and Bess nodded.

Dax, as always, hit the nail on the head.

"I wasn't."

Dax reached over and gave Bess a friendly pat on her knee, the touch sending waves of emotion through her. Something she should not be feeling if she was trying to put her all into dating Jon.

"Um, I better go," Bess said as she moved to open the car door, her gaze still on where Dax had touched her knee.

Dax cleared his throat. "Yeah, you probably should."

Bess looked back at Dax, startled that he hadn't argued to spend more time with her. That was what Dax typically did. But as she looked into Dax's eyes, it was easy to see the desire there. And because of that, he was letting her go. The way a good friend should.

Bess nodded and then opened the door.

"It was good to see you, Dax," Bess said, unable to leave the car on the awkward note they'd come to.

Dax swallowed. "It's always good to see you, Bess."

Bess nodded again. She lacked the brainpower to come up with the right words to say in that moment. Dax was supposed to just be a friend, and when they texted, it wasn't hard for him to stay that way. But in person ... and when he touched her? Bess knew this had to be the last encounter of its kind. It would be disloyal to Jon if it wasn't.

"I ..." Bess began, and Dax nodded.

"I know," Dax said, his voice low, husky and all too appealing.

"I'm sorry," Bess said, feeling guilty that she had put them here. If she'd been strong enough to push Dax away completely, they wouldn't be in this position.

"Don't be, Bess. I thought we could work as friends too," Dax said.

Bess nodded. It had been a foolish hope. There was far too much chemistry between them to ignore. But Bess had to ignore it.

"I guess I'll see you around?" Bess asked, and Dax nodded.

They both knew even the texting between them had to stop. It wasn't fair to Jon ... or to either of them.

"Do you want my umbrella?" Dax offered.

Bess shook her head. She was a Whisling native. And you didn't become a native of the Pacific Northwest while being afraid of a little rain.

"Make sure he's good to you, Bess," Dax said as Bess stepped out of the car and into the drizzly day.

"Good bye, Dax," Bess said, and Dax nodded as if he couldn't say the words back. Bess didn't blame him. She hadn't relished saying them either.

Bess finally got all the way out of the car and closed the door behind her.

She took a deep breath before walking to her own car. She was doing the right thing. She knew that she was. But then why did it hurt so badly?

CHAPTER ELEVEN

DEB BEAMED as she stepped into the space that would become her very own art gallery.

She proudly took in all of the room's features. The floors and three of the walls were all made of the same gray concrete. She knew that her paintings and the paintings that she acquired would stand out on the plain backdrop. The last wall was made of glass and showed the inside of the gallery off to all of the many tourists who walked along Elliot Drive. It was a pristine spot, and it was all Deb's.

"I'm so proud of you," Luke said, joining Deb in the middle of the room. In the middle of *her* gallery.

"What are you thinking?" Luke asked as he wound his arms around her waist when Deb stayed quiet. Deb wasn't the type to stay silent for more than a moment if she wasn't thinking hard.

"I'm thinking I'm so grateful for you. I would've never dared to do this without you," she responded. She spun in his arms and stood on her tiptoes, placing a kiss to Luke's lips.

"Yes, you would have," Luke said with a chuckle. "You are the most daring woman I know."

Deb smiled. Maybe she would've. But she was glad she

didn't have to do it alone. Life was a whole lot more fun with Luke by her side.

"And I'm imagining what I want to put where," Deb said as she pointed to the space by the door. "I'm thinking a reception area there."

Luke nodded as he took in Deb's vision.

"We can just fill the existing walls at first, but as we grow, I'm hoping to put a partial wall in right here," Deb said, pointing down at where she and Luke stood. "And I'm going to put in skylights."

Luke looked over at Deb with a skeptical brow raised.

"I talked to the owner. He loves the idea. As long as I pay for it," Deb said, and Luke nodded with a grin. That sounded very much like the man Deb was renting the space from. It had taken months for Deb and her new landlord to agree on a price. But they'd done it. And they were both happy. Well, Deb was probably a little bit happier than her landlord.

"The place could use some more light," Luke said, and Deb nodded. Her art loved light. Then again, so did Deb.

"It sounds perfect," Luke said, dropping a kiss on top of Deb's head. She loved it when he did that.

"The only thing that could make my life more perfect would be if you'd move to the island already," Deb teased with a playful smile.

Deb teased because she and Luke had had this same conversation several times before, and she knew that Luke wanted to do things the traditional way. Date, get married, and then move in together. But Deb was ready for that last step now. She hated having to say goodbye to Luke every evening. She was ready to not only share her home but every part of her life with him.

"I couldn't agree more," Luke said as he kissed her head again.

"Then let's do it," Deb said as she turned to look up at Luke.

"I want to, Deb. But you know how I feel about having the wedding first," Luke said.

Deb nodded. She understood Luke's reasons for his traditional thinking. One, Luke was just a more traditional person than Deb was, and she loved him for it. But she also knew that Luke hoped his example would help his daughters to make the same decision when the time came for them to get married. He didn't like the idea of his little girls living with men before they'd tied the knot. And Deb admired that about him as well.

"So then let's have the wedding. This weekend," Deb said, and Luke gave her a look that she knew well. He thought she'd gone crazy.

"I've been dreading planning a big to-do anyway. We both already had that kind of wedding. I don't need all of that again, do you?" Deb asked, looking up at Luke. When he shook his head, she went on. "What if we did it right here, in the gallery? I could get some of my favorite pieces up by then. We wouldn't have the sky lights yet, but—" Deb stopped, realizing she hadn't thought this through all the way. Would Luke want to be married in an art gallery? Deb knew she would love it, but she and Luke had never talked about where they wanted to get married. And now that Deb thought about it, Luke seemed like he was a *get married in a church* kind of guy.

Luke looked around at their surroundings and then down at Deb.

"Deb, the *where* and *when* of our marriage doesn't matter. The *who* is all I care about," Luke said with a sweet smile, and Deb felt one of her own spread over her lips.

"Really?" Deb asked.

Luke nodded. "Really. Besides, this does kind of feel right. But this weekend?"

"I'm sure I can find a dress, and Bess will take care of the food. My parents love a spontaneous trip."

"Mine don't. But they do love a free trip. As long as I spring for the tickets, I'm sure they can be here as well."

"I'll talk to Bailey and Wes," Deb said with a wild grin. They were really going to do this.

"And I'll need to talk to the girls. This will mean that Clara will have to commute back to Seattle for the last month of her senior year," Luke said.

Deb had forgotten about that one hiccup.

They'd planned to get married this winter, after Clara had already graduated. Grace was more than happy to move to Whisling for her own senior year—evidently she didn't love their school in Seattle—but of course Clara wanted to finish out her last month of high school with her friends.

"Do you think she'll mind?" Deb asked.

Luke shook his head. "We can make the commute together. It'll be fun," he said, and Deb's grin was back.

"Really?" she asked, her heart racing from the excitement of all of this.

"Yeah. I think we should go with your crazy plan this time," Luke said.

Deb laughed again, her entire being full of joy. She was getting married ... to the man of her dreams ... this weekend.

Deb needed to find a dress.

DEB WAS NEARLY SMASHED against the sink in the bathroom of her new gallery. Bailee stood behind her, putting the finishing touches on Deb's hair. Also in the small room were Deb's mom and sister, and Bess. Luke's girls had just left to greet their grandparents.

Bess had a look on her face that told Deb she wanted to leave the tiny space to the family, but Deb pinned her best friend with a look that she knew Bess wouldn't mistake. Bess was going to stand with Deb for the entirety of the day. Deb loved her family, but Bess was her female soul mate. She needed Bess in a way that no one else could fill.

Bess smiled a tight lipped grin that made Deb laugh out loud. It was going to be a good day.

It had taken some round-the-clock work, but the space was now exactly how Deb had imagined it for her wedding day. She had some of her favorite pieces that she'd made over the years installed on the walls. Although Deb had hoped to acquire a few paintings created by other artists, getting them to the island in such a short time had proved impossible. But the walls were full of Deb's favorite vibrant colors, so she was pleased.

Luke had put his daughters in charge of flowers, and they'd knocked it out of the park. First, they'd been sweet enough to not only ask Deb what she wanted for the day, but dear Clara had even taken notes. Deb had decided, because her paintings had so much color, that she just wanted greenery. The girls had found large potted plants, and they were dotted around the room in a way that only Clara could've done. The piece de resistance was a wooden arch that had vines of green intertwined throughout it. It was absolutely beautiful.

In front of the arch were two rows of chairs, plenty to seat the few guests, and on the other side of the gallery were a couple of round tables and chairs for the luncheon Bess and Alexis would be putting on after the main event.

Deb put her hand to her stomach and felt none of the butterflies of worry she'd felt when she'd married Rich. She had been so nervous about every detail that day. She'd wanted it all to go off without a hitch and for the day to be absolutely perfect. And it had been.

But today, when Deb touched her stomach, she felt a calm and surety that she was doing the right thing in a way she never had before. Because she wasn't scared about anything going wrong. Nothing could go wrong as long as Deb and Luke could weather it together. Things might not go according to plan, but they wouldn't go wrong. And it was because of that knowledge that Deb just felt utter giddiness that she would soon be Mrs. Luke Jordan.

"You look beautiful, Deb," her mom said as she patted her own cheeks that were wet with happy tears.

"Mom, don't start," Nora, Deb's sister, reprimanded, waving a hand in front of her own eyes.

"It's just ... we've waited a long time for you to be this happy," her mom added.

Deb watched as the women around her all nodded, Bailee included.

"Luke is a pretty lucky guy," Bailee added.

"I'm pretty dang lucky too," Deb said, and now every person in that tiny bathroom was waving their hands over their eyes, trying to keep the tears at bay.

A knock sounded on the door.

"The pastor just got here," Wes said through the door, and then his footsteps faded away quickly. Deb was sure that her boy wanted to be as far away from all the estrogen in that bathroom as possible.

"I guess that's our cue," Nora said as she and Deb's mom turned toward the door.

"You'll knock his socks off, sister," Nora added with a grin, escaping the room with her mother on her heels.

"You really do look amazing, Mom." Bailee reiterated her aunt's words as Deb took one last look at herself in the mirror.

Deb wore a fitted, white, knee-length dress that had fluttery sheer long sleeves. The moment Deb had seen the dress while shopping in Seattle, she'd known it was the one. She'd gone with a light smoky eye but had opted for no eye liner, going heavy on the mascara instead. The rest of her makeup look was light, and Deb had made sure to keep her lips free of any product but lip balm. With the amount of kissing she was planning on doing that day, bold lips were not possible. Bailee had curled Deb's brown hair so that it fell around her shoulders, giving Deb a dressed up but casual look—the exact contradiction she hoped this whole day would have.

"Thank you, Bailee," Deb said, giving her daughter a kiss on the cheek. Her little girl looked quite smashing herself in the blush pink dress she wore. But Bailee was proving to her mother and to the rest of the world that she wasn't so little anymore with the figure hugging attire that was a bit too low-cut for Deb's taste. Deb knew, though, that the turtleneck she wanted her daughter to wear wasn't exactly appropriate either.

Deb turned her gaze to Bess through the mirror, who winked in response. This was it.

"Are you ladies ready?" Deb asked as she extended both of her arms so that she could loop them with her daughter and best friend. She had initially asked Wes to walk her down the aisle with Bailee but had immediately seen that her adorable son wasn't exactly fond of the idea. That was when Deb had decided to put Wes out of his misery and asked Bess to take his place. If anyone should "give Deb away," it was her children and Bess. They'd been the ones to endure the day-to-day after Deb's life had fallen apart. They had been there to pick up the pieces, and they had been there to see Deb's life fill with light again.

"I sure am," Bess said as Bailee nodded, both intertwining their arms with Deb.

They walked out of the small bathroom and stood behind a makeshift wall that Deb's dad and Wes had made out of PVC pipe and some white curtains. Deb couldn't wait to see the group gathered on the other side of that wall. She knew she loved each and every one of her guests because the only people at the wedding who weren't like family were the pastor, the photographer, and the violinist Deb had hired to play as she walked down the aisle.

Bailee peeked around the curtain to give the violinist a thumb's up, the cue that Deb was ready to walk down the aisle, and the violin began to play the first strains of the wedding march.

Bess swiped under her eyes as Deb grinned. She loved seeing that this day meant so much to her friend, but Deb wasn't going to join Bess. She was too full of hope, love, and happiness to let any tears get her today. Well, at least so far. She and Luke had written their own vows, and she had a feeling the tears might catch up to her there.

Bailee led the three of them around the curtain, and then they walked in unison down the short aisle.

Deb looked to her left and saw Luke's parents with Luke's daughters. The cute girls had been more than okay with moving to Whisling sooner rather than later, and Deb adored them even more for it. She had always wondered how step-relationships worked and had marveled at people who created good ones. But Deb now felt what she hadn't understood before: an overwhelming motherly love for children she hadn't born. Luke's daughters were just as much a part of her heart as her own children were. Because when she'd decided to love Luke, loving his daughters had come naturally. They were a part of him and, now, a part of Deb.

Deb was about to look to the other side of the aisle where she knew Wes, Nora, and her parents sat, but she was caught by the sight of Luke standing at the front of the room next to the pastor.

Luke held her eyes in a way that told Deb he'd only been watching her since she'd come into the room and would forever only have eyes for her. She felt her heart flip at the intense gaze

of the man she loved and then took in the navy blue, fitted suit
her soon-to-be husband wore. Her man sure knew how to fill out
a suit.

Luke grinned as if he could read Deb's thoughts, and before
she knew it, she'd left Bailee and Bess to stand across from Luke,
her hands held by his.

The pastor began to speak, and Deb really tried to pay
attention—she knew the ceremony was important to Luke—but
all she could think about was how lucky she was to be marrying
this man who held her.

"I do," Luke suddenly said, and Deb tried not to look as startled as she felt.

"Deb," Luke began, and Deb realized it was time for their
vows. "You are my sunshine." Deb grinned when she realized
they'd started their vows in almost the same way.

"You are the most thrilling waves in this sea that is my life,
and I can't imagine spending another day without you by my
side. You are my partner, my equal, and my best friend. You are
the first face I want to see in the morning and the last lips I want
to kiss each night. I know that life will have some ups and downs
because I've weathered some rough ones. But as long as we are
together, the downs don't seem as daunting, and I have a feeling
the ups will rise beyond my wildest dreams. I love you."

Deb felt tears streaming down her cheeks. She knew Luke's
words would get her, but it wasn't just his words. It was the
sincerity behind them, the way his eyes gathered her in and the
tender smile on his face.

"Deb, it's your turn," the pastor said, and Deb nodded.

"Luke. You are my rock. But I'm not as good at words as I am
with my paintbrush. So I have a little help."

Wes stood on cue and took the white sheet off of a painting
that hung right in Luke's line of sight.

Deb knew the piece was good. She had put her heart and

soul into it. But by the way Luke's eyes warmed and his grip tightened on hers, she knew the painting had done just what it was supposed to do.

A big, bold rock stood in a way that looked like it could be alone. But with a second glance, one could see that the rock wasn't alone. One of the waves from the ocean had lapped up against the rock, standing next to it. Denying the pull of the rest of the ocean to go back to where it had once belonged.

"I've always been like the waves. Maybe I was thrilling, but I was also ever changing. Never sure where I stood because the ground beneath me was never steady. And I'm still that wave. But now that I've found you, my rock, I know exactly where I'm supposed to stand. Beside you. Always here and safe. I don't love you despite our differences. I love you because of them," Deb finished, and she caught a rogue tear falling down Luke's cheek with her thumb before regrasping his hands.

Luke grinned down at Deb as the pastor began to speak again. She knew her returning grin was probably goofy-looking, but she didn't care.

"I now pronounce you husband and wife." The pastor got Deb's attention with that phrase. "You may kiss the bride."

And there were the words Deb had been waiting for. She threw her arms around Luke's neck and tugged him down impatiently, their lips meeting with force as Luke's arms wound their way around Deb's waist, pulling her flush against him.

"Mom, mo-om!" Bailee called out, and Deb realized their kiss might've been a bit much for a ceremony. But Deb was now Luke's wife. And she wasn't going to waste a moment of that precious time.

Deb pulled away from their kiss to the horrified faces of their children and the laughter of the adults.

Bess had an arm around Bailee whose eyes were still wide

from the presumed horror of watching her mom make out with her new husband.

"I guess it's time to eat?" Deb asked, not too worried about her children. She'd caught them in just as passionate kisses, and they weren't married. It was basically law that now Deb needed to have fiery kisses with her sexy, new husband every day. And that was one law Deb was more than pleased to follow.

CHAPTER TWELVE

"MOMMA!" Amelia called out from her crib. The baby girl had never been very patient, and now that her father wasn't around to carry half of the load anymore, she seemed to feel an even more urgent need to be with her momma every moment of every day. But Lily didn't mind. She needed her baby girl just as much as Amelia needed her.

Lily put on a bright smile as she rushed to the room she was sharing with Amelia now that they were staying with Kate.

Lily was living with Kate. Away from her husband. The idea still stunned her.

When Lily had returned to the hospital to take her husband home, Allen had asked that Lily and Amelia stay somewhere other than their home for the foreseeable future. The words had been said cordially, as if Allen was breaking off a business arrangement. While on the other end, Lily had been bowled over by the request. How could Allen turn her out of their own home during a time that he needed her most? Even if he was mad at her for what she'd done—heck, no one could hate what Lily had done more than herself—he could be angry while they still lived together. There was no need for her to move out. She wasn't giving up on them, and Allen needed to know that. So she'd told her husband as much.

However, Allen's mother had intervened, telling Lily that Allen needed his space and she had to respect that. Lily had wanted to tell Allen's mother just what she could do with her space, but she'd looked at Allen sitting oh-so-still in the hospital bed behind his mom, and something cracked in Lily.

For the first time in their marriage, Allen didn't want her. And as much as she wanted to fight that, she had no idea what to do. Allen had always fought for her. It had always been the two of them against the world. But now ... he'd left her. Literally and figuratively.

So Kate had stepped in to help Lily move her things out of the home she'd shared with Allen and into Kate's two-bedroom apartment. Kate had been a godsend, not only helping Lily with Amelia but also being the shoulder Lily cried on nearly every night. Lily would not have survived this without her sister.

But now, months later, Lily was still at a loss as to what to do for her husband ... with her husband. See, she didn't even know how to phrase what they were going through, much less what to do.

She'd tried to go to the house about a month before—she knew they had to work together or at least speak to one another if he was ever going to forgive her—but Allen's mom hadn't even let Lily set foot in her own home. So then Lily had tried the school Allen had worked at and had been told Allen had quit his job.

And finally Lily understood. She had to continue to give Allen the space he so desperately craved. Because what else could she do? Allen was pulling away from everything he loved. Lily knew that he blamed her for all that had happened. And Lily got that he was hurt. He felt broken. But how was he supposed to heal, how were they supposed to ever get beyond this, if he pushed everything good away? Lily had decided it wasn't up to her to make that decision for Allen. So she'd gave him more space.

Now another month had passed, and Lily had had time to truly dig into her own issues surrounding what she'd done to her husband. Although she was far from forgiving herself, she was done punishing herself. She might still be lost as to what to do, but she knew they had to do something. It was time to get to work. So Allen had better be over needing his own space. She was going to go back to their home and take back her husband and her life. What she had done was terrible, but she hadn't meant to hurt Allen. If she could change that whole day, she would. So because of that, she figured even if she could never be forgiven, at least she deserved a chance to make things right. Allen, Lily, and Amelia needed to be a family again. And if Allen's mother wanted to stay as well, she would just have to deal with Lily. Lily had given in to Allen's wishes for two months—she figured he deserved that after what she'd done and the trauma he'd experienced—but she was done giving in. She had to step up. Even if the guilt that this was all her fault made her want to curl into a sleeping ball and never wake.

Lily debated whether she should take Amelia with her when she went back to their home. On the one hand, she figured Allen and his mother would have a much harder time turning Amelia away. But on the other hand, if things got ugly— if Allen told Lily he didn't want them again—Lily couldn't bear for Amelia to hear those words out of her father's mouth, even if she was too young to understand them.

So in the end, protecting her daughter won, and Lily waited patiently for Kate to come home from her job at Gen's salon so that Kate could babysit while Lily set off to win back her husband. Or demand him back. Either way, she was getting him back. She may have let him win the last couple of fights, but Lily was about to win this war once and for all. Allen needed her, and she needed Allen. They'd figure out the rest together.

Lily heard the lock turn on Kate's front door, and Amelia looked up from where she was crawling in Kate's living room. She knew what that sound meant.

Kate opened the door, and Amelia sat back, clapping her hands in glee.

"Oh why hello, my little Lia." Kate went straight to her niece and gave the baby a gigantic hug.

Kate sniffed the air as she hugged Amelia. "Did you make dinner again?" Kate asked Lily, and Lily nodded in response. It was the least Lily could do considering Kate wouldn't allow Lily to pay rent. And Lily knew finances were tight for her sister. Gen paid Kate a generous amount as her salon manager, but even a generous amount didn't go far in Whisling, especially since Kate had a cute two-bedroom condo to make payments on. Lily had thought about crashing with her parents instead, but Kate had insisted, and Lily had felt right about the move in the moment.

But two months later, Lily knew she could no longer rely on her sister's help. She needed to go home. In the meantime, she'd continue making meals for Kate every night so that Kate didn't have to spend money on the take-out places she frequented when Lily wasn't around.

"It was an easy one," Lily said, realizing she needed to stir the stew again. Beef stew was a comfort food for Lily, and if she was going to win her husband back tonight, she needed some comfort food in her belly.

Lily hurried over to the white stove where the stew bubbled away in a sterling silver pot and mixed it while Kate went back to her room to change. Kate hated being in her business attire any longer than absolutely necessary. Lily was pretty sure Kate would live in sweatpants if she could.

Sure enough, Kate emerged from her room in a pair of sweatpants and an oversized, baggy T a moment later.

"How was work?" Lily asked as she served Kate, herself, and Amelia a bowl of stew. She then broke off a piece of the crusty bread she'd baked earlier that afternoon and placed it on top of their stews. They all enjoyed dunking their bread, so there was no need for an extra plate.

"It went well. No big hiccups with scheduling. We did run out of Mrs. Hellman's favorite conditioner, and there might've been a bit of a fit thrown because of it," Kate said as she leaned against one of her light, pinewood cabinets.

Lily suppressed a chuckle. She knew it wasn't fair to laugh at Kate, yet Mrs. Hellman really did throw some epically tragic but hilarious fits when she didn't get her way. She was infamous for them.

"Go ahead and laugh. I did. As soon as she left the salon," Kate said, and Lily gave in to her laughter.

When Lily continued to laugh, Kate said, "Okay, it wasn't that funny."

Lily bit her lip in order to stop laughing, and Kate walked to the counter to grab her bowl of stew. She took her stew to the small white table that served as both a kitchen eating space and a dining table, and then she sat before looking up at Lily.

"What?" Lily asked as Kate stared at her. They'd been sisters for nearly thirty years. There wasn't a look that Kate gave that Lily didn't understand. And this one was her stalling face. Kate had something to say but didn't want to say it.

"Maybe we should wait until after Amelia's in bed?" Kate said as she looked toward the living room where Amelia was playing happily with her blocks.

Lily followed Kate's gaze and realized Allen had yet to see Amelia pull herself up to stand and grab a block from the couch, the way she was doing now. The last time he'd seen her, she'd been confined to the ground, crawling well but without enough leg strength to stand. In the past two months, Amelia had changed so much that she was now nearly walking. She'd taken a few tentative steps the other day, much to Lily's glee. But Allen hadn't seen any of it.

He had missed out on so much, including Amelia's first birthday. That was something Lily had been sure Allen would attend. But he'd texted the night before, telling Lily he was in too much pain and couldn't bear for Amelia to see him like that. And Lily had understood. She really had.

So she and Kate had put together a last minute, once-in-a-lifetime outing to Seattle for Lily's dear, sweet daughter. They'd been planning on a simple picnic at a park on Whisling—low-key for Allen's sake—before he'd bailed. But since Amelia would be missing her dad on her special day, Lily felt the need to make up for his absence. It had been a day full of too many sweets and so many hours at Amelia's favorite play place. Amelia had loved it.

Lily had been sure that after missing Amelia's actual birthday, in the next day or so Allen would be demanding to see his newly one-year-old daughter. But he hadn't.

And for what? Lily got that Allen was upset with her. She even understood why he didn't want to see her. Who wanted to see the person responsible for their paralysis? But to not want to see Amelia? That wasn't like Allen at all. Granted, holding something against Lily wasn't like him either. But then again, Lily had never done anything like this.

Part of her ached at the thought that Allen might never be able to forgive her. And then what? But she couldn't stop fighting for him. He might not want her, but she knew deep down he needed her. And that would be enough until he forgave her. Or if he couldn't do that, it would just have to be enough.

"I was actually hoping to go to my house after Amelia went to sleep tonight," Lily said, feeling even more resolve to do what she had to that evening.

Kate's spoon stopped on her way to her mouth, pausing in the air, her lips drawn down and her face full of pity.

"Um, Lily," Kate said at the same time Lily's phone beeped with the signal of a new text message.

"Can I get this?" Lily asked. Kate seemed unsure, so Lily just glanced at her phone that was on the butcher block countertop beside her instead of picking it up.

Allen. Her heart leapt when she saw his name. He was reaching out to her!

Had he felt as strongly as she had that this was their day to reunite? She wouldn't be surprised. She and Allen had always had such a deep connection. She often felt what he felt and vice versa.

"It's Allen," Lily said excitedly as she unlocked her phone so that she could read the message.

"Wait, Lily," Kate said, but her voice suddenly sounded far away as Lily read Allen's message.

Lily felt her body go limp, and her phone clanked against the white tile flooring in Kate's kitchen.

"Lily," Kate called out as she ran to Lily's side and helped her sister to the couch.

As Lily sat, she was somewhat aware that tears were streaming down Kate's face. But she couldn't acknowledge them as her mind was too full of the information Allen had just sent ... in a text message. The man was leaving her, and he hadn't even had the decency to call.

Lily swallowed, trying to get past the lump in her throat. Her body felt foreign to her as it swirled with emotions of betrayal, anger, and oh so much sadness. But she somehow felt hollow at the same time.

Allen is leaving me. He was moving back home to Alabama with his mom and leaving the house to Lily. He'd had the audacity to tell her that he would continue to pay the rent for the foreseeable future. Allen was going to pay the rent? With what money? Lily and Allen had lived from paycheck to paycheck, and Allen no longer had a job. Lily knew just who would be footing that bill: the same woman who'd probably talked Allen into leaving Lily.

Suddenly anger became Lily's winning emotion.

"He can't leave me," Lily said forcefully, and even Amelia looked up from where she stood next to where Lily sat on the couch. "I was going to win him back. I'm going to win him back. I just need to get there in time. Can you feed Amelia her stew?" Lily asked as she moved to stand, her thoughts going too fast for her to keep up with. "I've got to get to the house before he leaves ..."

"He's gone," Kate said quietly, and Lily felt as if an actual tangible object had torn her anger away.

"What?" Lily asked as she fell back against the pillows of the couch. With anger gone, all Lily was left with were betrayal and sadness, and neither gave her any kind of strength.

"That's what I was going to tell you. Carly Ashburn saw Allen and his mom boarding the ferry early this morning. Each had enough luggage with them to last months." Kate said the words Lily didn't want to hear, and Lily was willing to bet Kate didn't want to say them.

"Carly?" Lily asked.

There were tons of gossips on the island, but Carly wasn't one of them. She'd been Kate's good friend for years and wouldn't have made the story more salacious just for her own entertainment. If Carly had seen lots of luggage, there had to have been lots of luggage. Carly wouldn't have lied or even exaggerated.

"She didn't want to call me with the news, so she came straight to the salon after she got back to Whisling this afternoon. She promised me she didn't tell another soul the news."

That didn't matter to Lily. Who cared who knew that Allen had left her. All Lily cared about was that Allen *had* left her. She did feel a small tinge of gratitude to both Carly and Kate for trying to save her standing in the community, but Lily's reputation wasn't what was really in danger. Lily was.

Lily felt tears begin to pour down her cheeks as reality set in. Allen had left her. He had left the island. He had left Amelia. He had left Lily.

HER HUSBAND HAD LEFT HER.

But somehow Lily had found a new normal. She'd decided to stay with Kate. Thankfully, Gen's maternity leave was up, so Lily was back to her babysitting gig a full three days a week again. During the past couple of months, she'd been helping Gen out here and there, taking Maddie on some days when Gen felt overwhelmed. But nothing was quite as satisfying as doing her full job again. Watching three little girls ages three and under was harrowing at times, but Lily wouldn't have it any other way. She was typically so busy during the days when she had Gen's girls that she didn't even have time to think about Allen. Okay, that was a lie. Lily never stopped thinking about Allen, but she was too busy to wallow.

Gen had only gone back to work three days a week, but she still paid Lily the amount a full-time nanny would get. Lily had tried to argue with Gen that the payment was too much, but Gen had countered that she paid all of her employees well, and Lily had the most important job of all. Of course Gen had to compensate her the best. Lily would've argued more, but she really needed the money.

Lily had insisted that if she was going to stay with Kate, she pay half of Kate's mortgage. Especially because Lily wasn't just living with Kate; she was working out of Kate's home. The mortgage wasn't cheap. And neither were diapers, food, and the clothes Amelia was constantly growing out of.

Allen sent a check to Lily every week since she'd called him and left a message with the news that she wouldn't be keeping their bungalow.

The day after that initial text that Allen was leaving her, Kate, Kevin, and Lily's mom and dad had gone to pack up everything left in the home she'd shared with Allen. Kate had somehow shown back up at her condo with everything Lily would need for the foreseeable future, and the rest of it had been stored at her parents' home a few blocks away. Her family had been her salvation.

But Lily had yet to cash a single check from Allen. She couldn't do it. It felt like giving in, like telling Allen she was okay with this new arrangement. And she sure as hell wasn't. The checks felt like what happened after a divorce settlement. And Lily wasn't getting divorced. She was mad as a ticked off hornet that Allen had left her, but all that anger wasn't enough for Lily to give up on them. Nothing would be.

"Lily," Maddie called loudly from outside of Kate's condo, and Lily went to open the door. It was best to let Maddie in immediately or else she'd ask Lily the rest of the morning why she hadn't been ready for her to come and play. It was cute but got annoying after the first half hour or so.

"Hi, Lily," Maddie said happily, pulling Lily out of her melancholy thoughts. Money was tight, Allen was gone for now, but Lily was managing. All with a broken heart.

"Hi, Maddie," Lily said as Maddie went straight for the

kiddie kitchen Gen had brought over when Lily had decided she was going to stay with Kate.

"Oh hi, Amelia," Maddie said belatedly to Amelia who still sat in her high chair, finishing off the pieces of toast and blueberries Lily had served her for breakfast.

"Hey, Lil," Gen said as she came in, holding a napping Cami in her car seat. The baby loved her car rides, and that was often the only way she fell asleep. Lily tried to plan a longer car ride each day just in case she had a hard time getting Cami to sleep any other way.

"She hasn't really been up today. We took her straight from her bassinet to the car. Her diaper will probably need to be changed as soon as she wakes up and—"

"She'll need her bottle. I've got you covered, Gen," Lily said with what she was sure was a tired-looking smile. But tired-looking was as good as it got for Lily these days.

"Did you talk to Allen?" Gen asked, and Lily nodded.

That was another knife to Lily's gut. After she'd left that initial voice message, Allen now took her calls with ease. And he was seemingly unaffected by Lily's tears. He would listen to her cry and then try to get to the crux of the matter of why she'd called. Yesterday it had been because of an issue with their car insurance. Allen had assured Lily he would take care of it and then ended the call, all without a single ounce of emotion. The same way every other call had been. He'd even listened to her beg for him back, responding emotionlessly that this was what had to be done.

"The car insurance stuff will be taken care of," Lily said, trying to keep the level voice Allen had.

"Well, that's good, right?" Gen said. Bless her for trying to look on the bright side. But there was no bright side for Lily anymore. Besides Amelia, Maddie, and Cami.

"I guess." Lily dropped her eyes to the carpet. "I should've gone after him a day earlier. One day and I might've been able to talk him out of it."

Lily had gone over and over the timing of it all. How cruel it had been. But the honesty had hit her in the gut. Allen would've left her anyway. She knew the man well enough. He wouldn't have been dissuaded by a mere conversation or even by Lily fighting against him. But that didn't make the irony of the timing any easier.

"Let me pay for your ticket to go out and see him," Gen pleaded with Lily. "We can call it a bonus."

Gen knew Lily ached to go after Allen. To plead with him to come home in person. But Lily couldn't afford a plane ticket. Not with all of her newfound expenses. She knew she could always cash one of Allen's checks, but that didn't seem right either. Nothing seemed right, and everything was hard these days.

"Maybe one day," Lily said, and Gen nodded, seeming to understand that Lily needed more time to plan if she was indeed going to go after Allen. Allen seemed to be too okay without them. Going to Alabama would be a last ditch effort, a hail Mary. And Lily didn't want to use her hail Mary too soon.

Gen gave Lily a quick hug and then turned to go out the door, closing it behind her.

"So, what are we going to do today?" Lily asked Maddie, Amelia, and Cami once Gen had gone. She tried to sound as happy as these sweet little girls helped her to feel. But it was hard for Lily to show her happiness these days because all of her emotions felt muted by the overwhelming depression that Allen's absence held over her.

But this was Lily's life now, and she had to accept it.

CHAPTER THIRTEEN

"I'M STARVING," James said as Bess's kids, Jana, and Jon all piled into her kitchen. They'd squeezed into one car for Sunday dinner that week and, therefore, descended on Bess all at one time. Not that she minded. Bess adored Sunday dinners as a family and had actually looked forward to seeing Jon as much as she'd looked forward to seeing her children. Which, considering how much she missed her children and the fact that she'd seen Jon on their date just the evening before, was no small thing.

"You're always starving," Lindsey said as she surveyed the food offerings.

Bess had gone with some carne asada fajitas that evening. Stephen had recently told her that Jana's favorite kind of food was Mexican, and since Bess was trying to expand her cooking horizons, she figured this was a good way to challenge herself. Besides, with Jana and Stephen officially setting a wedding date for October, Bess figured this was a good way to butter up her future daughter-in-law.

Lindsey swiped a yellow pepper slice from the frying pan full of meats and veggies that Bess had just turned off.

Bess swatted at Lindsey's hand, warning the rest of her

family away from picking at their dinner, and Lindsey hopped out of Bess's reach.

"Oh, Mom. You nailed fajitas too," Lindsey said as Jana began to fill glasses with ice and the rest of the family helped to set the table.

"Really?" Bess asked, feeling weirdly self-conscious about her cooking for the first time in a while. The kitchen was the place she felt most at ease, but Tex-Mex fare wasn't her specialty. Sure she'd cooked it before, but she was no expert.

"Really," Lindsey said as she moved toward the pan again. But Bess's glare caused Lindsey to change her direction.

Soon they were all seated at their meal and everyone, including Jana, sang Bess's praises. After Bess took her first bite of tortilla stuffed with carne asada, peppers, onions, avocado, sour cream, and cheese, she had to agree with her family. She might even think about making this meal a special on the truck.

The family, especially Bess's guys, scarfed down the food, and before she knew it, Stephen and Jana were cleaning the dishes as Jon, Lindsey, and James cleared off the table and cleaned the countertops. Jon had insisted that Bess relax after making their meal and had rallied the troops to get the work done.

Bess smiled from her spot on the couch as she listened to her family. Things were going well with Jon. Really well. They had started really kissing again, and if Bess was honest, it had been hard to send him home last night. But she had. Even though she and Jon had shared more than just kissing in their past, Bess wasn't ready for that huge step yet. She wouldn't be until she and Jon were back together for good. Married.

Bess felt her eyes go wide with that thought. This was the first time Bess had thought about that word in association with Jon since their divorce. Would she get remarried to Jon? It felt silly to remarry the same man—she could imagine the way Deb would've ridiculed any other woman who'd done the same—but if she and Jon were going to be in it for the long haul, they would have to get remarried. Bess couldn't see herself in a long-term relationship if it didn't end in marriage.

So marriage was the end goal. It felt good for Bess to finally put a word to where she wanted her relationship with Jon to go. Because she loved him. There was no mistaking that. After beginning to date Jon again, it had been easy to see that the love she'd had for him had never gone anywhere. It had maybe been buried a little deeper, and it had been hurt, but it was there. These months of dating had reignited that love, and she felt it growing stronger each day. But Bess still felt a ways off from being *in* love with Jon and actually marrying him again, even if that was her end goal. Having love for Jon hadn't been the issue for Bess. Trusting him had been. And it still was.

She was pretty sure her trust was being restored, but it felt weak at best. However, she was working on it, hard as it may be. And it wasn't like she'd been perfect in everything. She remembered her last interaction with Dax. Part of building their trust again would be telling Jon the whole truth behind what she'd felt for Dax. She knew she needed to trust in Jon completely, trusting him enough to tell him all of her truths, if they were going to succeed. And if she wasn't willing to put the work into trusting him again, well, she might as well give up on them now. But Bess didn't want to do that.

"Hey there," Jon said as he took the seat beside Bess and then put an arm around her shoulders. Her heart flipped at Jon's touch, the one that used to be so natural, it was second nature.

"So this is what it's like now?" Lindsey asked as she joined them in the living room and sat on the other leg of the sectional couch.

"What's like what now?" James asked as he joined his sister.

Lindsey looked from the arm behind Bess's back to her brother.

"Oh," James said, and Bess wondered if they needed to explain what was going on to their children.

Things had been so tentative between her and Jon for such a long time. And then Bess had wanted to take things slowly. But now, although things were still going slow, they were moving forward to a good place. These past few weeks with Jon had been full of meaningful conversations about their past and their future, leaving Bess hopeful. They'd also been full of so much fun.

Remembering the way she'd looked forward to seeing Jon at their family dinner also told Bess a lot. Her feelings had grown for her ex-husband, and maybe it was time to tell their children.

"Your dad and I—" Bess began to explain before being interrupted by a chorus of, "No, no, no," from all three of her kids.

"What?" Bess asked, looking from Lindsey to James and then to Stephen, as he and Jana joined them in the living room, sharing a single armchair together.

"You guys are dating again. That much is obvious. Besides that, I don't need to know anything," Lindsey said, her face puckered in disgust. Her brothers nodded in agreement.

Okay. Well, that was easier than expected. And Bess was all too willing to take the easy way out for once since all of her children seemed just fine with the situation between herself and Jon. Satisfied, Bess leaned into Jon, loving the feeling of her family all around her once again.

"I will take credit for this though," Stephen said, looking between his mom and dad with a cocky raise of his eyebrows.

Bess felt Jon stiffen next to her, and she wondered what had caused Jon's reaction.

"If I hadn't told Dad about that guy from next door, he

would've never gotten up the nerve to ask Mom out," Stephen said, and Bess felt her own spine go straight.

What? Jon had only pursued Bess after hearing about Dax? After being jealous? Bess knew that alone shouldn't cause her hackles to raise in the way they had, so she tried to really think things through. Sure, it would've been nice if Jon had acted of his own accord, but that wasn't what was bugging Bess.

Jon had only asked Bess out after being jealous over her date with Dax, and yet he'd said nothing to Bess about that. In fact, she remembered an exact conversation when she'd asked what had prompted Jon to go beyond just saying he would always care about her to really pushing for that second chance and asking her out on Valentine's day. Jon had told her he just couldn't stand another moment without her. That was what had driven him to beg for her to give them another chance. Nothing about jealousy. Nothing about Dax.

She swallowed, willing the turning of her stomach to calm. Was she overreacting?

"Bess," Jon whispered, but Bess refused to respond. She couldn't until she thought things through. She needed more time.

Bess stood suddenly. "Is there time for dessert?" she asked, knowing she had some tiramisu in her fridge. She hadn't planned on having it for dessert because their meals usually took until the time they had to return to the ferry, but she had to do something so that she could escape the living room. She couldn't remain under Jon's arm like everything was okay. Her tenuous trust had evaporated. Jon had lied. That was the big problem. A lie of omission was still a breach of trust. Maybe it wasn't about something important to him, but at this point, any lie was a deal breaker for Bess.

She swallowed back her pain as she waited for her children

to respond. For the first time ever, the ferry couldn't come soon enough. She needed them all out of her house.

"I don't think we have enough time," Lindsey said as she looked at her watch.

"But we could always take it to go," James offered, and Bess tried to smile. She wondered what her expression looked like, considering her thoughts were so harried.

"I'll get it ready," Bess said as she went into the kitchen and took the tiramisu out of the fridge. She found a disposable tray and five plastic forks.

As she moved the tiramisu into the throwaway container, she felt a presence with her in the kitchen and knew that it was Jon.

"Not now," Bess whispered before Jon could say anything.

"Bess, I didn't mean—" Jon began.

"Not now," Bess reiterated as strongly as she could. She would not hash this out in front of their children.

Bess handed Jon the container and the forks.

"Thank you for dinner," Jon said, and he looked like he was going to move in to make some kind of physical contact. But Bess pinned him with a killer glare that Jon knew better than to ignore.

"Yeah, thanks Mom," Stephen said as he walked through the kitchen and toward the front foyer, thankfully oblivious to the tension in the kitchen.

Bess followed Stephen into the foyer where she gave each of her kids and Jana big hugs, continuing to ignore Jon. She couldn't even look at him. How could he lie? Sure, it wasn't a big thing, but that was why the lie had been so unnecessary.

"Jana and I can't make it next week," Stephen said, and Bess nodded. She typically took the news that her kids would be missing Sunday dinners hard, but tonight was the exception. She had already been hit too hard for anything else to register.

"Got it," Bess said, and Stephen gave her a look that said he knew she was trying to put on a brave front. Which Bess was. Just not about what Stephen was thinking.

"I'll be here," James said, and Bess genuinely grinned. She couldn't stay too upset when her kids were with her.

"Me too. Even if my hand is still hurting from where you swatted me," Lindsey said with a teasing smile.

"I didn't even touch you," Bess said, remembering that she'd missed said swat.

Lindsey nodded. "But it was the thought that hurt, Mom. You wanted to hit me," Lindsey said with a sassy tilt of her head, and she had to jump out of the way in order to keep Bess from swatting her once again.

"See, that hurts," Lindsey said as she giggled, running toward the car. The boys and Jana followed, leaving Bess with Jon.

"You need to go," Bess said without looking at Jon, her attention still out the door where her kids were piling into Stephen's car. Probably because Jon had bought that stupid truck, and all five of them couldn't fit in the truck's cab.

"Bess, please—"

"Why did you buy the truck, Jon? Midlife crisis?" Bess asked. It was something that had been bothering her, but she'd told herself she was making a mountain out of a molehill. Now Bess wondered if she had been. Had she ignored her better sense again, just to be blindsided? Well yeah she had, considering how she felt about the news that Jon had lied.

"It's just a truck, Bess," Jon said as he rubbed his hands over his face. As if *he* was frustrated. Where did he get off being frustrated?

"It's a huge purchase unlike anything you've bought before," Bess said as the car's horn blared. She knew her kids were just being playful. They couldn't have any idea that the conversation between Bess and Jon had turned so serious.

"I've been wanting one for awhile...."

"Why not tell me then? If you've had it on your mind for a while."

"You weren't around, Bess."

Bess stepped back. The accusation in Jon's words was easy to hear, as if her absence in his life was her fault. As if she'd been the one to choose their circumstances. It would've hurt less for Jon to have slapped her.

"That isn't what I meant. I know why you weren't there. It was all my fault."

Jon was saying the right thing, but for the first time in some months, Bess was doubting Jon's words.

"So all thoughts of a truck only came after you moved out? You never thought about it while we were together?" Bess asked, needing to finish the conversation about the truck before moving on to why she was no longer trusting Jon's words.

"I did. I mean, I guess I always wanted a truck. But it wasn't practical with three kids," Jon said.

"And you never said a word to me," Bess said.

"You told me about every wish you had?" Jon asked, his arms crossed over his chest as if he was trying to hold back the emotions he was feeling towards Bess. But that was the problem. He needed to let those emotions out. He needed to let Bess in. This had been their initial problem, and nothing had gotten better. Not even an affair, a divorce, living in different zip codes, and starting to date again had helped. Could anything help?

"No, I didn't," Bess said, thinking about the food truck. "You would've laughed at my dream."

Jon took a step back, his eyes narrowing. "Do you really think that?"

Bess nodded. "I'm sure of it." Bess thought about the man she'd been married to. He would've chuckled and then told her there was no need for her to take such a big risk. He had a great income, so she could just focus on her charity work.

"You'd better go," Bess said, knowing Jon and her kids would need to race to the dock or they'd miss the ferry. "And don't get mad at Stephen for saying anything about Dax tonight. This isn't his fault."

"I know how to treat our children, Bess," Jon said with an exasperated sigh.

"Great," Bess said with far too much sarcasm.

Jon turned and walked out the door.

Bess closed the door immediately behind him, not even waiting for him to get to the car. It was unheard of for Bess not to wave her children off until they were all the way down the street, but she had to close the door on Jon. She needed him out.

She leaned her back against the closed door, refusing to cry. She'd already cried so many tears for this one man, for this one stupid relationship. Only to have Jon shatter her trust once again.

She drew in a deep breath. Was she being too hard on Jon?

Bess shrugged as an answer to her own question. Maybe. Maybe not. That was the hard part of having so much history. She and Jon had this whole past they were trying to move beyond, but it would always be there. Them saying it was a fresh start didn't do much.

Bess thought about what she *did* know, and she knew this much to be true. She no longer trusted Jon ... again. Putting together a shattered trust had been nearly impossible the first time. Bess was almost certain the tiny fragments were now too small to ever assemble again.

CHAPTER FOURTEEN

THERE SHOULD BE classes for days like this. Some kind of prep. She was going on her first date since her junior year of high school. Where did she even begin to prepare?

But her girls thought it was one, big, wonderful adventure, so for that, Olivia was grateful. While Olivia was busy trying to bite her professionally polished nails—something she hadn't done since she'd been married to Bart—Rachel was scanning through Olivia's closet for the perfect date night dress, and Pearl had strewn Olivia's eyeshadow palettes all over their bathroom counter, helping her mother perfect a makeup look. Olivia guessed she should blame YouTube for her daughters' extensive knowledge about all things fashion and makeup. She had been a terrible example in those two arenas ever since she'd left Bart, and she didn't feel the least bit sorry about it. She wanted both of her girls to know their worth didn't come from an item of clothing, the best skincare, or even because they were beautiful. They were both worth more than they could ever imagine just because they were children of God.

But Olivia figured it was fine and dandy to dress up and feel pretty every once in a while. And for her, tonight was that night.

"You aren't going to wear black, are you, Mom?" Rachel asked as she stood in front of Olivia's selection of four dresses, three of which were black. Olivia had down-sized her wardrobe to about a twentieth of what it used to be.

"Um ..." Olivia said as she joined Rachel in her bedroom.

"Do you remember the pink dress with the tutu skirt, Mom?" Rachel asked, her eyes lit up by the memory as Olivia smiled with her daughter. Olivia had loved that dress as well. It wasn't exactly a tutu skirt, but she could understand why Rachel, who had to have been about five at the time Olivia had worn it, would've thought so. She remembered the day she bought it, thinking she would finally knock Bart's socks off. She had never worn anything like it, and when she'd slipped it on before the charity dinner she and Bart were attending, Olivia had felt gorgeous. But Bart had come home moments before the event started, given Olivia a once-over, and then told her she looked like Rachel attempting to play dress-up. And it wasn't a good attempt. He'd demanded she change and even went so far as to throw away Olivia's dress. She felt hot tears prick her eyes as she remembered how worthless she'd felt that evening, hardly even able to hold her head up as she wore a navy blue dress that showed off her svelte figure.

Showing off his wife was all Bart had ever wanted to do with Olivia. As soon as she'd done her job for him in public, she'd been left home ... alone ... until the next time he needed her. It was a poor existence. Olivia had always been so sad, she'd hardly had the energy to be angry. But Bart had behaved deplorably, and Olivia had every right to be mad. So she took a few seconds to be mad for her poor past self, and then she moved on, ready to live her current, beautiful life to the fullest.

"I do," Olivia said, turning her attention back to her closet. "But I don't have it anymore."

Rachel scrunched her lips. "I know. You only have black stuff."

"To be fair, I usually only wear my dresses to work. Black makes sense," Olivia said, unsure of why she felt the need to defend her wardrobe choices to Rachel. But she did.

Rachel frowned as she tilted her head and examined Olivia's closet. "We'll make something work," Rachel muttered, and Olivia bit back a laugh.

"Mom!" Pearl called out from the bathroom all three of them shared.

"Go, go," Rachel said, shooing Olivia out of the room. "Take care of that face, and then we'll get back to this."

"Rachel, you better be channeling some crazy fashion lady, not the new Rachel," Olivia said, somewhat teasing but kind of a little scared that her daughter had become the girl who took clothing too seriously. "The dress will just wrap the body, which protects the soul. The soul is the important part, Rach."

Rachel nodded, appearing to understand Olivia's message. "I know. But I still like dresses a lot."

"That's fine. It's great even, Rach. I love that you love pretty clothes. But I need you to remember what's important," Olivia reiterated. Olivia knew all of the stats about girls who were raised by abusive men and the kind of men those poor girls tended to choose for themselves. The stats weren't in her girls' favor. So Olivia had to make sure everything else was. She wanted Pearl and Rachel to feel so loved now that they would feel a gaping hole in the future if they ever dated an abusive man. They would know immediately that something wasn't right. And for that, they had to know their worth. Where it came from. What it made them: incredible.

"I do, Mom. I promise," Rachel said, and then she shooed Olivia right on out of her own tiny bedroom.

Everything about Olivia's bungalow was tiny, but she still

loved it. Maybe because she personally brought home the paycheck that paid for everything they had in their lives these days. Or maybe she loved it because the home was full of love and kindness, along with the occasional argument. It felt nothing like the arctic environment that pervaded Bart's home. Either way, this bungalow was her and her girls' home, and she was grateful for it.

Olivia moved from her tiny bedroom down the short, white hall to their tiny bathroom. All the walls in the bungalow were a bright white. Olivia loved the brightness, and the white helped the space to not appear so small, along with the many mirrors she had used to decorate.

As Olivia joined Pearl in front of the countertop that was mostly just sink, she knew this space was all they needed. They had a few drawers under the sink, along with a cabinet where she kept her cleaning supplies. The toilet sat immediately to the right of the sink, and the shower/bath combo was right next to the toilet. Olivia liked to joke that she could literally do anything she needed in the bathroom, all while seated on the toilet. But the room functioned, and it was cute.

Olivia wondered what Dean would feel about the picture she'd put up behind the toilet of a gray bear in a purple tutu. She smiled. She doubted her landlord would agree with most of her cutesy decorating touches, but she liked that their little house reflected that it was the home of three girls. And she knew Dean wouldn't mind. He loved that Olivia had made the place her own. He was really the best kind of person.

"Mom, stop daydreaming and let's do your makeup. Grandma will be here any minute," Pearl said in a bossy tone that was unlike her at all, and Olivia took a step back, banging into the wall behind her.

Pearl must've noticed that she'd startled her mom because her fierce drill sergeant look immediately became apologetic.

"Sorry, Mom. I'm just worried about tonight. It's our first date," Pearl said, and Olivia leaned down to give her adorable daughter a huge hug.

Olivia's date was why Pearl and Rachel were so on edge? But then again, it made sense that they considered this a first date for all of them. This was a huge step in all three of their lives. And if things worked out with Dean's friend, Noah, it would be a change for all of them. She now understood the girls' weird moods and called Rachel into the bathroom.

"You two know this is just a first date," Olivia said as she took a girl in each of her arms.

Pearl nodded.

"But a first date could lead to a second date and then a third and a fourth," Rachel said.

This time Olivia nodded. "And this is a man Dean likes. Dean is the best kind of guy, right? You said that."

Had Olivia said that to her girls? She guessed she could've. Dean had been so good to all of them, Olivia may have said that any of the numerous times he'd helped them or saved them.

"He is," Olivia said honestly.

"So if Dean likes Noah, he is probably the best kind of guy too, right?" Rachel asked.

Her logic made sense.

"He could be," Olivia said, refusing to raise the hopes of her daughters or herself.

"This date is a big deal, Mom," Rachel said, and suddenly all of the butterflies that had taken a brief intermission while Olivia talked with her girls came back in full force.

Olivia smiled, trying to ignore the flurry in her belly. "You girls are the best, you know that?"

Rachel nodded, and Pearl smiled.

"But I think it's time Mom got ready on her own."

"But I found the perfect slacks and top combination...." Rachel began, but Olivia shook her head.

"You girls have given me the confidence boost I needed, but this is a momma task." Olivia used the phrase she'd coined whenever she had to do anything on her own. With their family just being the three of them, sometimes the girls wanted to stand by Olivia's side to do tasks that were too adultish for them. So she had to protect her daughters. She realized that now was one of those moments. Both of her girls were too invested in this date. They needed to take a step back, realize it wasn't a big deal. And know that possibly nothing would come of this night.

"This could be just a first date, you know," Olivia said.

"Why wouldn't he ask you on a second date?" Pearl asked with wide eyes, her little hand placed adorably on her chest.

"Maybe we don't click. Maybe he has a huge wart on the end of his nose," Olivia said to make her girls laugh. A huge wart would not be a deal breaker in Olivia's book. At least not anymore. But the sentence had the desired effect, and the girls laughed as they walked down the short hall into their main living space.

"Dean wouldn't pick a guy with a big wart on his nose," Rachel said with confidence.

"Maybe he would. If he's really nice," Pearl said.

But then the conversation moved on to what the girls wanted to do with their grandma that evening, leaving Olivia very alone in her thoughts. Noah *was* a guy Dean liked. The girls were right. That put more pressure on this date. What if she ruined it?

However, she talked some quick sense into herself. She couldn't ruin it by choosing the wrong outfit or by not doing her makeup well. If she did, she wasn't really ruining anything because that was not the type of guy she wanted.

So Olivia quickly dressed in one of her black dresses, which was sleeveless and fairly form fitting. She paired it with a turquoise sweater, hoping the color would appease Rachel and knowing she'd need some sort of cover-up. The island still got pretty chilly in the evenings, even in May.

Olivia finished a simple makeup look that she liked because it felt natural, unlike the makeup looks Bart would ask her to do. He loved really smoky eyes, heavy lip liner, and even heavy blush and bronzer. Basically anything to make Olivia look less like Olivia.

But the light dusting of coral eyeshadow that really made Olivia's blue eyes pop felt like the right move, especially since the bright color matched her bright sweater well. The rest of her makeup was much more subdued, and Olivia basically looked just like Olivia with a little more color.

Olivia completed her look by putting her dark red hair up in an easy French twist. Elegant but simple. And she was ready to go.

She heard a knock on her door and knew her mom had arrived. This was it. Olivia was going on her first date as an adult.

She swallowed back the fear she suddenly felt rise up within, the terror at letting a man anywhere near her life again. The move had stung her so badly the first time, it was no wonder she might not feel ready to do it again.

But she could do this. She would move on. For herself but also to show her girls just how powerful their mother was. Olivia could face down this fear and any other as well. She was strong, intelligent, and deserved good things in life.

Olivia closed her eyes as she heard her daughters let in her mom. Bart had undone all of the good her parents had done while Olivia was growing up. The man who'd promised in front of God and many family members and friends to be the one to protect and cherish her had made it his life's mission to bring

Olivia down. And she'd fallen. So much so that believing she was anything good, even over a year after Bart had been out of her life, was really, really hard.

But she could do it.

"I HAD A GREAT TIME," Noah said in his deep voice that Olivia found attractive as he walked her to her car. They'd met at a quaint seafood restaurant on The Drive, Olivia's suggestion. Noah had wanted to pick her up from her home, but Olivia didn't want her girls to even see Noah yet. Maybe it was a bit too protective, but she needed to keep a barrier up with this and any first date. She would hopefully let it down one day, but only when she was good and ready. And only when the man proved himself worthy of Olivia and her girls.

"I did too," Olivia responded to Noah honestly. She really had.

She hadn't been so sure when she'd walked into the restaurant and seen how good looking Noah was. Part of her had wanted to turn around and pretend she was sick. But before she could back out, Noah made eye contact, a look of recognition in his eyes. Her red hair was probably a dead giveaway. Olivia warily took in Noah's broad shoulders and his thick black hair. He had intelligent brown eyes that also made her crave dark chocolate. Basically he was yummy, and Olivia was unsure.

But their conversation was stimulating. Noah asked her about growing up on the island and then answered her questions in a way that was open and refreshing. They spoke about their dream vacation destinations and even delved a bit into religion, dangerous but necessary in Olivia's book. Bart hadn't believed in any kind of higher being, and Olivia felt that made him think he was the highest being in his world. Olivia wouldn't endure a man like that again. Fortunately, even though Noah wasn't exactly religious, he believed in God and he believed in goodness. For now, that was enough.

Now the evening was done, and it had gone too fast. Who would've thought that Olivia would enjoy herself enough that she'd want their time together to go on?

Olivia's stomach tumbled in anticipation when Noah took her hand as they both stood in front of the open door of her car.

"We should do it again," Noah said, his gaze on where he'd clasped Olivia's hand, and Olivia smiled.

"Was that lame?" Noah asked, raising his eyes to meet hers. "I did mention I was out of practice, right?"

Olivia giggled. She actually giggled. What was going on with her? But she loved how Noah was just as nervous as she was, even though he had no reason to be. He was practically a Greek God in looks but a sweet Labrador in demeanor. A dream man for any woman, right?

Olivia nodded, reassuring Noah, because she understood. Noah had also been in a long term relationship for many years and had just gotten out of it the year before. So he hadn't had quite the dating hiatus Olivia had, but it was close. And though they had bumbled through this date together, Olivia had had a wonderful time.

"We *should* do this again," Olivia said, feeling an inner confidence she'd been lacking for a long time.

"Good," Noah said with a broad smile that showed all of his perfectly white teeth. Seriously, how was this man still single?

"Maybe next weekend?" Noah asked hopefully.

Olivia nodded. She was actually wishing to see Noah again even sooner but knew life would come at her full force on Monday. Waiting until next weekend was the smart thing to do.

Noah let his thumb trail over each of Olivia's fingers, and she felt her breath hitch in excitement.

"I could come to Seattle," Olivia offered.

"Sure, if you want. Or I can come here. I love your island," Noah said sincerely.

"I wish I could lay claim to all of it. But I just rent a tiny piece of this paradise," Olivia said, hoping that Noah wouldn't be turned off that Olivia had so little to her name, even though she was well into her thirties. But it was the truth, and Noah needed to know the truth.

"Just a tiny piece is all I would need. Besides, any part of paradise is better than spending sixteen hours a day in an office," Noah said flippantly, as if working for sixteen hours straight wasn't a big deal.

And there it was. He had to have a fatal flaw, right? Noah had just been too good to be true.

"Workaholic?" Olivia asked, her heart dropping. It wouldn't be a deal breaker if he was, but Olivia would be lying if she said she didn't feel concern.

"More like the way I self-medicated after my breakup," Noah said as he leaned against Olivia's open door, still holding her hand.

Olivia nodded, her heart feeling a bit of hope. She could understand that. If it hadn't been for her girls, she wasn't sure how she would've dealt with her divorce. Even with her girls, she hadn't handled everything in the way she should've.

"I'm trying to cut back my hours. But my clients have gotten used to me being in the office any time they need me," Noah said with a laugh.

Olivia swallowed. She knew that kind of work. It was the kind of work Bart had done. But she wasn't going to run at the first sign of trouble. Noah had proven he wasn't a man like Bart in most ways. Olivia would give him the benefit of the doubt here. But she was going to do a bit more digging.

"Be honest. How many emergency phone calls have you

received since arriving at dinner?" Olivia remembered that the very few times she and Bart had actually gone on dates, he'd often been outside of the restaurant taking those emergency calls.

"Honestly ..." Noah paused as he met Olivia's eyes. "I don't know. I haven't checked my phone. But it has been buzzing quite a bit," he said with a laugh.

Olivia couldn't laugh. She was too touched. Noah had ignored important people. For her.

"I've scared you, haven't I?" Noah asked.

Olivia wasn't sure how to respond. He hadn't scared her in the way he thought, but was she ready to reveal so much about herself?

"Not really scared. I just ... my ex made sure to let me know where I was on his list of priorities. And it was nowhere near the top. I feel like you've told me where I am on yours. And you owe me nothing," Olivia spilled before she could talk herself out of it.

"First off, I think I owe every human being common decency, especially one as charming, smart, and kind as you are. But second, yeah. The woman in my life is at the top of my list. It's the only way a relationship makes sense to me," Noah said. His brown eyes were so full of sincerity that Olivia couldn't help but believe him.

Noah pulled softly on Olivia's hand so that she took a step closer to him. "I really, really want to kiss you."

Olivia felt her stomach flip and her eyes went wide. No part of her didn't want the kiss Noah was offering, even if she was practically scared to tears.

"But ..." Noah dropped his head over Olivia's hand, his lips gently kissing it. Olivia's heart beat faster than was safe, and her whole core warmed.

"I'm trying to be patient. I have a feeling you are one woman worth waiting for," Noah said as he put his other hand to Olivia's waist and guided her into her car.

Are you sure you don't want to kiss me? Olivia wanted to ask. But she was in her car facing her steering wheel. The chance for a kiss was gone. At least for the night. She had a feeling she would have another opportunity soon. And boy was she looking forward to it.

"Drive safely, Olivia," Noah said as he leaned into her car and then pulled back, closing her door.

Olivia took a few deep breaths before even turning on her car. Olivia hadn't been so affected by a man in ... well, maybe Dean, but he didn't count. Dean was a class all of his own.

But Olivia hadn't realized another man could churn so many of her womanly feelings. She *really* liked Noah.

Olivia finally felt calm enough to reverse out of her space and start on her way home. The drive went by far too quickly as Olivia relived every part of her date, and she pulled into her driveway.

She grimaced when she saw that every light was still on in her bungalow. The clock read ten-thirty, well after the time her girls should be in bed. But she should've known her girls would be too excited to go to sleep before Olivia came home.

Olivia got out of her car and entered her home to a barrage of exclamations.

"How was your date, Mom?" Rachel asked at the same time Pearl called out, "Miss Charlotte got so mad at Dean, Mom!"

Olivia somehow also managed to hear her mom's apology that the girls were still up.

"First off, why are you two out of bed?" Olivia decided that was the most important thing to address. Her girls were rarely up after nine pm.

"Because of Miss Charlotte yelling," Rachel said as Pearl added with a grin, "And we want to hear about your date."

"We wanted to make Dean feel better, but Grandma said we had to wait until you came home before we could go see him," Rachel said.

Olivia looked to her mom, Kathryn, for clarification.

Kathryn gave a side-eyed glance at the girls before meeting Olivia's gaze, telling Olivia what Kathryn needed to say was better done in private.

"Okay, you two go brush your teeth and get ready for bed. We won't be seeing Dean tonight," Olivia declared to a chorus of moans and groans.

"But Mom, he's sad," Rachel said.

"Miss Charlotte said mean things," Pearl added.

"I'm sorry about that. I really am. But it's late, and you can see Dean tomorrow if he wants to see us. We might have to give him some space. Sometimes after people are mean to us, we want to be alone," Olivia said.

"Dean wants to see me," Pearl said, and her tone told Olivia there would be no way to talk her daughter out of that declaration.

"If you go get ready for bed, I'll come in and tell you about my date before you go to sleep," Olivia promised since she wasn't sure what else to say about Dean. Thankfully that was enough for her girls because they squealed as they ran down the hall. Thank goodness. But she knew the discussion about Dean wasn't over.

Olivia turned to her mom. "What happened?" she asked, feeling thoroughly confused. Charlotte and Dean had been dating for a long time, and Olivia hadn't heard either one of them yell, especially loud enough to be heard in her home.

"I couldn't pick up on everything because Dean never raised his voice, but I think he broke up with Charlotte," Kathryn said with a frown.

Olivia felt bombarded by emotions, but mostly she just felt

sorry for Dean and Charlotte. They had seemed so good together.

"Oh no. Why?" Olivia asked, even though she was pretty sure her mom wouldn't be able to answer that question.

Kathryn shrugged as she said, "But I do know that Charlotte wasn't happy about Dean's decision to break up with her. She may have said a few things not okay for sensitive ears," Kathryn said, looking down the hall toward the bathroom where the girls were brushing their teeth. "I tried to turn on the TV, but the girls weren't having it. They were worried about Dean, and it took everything in me to keep them inside."

"Thanks for that," Olivia said, imagining how badly things would've gone if her girls had appeared during Dean and Charlotte's breakup scene.

"One more thing. Charlotte mentioned you," Kathryn said reluctantly.

"What?" Olivia asked, her eyebrows raised in disbelief. "What about me?"

"She said Dean was breaking up with her because of you. Dean said something quietly that must've been along the lines of the fact that he was setting you up with another guy when Charlotte laughed a crazy laugh. She told him he'd only done it so that you could have another guy be your rebound and he could be your forever. She said he was waiting for you to be ready for him and using Charlotte in the meantime."

"Oh," Olivia said, putting a hand to her forehead. "The girls heard all of that?"

"I tried to talk over it, but probably."

Olivia groaned.

"I know the girls need to see him, but I'd just be careful going over there," Kathryn said.

Olivia nodded. She'd already been thinking Dean would

probably want to avoid her for a while after that kind of an embarrassing scene. But the question was, should she let him?

"Good night, Olivia," her mom said as she hugged her daughter and then went back to give her grandgirls hugs as well.

Olivia had a few more minutes to herself as the girls changed into their pajamas.

Dean was single. And so was Olivia. She knew she had feelings for him more than friendship, but then Noah came to her mind. He was a really good guy. And he didn't deserve the back burner while Olivia figured things out with Dean. She had to pick one or the other. And so far, Dean hadn't even thrown his hat in the ring. But Noah had. Didn't that make Olivia's decision clear? She had to give Noah a real chance. Dean was her friend, the way he'd always been. It didn't matter what Charlotte had said.

With that resolve, Olivia told the girls a bedtime-story-appropriate version of her date and then fell into her own bed, her dreams full of two tall, dark, and handsome men.

CHAPTER FIFTEEN

BESS RANG GEN'S doorbell with a smile on her face. She'd been surprised when Levi had called her, asking that she come watch the girls for a night. Gen and Levi were pretty self-sufficient when it came to keeping their home. They weren't ones to solicit help, so when Levi made the request, there was no way Bess was going to say no. Not only did it mean Bess was very needed, it was also finally a chance for her to give back to her sweet sister.

"I know I look terrible," Gen said as she opened the door with dark bags under her eyes and her hair in a top knot. But Gen's terrible was still pretty dang gorgeous, if you asked Bess.

"You look like a new mom," Bess said comfortingly.

Gen nodded. "Terrible."

Bess laughed as she walked into Gen's home, a place that she'd only seen in pristine condition. However, even just in the foyer, Bess had to sidestep a tricycle and four dolls. As Bess walked in further, she saw a sink overflowing with dishes, dirty countertops, game pieces and plastic food all over the living room floor, and a dirty diaper right next to the trash can. Bess figured there was probably a story Gen didn't want to tell behind that one.

"Levi is getting us packed, but I don't know if I can do this," Gen said as she looked at Bess, her eyes full of fear and longing. Bess understood.

"I know your girls and they know me, Gen. I've got this. And you need this," Bess said.

Gen didn't look so sure.

"Start with a shower," Bess said.

"A what?" Gen joked as if she'd never heard the word.

"Take a shower. If things fall apart when you're in there, you can stay," Bess said with a nod.

Gen pursed her lips as she watched Bess. "Fine."

Gen walked toward the back of the house, and Bess knew she had minutes to prove to Gen that she should go.

Bess found Cami's carrier and wrapped it around her shoulders and back. She slipped a fussy Cami into the carrier, who calmed nearly immediately. Bess knew Cami was only content while being held.

"Maddie, do you want to play a game?" Bess asked the little girl who was intently reading a board book.

"Okay, Aunty Bess," Maddie said as she slid off the couch.

"I need your help. So we can help your momma," Bess said, and Maddie nodded with all the seriousness a three-year-old could muster.

"Can you clean up your kitchen food and dolls? Aunty Bess is going to wash the dishes. We'll race," Bess said.

Maddie's eyes lit up. "Okay. And then we help momma too," Maddie said.

Bess grinned. "That's right," she said, but Maddie had already moved on.

"Ready, set, go," Maddie declared, and both of them got to work.

Bess started on the dishes. When the dishwasher was full and running, she moved on to the counters. There were a few big pots left in the sink, so Bess scrubbed those and put them in the dishrack just as Maddie ran into the kitchen.

"I'm done! I win!" Maddie declared, and Bess looked toward the living room to see it void of toys. The girl was good.

"What about your tricycle?" Bess asked about the foyer she couldn't see from where she stood.

"I did it," Maddie said, and Bess was impressed.

"I'm almost done too. But you win, Maddie Moo," Bess said, and Maddie beamed.

Levi and Gen came out of their room just as Maddie's smile was at its largest, and Gen's eyes went wide.

"How ... what?" Gen asked as she looked around the nearly clean area.

"Maddie did it," Maddie declared.

"Thank you, Maddie," Gen said, still looking bewildered as she bent down to give Maddie a hug. Then Gen looked at Bess with wide eyes.

"It's so much easier to walk in and make things happen when you aren't at it all day," Bess said.

Gen shook her head. She wasn't used to not being able to do everything on her own.

Gen stood, lifting Maddie with her, and Bess noticed the way her eyes glittered. Bess knew her sister would miss her girls, but Gen needed a break. To leave the house and go somewhere other than work or an errand.

"Go," Bess encouraged. "Levi booked you the best room at Whisling B&B."

"You did?" Gen asked, looking at her husband.

"Where did you think we would get away to?" Levi asked.

"I thought we were leaving the island," Gen said, seeming

relieved as Maddie wriggled out of her arms and back onto the ground.

"No. We'll be right here. And Bess will be fine."

"Maddie be fine too," Maddie chimed in while hugging Bess's leg, and the adults laughed.

"Fine. You all win," Gen said as she took Levi's offered hand and started toward the front door.

"See you soon," Bess said, and Maddie chimed the same.

The rest of the evening was full of Maddie games and lots of Cami carrying. But Bess relished her role of aunt, grateful that she would have days after this to rest her aching back.

The next morning came quickly, and Gen and Levi were home an hour after the rising sun.

"You guys should've had a nice breakfast out," Bess admonished when they came in the door. Cami was still asleep, so it was just Bess and Maddie in the kitchen eating strawberries. Maddie's request.

Levi pointed to Gen who ran straight to Maddie. "I couldn't. I missed them too much," Gen said into Maddie's hair as she hugged her, strawberry stains and all."

"I missed you, Mommy," Maddie said as she pulled away and went for another strawberry.

Gen laughed at her daughter's priorities.

"This was exactly what I needed. Thank you, Bess," Gen said genuinely, and Bess grinned in response. "But now I never want to leave again. I missed them so much," Gen declared.

Bess laughed. She wasn't sure how long that feeling would last, but Gen seemed rejuvenated, exactly what Levi had hoped for.

"Being a mom is hard," Bess said to Gen as Gen nodded her agreement.

"But the best job in the world," Gen said, and Bess had to agree with that as well. As much as her food truck was her current passion, raising her children had been her first dream. It was only because the heavy lifting of that dream was done that Bess was able to put her attention elsewhere.

Speaking of the truck, Bess needed to get there ASAP since Gen was home. Alexis had said she'd cover the earlier shift as well as the prep for the day, but Bess figured she should get in there and help any way she could if she was no longer on aunty duty.

"So you two are set?" Bess asked, making sure she wasn't leaving too soon.

Gen nodded as she tried to hug Maddie again, but Maddie moved at the last second to go for yet another strawberry. The girl loved her food.

Gen and Bess laughed, but Levi had missed the scene since he'd taken their overnight bags back to their room.

"Thanks again, Bess."

"Hey, you did the same for me a number of times when my kiddos were little. Just be sure that you call me when you need me, k?" Bess said, and Gen nodded because she knew it was the truth. Gen had done overnights with all three of Bess's kids a handful of times and even more girls' nights with Lindsey. Gen and Bess's kids all still had extremely strong bonds because of those nights.

"Will do," Gen promised. Then she looked at the clock. "But shouldn't you get to the truck?"

"Alexis is opening, but I should probably go help," Bess said as she stood up next to Gen.

"Then get out of here," Gen said sassily with a hip bump, and Bess wondered, not for the first time, if that was where Lindsey got all of her sass from.

As Bess hit the road and drove toward her food truck, her thoughts went back to her own life and the mess that filled it. It had been easier to forget Jon's lie while she'd been so busy with her nieces—another reason why Gen should call her for help more often—but now she was back with her own worries. Jon had called a few times since that Sunday dinner and had tried to explain his side of the story, but it always came back to the same thing. He had lied. He admitted that he had purposely not told Bess about the real reason why he'd asked her out. There was no getting around that. He had agreed with Bess that there were many times since then he could've come clean, and yet he hadn't. He'd chosen to lie and continue lying. With how weak trust between them was, Bess didn't know if she could forgive that.

At one point, Jon blamed it all on Bess and Dax, saying he'd felt insecure about the friendship that Bess had insisted on keeping. Bess told him he should've told her. He should've said anything, but he'd chosen to stay quiet.

This all came out over the course of four calls, and then Bess couldn't do it anymore. It felt like the same conversation from right before their divorce. The only thing different was it was a year later. They should've learned so much more and grown beyond the exact same problems. So why were they still in the same place? That couldn't be a good thing.

As much as she fought against these issues being the end of her and Jon, she wasn't sure how to come back from this. She told herself she'd traversed the road before, so if she'd done it once, couldn't she do it again? But in the end, her thoughts came back to wondering if all of this was worth it. Because she and Jon might work their little tails off, clawing every inch of their way to a good place, only to have these same problems arise yet again.

So they had to solve these issues before Bess could convince herself to give their relationship another shot. It was the only way she could see herself willing to walk down the same road again. It was the only way she could see them making it. But how? Jon had suggested couples' counseling, and Bess wasn't opposed to it. *If* she wanted to work things out with him. But she'd done her own counseling with Dr. Bella for over a year now, and she wasn't sure she wanted to do it all again with Jon. She didn't want to give up, but she was also tired. A good part of her felt ready to be done.

Maybe this lie and the subsequent learning that they hadn't grown much as a couple just proved Jon wasn't right for her? Maybe keeping at this was beating a dead horse? Jon wanted to try again, at least he said he did. But when Bess had asked him to be honest with her about what he was feeling in that moment, he'd clammed up. The same way he always had when Bess asked him to voice his feelings. So that was the end of that call. Because Bess was finished with trying to push Jon. She'd never been so confused. And although she knew relationships weren't supposed to be easy, were they supposed to be this hard?

Bess's thoughts kept her busy the entire fifteen-minute drive, and when she got to her truck, she saw Alexis's car parked beside it. She didn't put her keys away since both women locked the truck until they were open, for safety reasons, and so Bess knew she would have to use her keys to open the truck. She got out of her car and quickly walked toward her beautiful, red food truck.

"Hey, Alexis!" Bess called out before she opened the lock to warn Alexis it was her on the other side of the door.

"Hey, Bess!" Alexis called back as Bess opened the door.

"I didn't expect you in so early," Alexis said, still focused on her chopping.

Bess smiled at her ever-vigilant employee. "Gen decided to cut her night away short," she said as she washed her hands and put on her apron.

"Missed her girls too much?" Alexis asked knowingly. Alexis might not be a parent, but she was one of the most caring women Bess had ever met. Alexis's empathy was a strong gift, and she seemed to understand and feel others' emotions almost as well as her own.

"On the money," Bess returned.

Bess took a quick glance around the truck, surveying what Alexis had already done that morning.

"Did you already prep all of the lasagnas?" Bess asked.

"I got here a bit early," Alexis said, her cheeks going red as if she were hiding a secret.

"Have a hard time sleeping?" Bess teased. She knew Alexis was dating a guy that she was really excited about. Bess had to think he was the reason for Alexis's sweet blush.

"He's so fantastic, Bess," Alexis gushed, and Bess grinned at her cute friend and employee. All full of the glow of young love.

This was what Bess wanted. But would she not get that since she and Jon had a past? Because they'd already been in love once? But she'd seen people who'd been married for years still excited about their partners, gushing about how wonderful they were. Granted, not every moment of every day, and Bess didn't need that. But she did want to feel overwhelming love or adoration or even respect for Jon. An all-encompassing feeling of emotion that would bowl her over at least at one point in all of this. Yet all Bess felt was weariness when it came to Jon these days. And that didn't seem right.

But this wasn't about Bess and Jon; it was about Alexis and her new guy. Bess made sure Alexis saw her smile so that Alexis would continue to tell Bess about her newfound love. Alexis seemed like she could use someone to gush to.

"I can talk to him all night about nothing and everything. He thinks I'm beautiful," Alexis added, her blush going even deeper.

Bess knew Alexis was insecure about her full figure, which Bess didn't really understand. Alexis *was* beautiful with her long black hair, big green eyes, and curves for days. Sure, she carried a few more pounds than the girls in the magazines, but that was meaningless. Bess herself carried a bit more weight than she would've liked. She was surely not the beauty Alexis was, and yet she still found herself somewhat attractive on most days. But, at fifty-something years old, Bess had had a lot of years to learn to love herself, and still, she hadn't mastered it. So as much as Bess thought Alexis should know for herself that she was gorgeous, Bess guessed that if Alexis wasn't feeling that way about herself yet, she could see why it was so gratifying for her to hear that compliment from her date. However, it was important to Bess that Alexis also know that her new man wasn't the only one to think she was a beauty.

"He should. Because it's true," Bess complimented.

Alexis smiled. "Thanks, Bess."

With that sentiment, Bess turned to the mound of vegetables still needing to be prepped for the day and got to slicing and dicing. The two worked in a peaceful quiet for a couple more hours, although Bess wished Alexis would speak about anything since the silence lent to Bess's thoughts dwelling on how she and Jon just weren't working and really debating the merits of counseling. Was the last ditch effort worth it? But then again, wasn't Bess's only other option ending it? And was she ready to end it? Who knew? She was still so mad at Jon for lying. At this point, deciding it was over for good felt like it might be a whole lot easier than working through yet another issue.

Bess glanced over at her companion and guessed Alexis's thoughts were much more pleasant in nature considering the huge grin on her face.

"So do you want me to take the lunch shift or dinner?" Alexis asked as the finished the final steps of prep for the day.

"You're already here. How about you take lunch, and I'll be back by two to take over?" Bess asked.

Alexis nodded. "Thanks, Bess."

"Thank *you* for covering for me and helping me with the day's prep," Bess said as she left the truck.

Part of her had wanted to stay and just continue working the entire day, but Cassie would be there soon, and the truck got rather squished with all three of them. And besides, there would be little need for a second chef during a Thursday lunch. It was one of their slow days.

So she drove home, trying not to feel so betrayed and angry at Jon. Trying to move on. But she wasn't sure how. The only answer seemed to be that she would have to talk to Dr. Bella about it at her next session. She wasn't sure why she was so reluctant to try couples' counseling when her own individual counseling was one of the best things in her life. She could only guess it had something to do with the fact she wasn't sure Jon deserved more of her time. But that was silly, wasn't it? If they were trying to make things work, shouldn't she be more forgiving? And she was back to needing to speak to Dr. Bella. The circles Bess's thoughts were making weren't helping her in the least, but at least she was almost home. She turned on to her street and slowly took the road to her home.

As Bess drew close to home, she felt a grin overtake her face, unable to help the way her heart leapt as she drove into her driveway and saw an unfamiliar car in the Penn's driveway. A rental car typically meant Dax was home.

Her reaction to Dax possibly being home quickly brought Jon's words that his lie was all her and Dax's fault to Bess's mind. He'd told her he would've been honest if she would've given up her friendship with Dax. And the irony in it all was that she and Dax weren't even friends anymore. She hadn't texted, called, or seen him since that conversation in his car. All out of respect for Jon. True, Jon didn't know that Bess and Dax were no longer speaking, but Bess didn't feel it was information Jon needed.

But maybe he did? So maybe some of this *was* her fault. But then again, her decision didn't make Jon's decision. Bess wanting to keep a friendship with Dax might've hurt her relationship with Jon, but that didn't give him the right to lie.

And it was that incessant circle of pondering that finally gave Bess the answer she needed. She needed to try couples' counseling. She had to try every last thing with Jon before forever giving up the possibility of them working. She hadn't come so far just to give up now.

She parked her car in her garage, feeling determined, and immediately texted Dr. Bella's receptionist, asking when would be the best time for her and Jon to meet with the doctor. Then she got out of her car, slamming the door behind her.

She avoided turning around and staring at Dax's car as she longed to. Why, when her mind was so determined to make a go at this second chance with Jon, did her heart not fall in line? Why did she miss Dax so much?

But this was her choice, her decision, and she had to stick to it. For the good of everyone involved. So Bess pressed forward, keeping her eyes in her garage and on the door that led to her kitchen.

However, just as she got to the garage entry of her home, she heard the front screen to the Penn's home squeak open and shut, causing her to pause a moment.

She shouldn't look. She should pretend she didn't hear anything, close her garage, and continue on in her new resolve. But she couldn't do that to Dax, the man who'd been everything Bess had needed this last year.

So she glanced over at the house, knowing she'd see Dax. She watched as his long legs made quick work of the distance between their homes, and then he stopped just outside of her garage, still giving Bess the space she'd asked for.

"Bess," Dax said, his friendly voice sounding a little gravelly, as if he'd just woken up.

Good. This was a friendly visit. Dax didn't feel any of the longing Bess did. That was good. Bess could do friendly. She'd asked for friendly. So Bess did what any friend would do.

"Late night?" she teased since she knew it was already almost noon, a bit late to be waking up for the day.

"More like really early morning. I got in at about six and then took a nap," Dax said as he gazed into Bess's eyes. Bess loved the way he always kept eye contact with her. As if what she was saying was the most important thing in his world.

"Must be something important that brought you home then," Bess said since she knew how much Dax detested early mornings. If he'd braved the first of the am hours for his flight, his purpose for being home must be significant. Maybe it was a big event in Rachel's life? Dax's last trip home had been to watch his niece, Pearl's, last soccer game of the season.

"I think so. Since the reason I came home is you," Dax said.

Bess felt her insides go to mush. Okay, so maybe his visit wasn't so friendly. Bess knew she should stop Dax right there. Tell him that she was still working with Jon and going to counseling soon. But she couldn't. She stayed silent, replaying the words Dax had just said and wondering if he'd really meant them.

"I know this might be too forward, Bess. But Olivia told me about the stunt that Jon pulled this time and ... he's an idiot," Dax said as he pushed a hand through his auburn hair that gleamed in the sunshine.

"But I was an idiot too. I should have fought harder for you when I had the chance. But I took a step back, thinking you needed to give Jon a shot. I didn't want you to have any *what ifs*. But he messed up again. I figure he had his chance, and I'm done stepping back. I want you, Bess. I need you. I want you to choose me. I don't want to just be your friend. I want to be your best friend. I want to be your love. I want it all, Bess. I want it with you."

Bess was at a loss for words. What did one say to such a declaration? Especially a declaration of love from Dax ... to her. This was all for her. The utter honesty behind his words hit her hard. He wasn't mincing anything. And he was fighting. For her. None of it was conditional. He knew very well she could throw all of this in his face. She'd already not chosen him once.

"This is the time you throw your arms around me and declare I'm what you've always wanted," Dax teased with a smirk, but it was easy to see how vulnerable he was behind his bravado.

See, this was how things were supposed to be. The racing heart, the honesty, knowing immediately. Her time with Jon hadn't been void of racing heart moments, but there had also been too many lies and so many insecurities.

"I don't know what to say," Bess finally said.

Dax's face fell.

"I think you said enough," he said, and Bess realized he'd misunderstood.

"I like you. A lot, Dax. My heart flipped when I saw your car, and I wanted to see you. So badly. But things with Jon ... he wants to try counseling," Bess said, knowing she was going to lose Dax with the choice she was making. What kind of man promised to wait around while you tried to make things work with another man, not once but twice. But she had to be true to herself. And that meant giving this last ditch effort with Jon. Even if she wasn't sure about anything with Jon. Even if she was almost sure she would regret giving Dax up.

Ugh! Why was this so hard?

"Okay," Dax said slowly, and then he gave Bess a firm nod of his head. "I was going to say you don't have to give me an answer right away. So if I was going to give you time to figure out what you wanted anyway, who am I to demand how you spend that time? Go to counseling. Be sure Jon isn't for you. But know this, Bess. I know I am for you. I know you are for me. And I'll wait as long as you need to know that as well," he said.

Bess closed her eyes against the onslaught of emotions. She wished she were free to give her heart to Dax, but she owed too much to herself to give her heart before she was ready. She suddenly and clearly realized this wasn't really about choosing Jon or Dax. It was about choosing herself. And Dax was not only allowing that, he was facilitating it. Would Jon do the same? Bess told herself she would make sure he would before choosing him. If she did choose him.

Dax walked purposefully into the garage, placed a soft kiss on Bess's cheek, and then turned to walk away.

"I don't deserve you, Dax," Bess said to his back.

Dax turned around, his eyes meeting hers. "The thing is, I know you do. You deserve the sun, moon, and stars, Bess. But if you'll settle for me, I'll be waiting."

Dax winked before turning back toward the Penns.

Bess waited until he was all the way back in his home before turning around and making her way inside. She really, really hoped she was doing the right thing. Because one thing she knew for sure: a man like Dax came around once in a lifetime.

CHAPTER SIXTEEN

LILY HAD GIVEN Allen another month to realize he'd made the biggest mistake of his life. To come home to her. But a month later, and she was exactly where she'd been before. The only thing different was now she had a second job at a local preschool on the days she didn't watch Maddie and Cami. The preschool was wonderful enough to allow Lily to bring Amelia with her while she worked. If it weren't for the whole situation with Allen, life would be good, maybe even great. But because Allen had been Lily's whole world, she felt like her life now was just a shadow of what she really wanted. Because her husband wasn't with her.

The night before, she'd had another call with Allen. He was still upset she wasn't cashing his checks. She told him she didn't want his parents' money; she wanted him with her. Without emotion, he told her that was impossible. That's when Lily lost it, resorting to a cross between yelling and crying that wasn't pretty. She ended up hanging up on him. She was just so tired. So very tired of fighting against Allen for Allen.

But she was not going to give up. She was Allen's everything. She knew it. She just needed to remind him of that.

Lily brewed her coffee as she gratefully remembered that this morning was a Gen morning. Lily appreciated her job at the preschool, but she really loved being able to stay at Kate's with just Maddie, Cami, and Amelia. The three girls helped to soothe her soul, and this morning, Lily needed some soothing.

"Oh, Lily," Gen said softly the moment she walked into Kate's condo. Maddie even stopped to look up at Lily instead of running straight to the toys, the way she normally did.

"You okay, Lily?" Maddie asked as she looked from her mom to Lily.

"I'm fine, Maddie Moo," Lily assured, and Maddie ran to her toys with a gigantic smile. If only Lily's problems could be solved with an *I'm fine* the way Maddie's were. Actually, she realized they kind of could. If Allen would just listen to her and they could feel together that things would be fine, Lily's problems would be solved.

"Really?" Gen asked as she took the open seat on the couch next to Lily.

"She's fine, Momma," Maddie reassured, causing Gen to smile.

"Well, if she says so," Gen whispered, and Lily felt a ghost of a smile on her lips. She really wanted to push past all of the mess with Allen and live in the moment, especially for these sweet girls, but she couldn't. The fact that Allen had moved away without even talking to her, that he'd refused to see her before that, that he'd asked her to move out—all of it was a dark cloud over Lily's head that she just couldn't budge.

"I talked to Allen last night. No, *talked to* is too generous a term. I talked at Allen, and he proceeded to ignore everything I was saying." Lily refused to cry again. She knew her eyes were red and puffy from the hours she'd spent doing just that the night before.

"I think he's hearing you, Lily," Gen said softly as she patted Lily's thigh.

Lily turned to look at Gen, more than willing to take any advice that she felt sure Gen was about to offer. Lily felt like she was in the middle of a pit of quicksand, and everything she did only made her fall into the mire faster. She needed help, and if Gen was willing to give it? She'd take it.

"Our situations are completely different, but I think I can kind of begin to understand where Allen is coming from," Gen said.

Lily leaned forward, closer to her friend. She could? Because Lily sure as heck couldn't.

"He feels broken. At least I think he must."

Lily agreed. She didn't agree that Allen was broken, just that he probably felt that way.

"It's a crazy thing to be physically broken. To have your body betray you in such a way. I can't imagine how frustrating it is to Allen that he can't do things that just months ago he took for granted."

Lily knew that must be the case as well.

"And the thing is, when you're broken, the last thing you want is to inflict your broken self on the person you love the most."

Lily tilted her head in confusion. If she was broken, the first person she'd turn to would be Allen. She told Gen as much.

"Allen thinks you're perfect, Lily. He's always put you on a pedestal."

Lily nodded. It was a place she'd tried to climb down from many times, but Allen wouldn't have it. At least until recently. Now she felt very much below the man she loved.

"He doesn't want you to feel held back by his physical limitations. He wants you to move on."

Lily shook her head, unable to fathom leaving Allen behind. "He has to know I won't do that."

"Does he, though? I wanted Levi to move on, to leave behind my broken uterus," Gen said, her eyes telling Lily she was lost in her memories.

"You knew Levi wouldn't though."

Gen shrugged. "I figured I would just have to get mean enough. Anyone will leave."

Lily thought back to all that Allen had done since the accident. Was that what Allen was doing? Pushing her away because he didn't want to hold her back? She fought the urge to scoff. If that was the case, he didn't know her at all.

A knock sounded at the door, and Lily looked at Gen with a confused expression. They didn't often get visitors at this time of the morning. It wasn't super early, but it was still before nine am.

Lily got up to answer the door and saw a man she'd never seen before on the other side of it.

"Lily Anderson?" the man asked, so Lily nodded. It was her name, after all.

"This is for you," the man said as he handed Lily a thick mailing envelope and then walked away.

Sure enough, on the front of the envelope was Lily's name with Kate's address. But it was the address on the upper left hand corner of the envelope that had Lily nervous. Brigham and Brigham, Attorneys at Law. Why were lawyers ...?

Lily's thoughts screeched to a halt. Who knew she was living here? Who would send her papers through an attorney?

She glanced up at Gen, not ready to actually know the truth. It was one thing to suspect that Allen had served her with divorce papers, but to see them? What was the idiot man thinking?!

"You never went this far, did you?" Lily asked Gen, holding the envelope out so she could see it.

Gen glanced over the envelope and then met Lily's gaze.

"I thought about it. But I always lost my nerve," Gen said as her eyes dropped back to the envelope again.

Cami chose that moment to wake up from her morning nap, and Gen took her out of her carrier while Lily continued to stare at the envelope. Allen wouldn't have, would he? Did he hate her so much?

Lily hadn't realized she'd voiced the last question aloud until Gen responded.

"He doesn't hate you, Lily."

"He says this was all my fault. I hurried him home. He was getting a ring ... for me. How could he not hate me?"

Gen shook her head. "I would bet big money that him telling you this is your fault is another tactic to get you to leave. He can't bear for you to be hurt by staying with him. He'd rather set you free."

Those thoughts had occurred to Lily at the hospital, but after everything Allen had done to her, was that really what he was doing? Was he still trying to protect her? If so, he was doing a horrible job of it.

"Even if it means hurting me more?" Lily asked, feeling the sting of tears. But she wasn't going to give in.

"He doesn't know that."

"Because he ran. Like a coward," Lily said, bouncing between two of the emotions she often felt. Guilt at her involvement in Allen's accident and frustration at Allen's pig headedness.

"He did," Gen said as she put her free arm around Lily's shoulders.

"I'm so mad!" Lily said too loudly, getting Maddie's attention. Maddie walked over to the women and climbed into Lily's lap.

"But I'm also so so sad," Lily said, cuddling Maddie and hating how vulnerable she was feeling. Allen wasn't supposed to do this to her. He was supposed to guard her from this. And yet, here she was.

"So what do I do now?" Lily asked Gen as she stroked Maddie's hair. Maddie turned to give Lily one last hug before slipping off her lap and joining Amelia who was playing with a set of blocks, oblivious to anything happening around her. Lily was so glad she was still so young. She was sure Amelia noticed her father's absence, but if Lily could make things right soon enough, Amelia would never remember it.

Gen looked down at the envelope.

Yeah, Lily guessed she had to open it.

She focused on the paper, anything but the meaning behind what this envelope could possibly hold. She tore it open and then with shaking fingers pulled out the stack of papers from the envelope.

"I can't," Lily said as she held out the first of the papers for Gen to look at.

Gen glanced at Lily before looking down and reading what the envelope held.

Gen looked back up at Lily, and she knew. The papers fell from Lily's hands to the carpet as a few errant tears fell down her face. She knew this had been coming and yet ... why did it hurt so much?

Lily fought back her emotions. She couldn't lose it here and now. She had a job to do, little girls who looked up to her. Lily took in a deep breath. She could do this. She would figure out how to fight this last step in the war for Allen against Allen later.

"You have to go to Alabama," Gen said as if she could read

Lily's thoughts. But Lily shook her head. Even with both of her jobs, she didn't quite have the money to spring for a plane ticket. And she sure as heck wasn't touching the money Allen was trying to get her to cash.

"Is it the money?" Gen asked.

Lily shrugged. She didn't want Gen to feel any more pressure to help her than she already did.

"Let me pay for it."

Lily shook her head again. She couldn't let Gen do that.

"You have to see him in person. Or at least try. Throw those papers back in his face. Be the woman you want to be, Lily. You can't do that here," Gen pleaded.

And it was the pleading that got Lily to pause and consider. She knew that if anyone understood fighting for her marriage, it was Gen. She'd waged an uphill war and won. Could Lily do that too? She couldn't if she didn't fight. And Gen was right, Lily couldn't fight from across the United States.

Although taking Gen's money was a blow to her ego, what did Lily care about more? Her ego or her family?

Lily finally nodded, knowing what Gen had said was true. Lily needed to swallow her pride, take help from her friend, and fight for her husband.

"I'll pay you back," Lily promised.

Gen rolled her eyes. "Just book that ticket."

So Lily did just that.

AS SOON AS Lily stepped onto the jetway, the humidity hit her. Whisling wasn't a dry climate by any means, but the south in June was something special. Alabama didn't mess around when it came to heavy, wet heat.

The air-conditioned airport was a small reprieve, but Lily

was soon back out in the warmth, maneuvering her way to the rental car pickup.

A nice man helped her find her tiny Prius rental, and then she was on the road in a familiar yet completely unfamiliar place. She'd driven down this exact stretch toward Allen's mom's home numerous times, but the circumstances couldn't be any more different than they'd been in the past. Allen had always been by her side before. Ready to slay the dragon. If Gretchen, Allen's mother, didn't play nice, Allen was always right there, letting Gretchen know that he and Lily were a team.

But now Allen sat with his mom, pushing Lily away. After talking to Gen, Lily knew that what Allen was dealing with wasn't as simple as that. She'd probably known before talking to Gen as well, but that didn't make Lily feel any less like it was Allen and his family against her.

Lily glanced into the backseat, half expecting Amelia to be there, but the backseat only held Lily's carry-on suitcase. Lily's parents had been more than happy to watch Amelia for the night, and since Lily had known this trip wasn't going to be pleasant, she'd left Amelia home to spare her from whatever the rest of this day held.

The car ate up the miles too quickly, and Lily found herself driving down the gorgeous tree-lined street where Allen's mother lived. Lily had debated calling Allen's mom to try to win her over before coming all the way out here but decided that was probably a lost cause. Someone had to be paying for Allen's divorce attorney, and if his mother was doing that, she was probably all for the divorce. So Lily had stayed mum. Besides, the element of surprise might actually work in her favor.

Lily drew to a stop in front of the brick palace Allen had always called home. His mother had won the place in her own divorce. A circular driveway led right to the massive, white double doors of the house, but Lily decided to park along the street instead.

She paused before looking up at the house. She had no idea if anyone would be home on a Saturday at noon, but if not, she could wait. She had nowhere else to be. Nothing else to do. She was there solely for Allen.

Lily glanced at the envelope on the driver's seat beside her. She'd read every single paper. She wasn't going into this war ignorant of her opponent's tactics. She hated thinking of Allen as the enemy, but it actually made all of this easier. It gave her courage, almost as if this was a game. The most terrible game she'd ever had to play.

She knew she only had twenty-eight days from when the papers were served to give the courts her own response, and Lily was going to stall for every one of those twenty-eight days. Gen had asked her if she wanted a divorce attorney suggestion, but Lily had refused. It wouldn't come to that. She wouldn't let it. Allen was not getting a divorce.

Lily turned off her car as soon as she put it in park, and immediately the heat of the afternoon began to seep into the tiny Prius. It was time for her to move.

She drew in a deep breath. Ready or not, she was going to invade the fortress.

Lily got out of the car and then retucked her pale purple blouse into her dark blue jeans. She watched as her white sandals stepped along the brick driveway, and she was finally at the front door.

She eyed the gold lion knockers on both white doors and knew this was it. There was no turning back. Granted, that had never been an option. As soon as Allen had fired the divorce paper shot, her course to this door had been set.

Lily gathered up every courageous bone in her body and lifted her arm to smack the knocker against the door.

She had chosen to arrive on a Saturday for multiple reasons, the two biggest being she didn't have to work and also she knew that most of Allen's mother's staff was off on Saturday. That meant fewer barriers between Lily and Allen. She was sure Gretchen's butler was under strict instructions not to let anyone in without approval, and Lily wasn't about to wait around to be approved.

The massive door finally quaked open, and a very surprised-looking Gretchen stood in front of Lily.

The shock only lasted for a second though, and Allen's mom began to close the door. She was about to bar Lily from entry. That wasn't happening.

Lily slipped past Mrs. Anderson—Gretchen had kept her married name, even after divorcing Allen's dad—and into the enormous foyer, which housed a flamboyant crystal chandelier. Allen had always hated that thing.

"You aren't welcome here," Gretchen said, trying to keep some semblance of southern hospitality on her face. Lily had counted on Allen's mother's well-bred manners to keep her from throwing Lily out on the street. But she hadn't anticipated the attempted slamming of the door in her face, so Lily had to admit she was a little scared of what Gretchen was capable of.

"I understand that. But I need to speak to my husband," Lily said, squaring her shoulders. She knew the Andersons never thought Lily was good enough for their Allen. It was the one thing the warring ex-spouses had always agreed on. Well that and their like of their shared last name. Lily had always thought it was strange that Allen's mother had kept her married name, but after having Amelia, she'd begun to understand. It would be enough to lose a spouse; no longer sharing a name with her child would be another hurt to add to the pile.

Allen's mom looked at the envelope Lily held and had the nerve to smirk. Well, if Lily had ever held hope that Allen's mom might take her side, there went that hope. But Lily didn't need her. She just needed Allen.

"He doesn't want to speak to you," Mrs. Anderson said.

"I understand that. But he gave me these. I think that at least deserves a conversation," Lily said as she held up the envelope.

"What about what my son deserves? He's asked you for one thing, and you can't even give him that. You have some kind of nerve showing up here as if my son owes you anything after what you've done to him." Gretchen somehow kept a sweet smile on her face as she voiced her callously cruel words.

Lily bit her lip to keep from spewing venom right back at the woman. Instead, she just narrowed her eyes. It was one thing for Allen to blame her for his accident, but this woman had no right. She hadn't been there. She didn't even know Lily because she never cared to get to know her. Now she wanted to pass judgement? Nope. Lily was not having it. Courage swelled within her. She wasn't going to say the unkind words that crossed her mind, but she was going to see her husband, whether Gretchen liked it or not.

Lily crossed her arms across her chest. "You can either tell me where your son is, or I will search every inch of this home until I find him."

That bold statement shocked the southern charm right off of Gretchen's face, and her scowl showed Lily just what she thought of that idea.

"I'm calling the police," Allen's mother said, her back rigid, before turning to go to her study just off the foyer. Now it was Lily's turn to be shocked. Gretchen wouldn't really, would she? Lily was her family. Or at least she should be. And Gretchen was of the school of thought that family matters should be handled privately. Calling the police sounded far from being private. Lily was about to call Gretchen's bluff when a voice stopped her.

"Mom!" Allen called out, and it was easy to hear from the proximity of his voice that he was close. Close enough to have heard everything that had happened. To have known the kind of abuse his mother had heaped on Lily. And he'd just let her take it.

Anger boiled within Lily. How dare he!

Lily stomped toward the sound of Allen's voice, right to the main floor living area. Her arms stayed crossed over her chest as she stomped. How could Allen allow his mother's treatment of Lily? He had promised to cherish her. This wasn't cherishing.

Allen sat in his wheelchair next to one of the huge bay windows that overlooked the driveway and the street, telling Lily that not only had he heard everything, he'd seen everything. He'd seen Lily park, wait in her car and walk the long way up the circular driveway. Mrs. Anderson might've been surprised by Lily's appearance, but Allen hadn't been. And yet he had just sat here.

She threw the envelope in his lap, fired up by her righteous anger.

"What the hell, Allen?!" Lily said in too loud of a voice. But the house was huge, the Anderson's closest neighbor too many yards away to hear what was happening in this room. And Lily was beyond sparing her anger for Mrs. Anderson's sake.

"What is this?" Lily continued, pointing at the offending envelope, when Allen said nothing.

"I thought that was self-explanatory," Allen said, his voice calm. Too calm. How dare he not care enough to raise his voice right back!

Well, Lily was about to change all of that.

"If you think you're getting a divorce, you have another thing coming, Allen Anderson. I did not make vows to throw them away. I did not wake up every morning of the last eight years choosing to love you to throw that away. I did not give birth to the most beautiful baby girl on the planet to throw our family away!"

Lily felt the angry tears rolling down her cheeks, but they sure felt better than the sad ones.

"Why are you here, Lily?" Allen asked, sounding exhausted. As if he had a right. Lily was the one who'd flown across the country to fight for them. Lily was the one raising their daughter on her own. Lily was the one who should feel exhausted!

"Why am I here?!" Lily screamed, and then she willed herself to calm down. Losing her head would help no one. She drew in a deep breath. "I thought that was self-explanatory."

Allen winced at having his own words thrown back in his face, and Lily took the small action as a victory. It was the closest thing to emotion she'd seen from Allen in a long time.

"I'm not giving up on us, Allen. You can't make me. I will hire the best attorney Gen's money can buy in order to keep us married," Lily said, even though she had no intention of taking Gen's offered money. But the only person Lily knew who could in any way stand up to the kind of money the Andersons had was Gen. And if it came down to it, Lily would take a loan from Gen just to be sure the divorce Allen was asking for didn't come easily. But Lily hoped with her entire being that it never came down to that.

Allen bit his lip, and Lily wanted to cheer. That meant he was thinking. He was hearing her and he was thinking.

"Lily, I think you should go." Mrs. Anderson entered the room, and Lily fought the urge to scream again. The fact that the woman had come in now, while Allen was caving instead of while Lily had been raging, proved that she didn't want to protect her son. She wanted to keep Lily out. Lily knew Gretchen didn't like her, but this was a new kind of low.

Even though Lily wanted to fight against this newest threat, she let it go. Lily wanted to see what Allen would do.

"Lily, did you hear me?" Allen's mother asked, her hands on her ample hips and her perfectly plucked eyebrows raised high on her forehead.

"I did," Lily responded, but she didn't move.

"I am telling you to leave my home," Mrs. Anderson said, moving her hands from her hips to across her chest.

"I thought you said it was *our* home, Mom," Allen said, finally speaking up.

"What?" His mother turned her attention to him.

"This is my home now too, right? You want me to always have a place here?"

Mrs. Anderson nodded quickly.

"Well, Lily is my wife. That means she has to have a place here as well," Allen said.

Lily felt her heart swell with joy and a new kind of tears prick her eyes. Allen was still standing up for her, still calling her his wife. She had known all wasn't lost.

It was only that pure and pleasant joy that kept Lily from smirking victoriously at Gretchen, whose mouth had dropped open in shock. She looked from Allen to Lily and then shook her head before walking out of the room.

Allen's attention went back to his wife. "I'm staying here," he said firmly, but then he looked down at the papers. "However, I'll stop this process."

Lily nodded. That was enough. For now. It was a just a single battle's victory, but Lily would take it.

Allen's face softened, finally looking again like the man she had married. Lily fought the overwhelming urge to run up to the man she loved and drop herself in his lap. Her husband was coming back. But Lily knew now wasn't the time to overwhelm Allen with her emotions. He wasn't ready yet. But that couldn't stop the flicker of hope that had been burning in her heart from turning to a flame. She knew he would be ready to fully love her again one day.

Lily waited patiently as Allen's gaze appraised her.

"Are you flying back to Whisling tonight?" he asked.

Lily nodded. She hadn't seen the point in staying overnight in Alabama. All she had wanted was to speak to Allen, make him see reason, and then go home to her baby. Flying out that evening instead of the next morning would mean a long redeye, along with too many layovers. But it also meant getting home to Amelia as fast as possible. So that had been Lily's choice.

"That means you don't need a place to stay tonight?" Allen asked.

Lily shook her head, trying to keep her face neutral even though she was thrilled. She could only imagine the kind of fit Gretchen would throw if Lily tried to finagle an overnight invitation to her home. But Lily would keep Allen's semi-invitation in mind for later. He was willing to let her stay in the Anderson home with him. That might be a card she'd have to play in a future battle.

Allen watched Lily, probably knowing most of the thoughts running through her mind. For years he'd been the one to spend the most time with her, the one to know her thoughts before she even voiced them. She guessed that hadn't gone away in their time apart. That thought gave her even more confidence. She returned Allen's gaze, waiting for him to speak. She didn't know what he was about to say, but she knew he wanted to ask her something.

"Why didn't you startle when you saw me?" Allen asked.

Lily knit her brows in confusion.

"I'm in this chair. You've never seen me like this. Yet you didn't even pause. You just came up, started yelling at me and then threw this at me," Allen said, holding up the envelope.

"You made me mad," Lily said honestly. He had. She had

been so very angry. Besides, why would him being in a wheelchair change how they communicated? Did he expect her to go easier on him because of that?

Maybe others would, but not Lily. She expected much more of Allen than he was giving at that moment, and she wasn't going to shirk her duty of telling him he needed to be better and do better because of his new disability.

Lily then added, "I know you're in a wheelchair, Allen. Believe it or not, I know a whole lot about your condition. I've been researching it nonstop since your accident."

Allen shook his head. "But that's not how you should be spending your time," he muttered.

Seriously? What did he expect? That he would go away and she would forget that he was her husband? That she cared for him more than anyone else on the planet?

"Okay then. How should I be spending my time?" Lily asked, frustrated at Allen's statement. What the heck did he mean by that?

"Doing things that pertain to *your* future," Allen said, his voice now firm as he spoke.

"You *are* my future, Allen," Lily said, the sadness that she had to say so trickling into her words.

Allen swallowed, and Lily wondered if he was going to waver, if he was finally going to stop pushing her away. But she had no such luck.

"But I don't want you with me," Allen said as he turned away from her and looked out the window.

"And yet that doesn't keep me from wanting to be with you," Lily said, feeling defeated once again. The shine of victory had been short lived. But she refused to let her eyes fall, keeping them on Allen, willing him to look back at her. And he finally did.

When Allen's eyes met Lily's, they pierced her soul the

same way they had the very first day they'd met. Lily had never believed in love at first sight—lust for sure but not love. Then Allen had come along, and she'd known from that very first moment that he was hers and she was his.

So this happening again, what did it mean?

"Is Amelia walking?" Allen asked, surprising Lily by the turn of conversation. She grinned at where Allen's thoughts had gone: to the daughter and life they shared.

And there was Lily's answer. That look had meant something very good. It had connected Lily and Allen again. She'd felt it; he'd felt it. And that connection was enough that whatever had been keeping them apart had crumbled, at least a bit. Enough so that Allen was asking about their daughter.

Allen staying away from Amelia had been the part of all of this that had bewildered Lily the most. Lily knew Allen loved their daughter with all of his heart. He'd always been the best kind of father. Lily had assumed the distance Allen had kept from Amelia was Lily's fault. But he was closing that space, and Lily knew this was a huge move in the right direction.

"Yeah, a few steps here and there." In Lily's mind, she could see Amelia's chubby little legs taking small, slow steps. "She doesn't want to let go of what she holds on to, but I know she has the stability. She just needs a little more faith in herself," Lily said, gladly boasting about her proudest accomplishment.

Lily watched Allen as she spoke, and it was easy to see the hurt in his eyes that he was missing so much.

She wanted to ask him why. Why was he staying away when he needed them and they needed him? But it wasn't the time. Lily could feel it. She wasn't about to ruin all of the progress they'd made that day, even if the question she had was the most important one of all.

She knew if Allen would just come home, all of their hurt would be gone. But for some reason he wouldn't. Maybe he felt he couldn't. And although Lily thought he was being stupid, that didn't stop the pain in his eyes from cutting into her soul. Lily hated to see her husband hurt, even if it was his own idiotic fault. She had to try to make it better.

"I can send you videos of her if you'd like," Lily said.

Allen gave her the tiniest smile on the planet, but it was a smile. "I'd like that," he said.

"I know you said you're staying here. I know you feel this is something you have to do. But I'm not going to pretend that I understand this, Allen. I don't like it. But I love you. And if you need this, I'll take a step back. But don't ever serve me with divorce papers again," Lily warned with all of the sternness she could muster.

Allen nodded.

And with that nod, Lily was satisfied ... for now.

"We miss you," Lily said before turning to leave. She'd said her piece and promised to give Allen space. She now had to honor that promise because she expected him to honor his.

"I love you, Allen," Lily said as she paused before exiting the room.

As Lily walked away, she swore she heard Allen say, "I love you, Lily Anderson.'"

CHAPTER SEVENTEEN

"ARE you sure you don't mind?" Olivia asked Noah as they drove toward her bungalow instead of to the fancy dinner reservation he'd set up for her fortieth birthday.

Olivia was forty. It was a big one. One that sometimes worried people. But not Olivia. Because she was happier than she'd been in years, and although the day had been filled with just simple pleasures, it was exactly what she'd wanted.

She and Noah had spent the day on her favorite beach with a picnic lunch packed by Bess. Noah was pretty close to being the perfect man, but apparently he didn't cook. Fortunately, Bess was more than willing to cover for that deficiency.

She and Noah had then walked hand in hand along the sidewalk in front of the shops and restaurants that lined the beachfront in town. Noah had bought them silly, matching straw hats that were much too flamboyant for Olivia to ever wear. But they'd had a blast trying them on, and Noah's desire to mark the day with something memorable was sweet.

And now that the pleasant day was over, the only place Olivia wanted to be was at home with her wonderful little family. Her mom was at Olivia's bungalow babysitting the girls, and she knew that her dad would join them soon. Olivia could think of nothing better than a simple meal at home with all of her favorite people.

This birthday would also mark another big event. After dating Noah for a few months and getting to know the incredible man he was, it was finally time to introduce her girls to him. Olivia's heart skittered in anticipation, knowing that everything would change after that evening. No more would she have to choose whether to spend a Saturday with Noah or with her girls. No more would she have to ask her mom to babysit each and every time she wanted to see Noah. Her girls would know more than just the man from Olivia's dating stories, and Noah would know the sweet girls who completed her life. Although this was a huge step that Olivia had wondered if she would ever be ready to take with a man, after careful pondering for probably much too long, letting him into her girls' lives tonight felt right. A family dinner with all four of them ... and her parents.

"I'm honored you want me to meet your girls," Noah said as he pulled into Olivia's driveway.

Olivia grinned. This was why she felt good about this move. Noah was probably more thrilled about the introduction than even Olivia was, and that was saying something.

"They're excited to meet you," Olivia said, her smile only growing.

Pearl had spoken about little else since Olivia had made the decision that morning that they would all be eating her birthday meal together. Rachel was a little warier—it was Rachel's way—but even she seemed ready to meet the new man in their mother's life.

"Is this Dean's place?" Noah asked as they drove past the large home to their left and then parked in front of Olivia's bungalow.

Olivia nodded, even though she hadn't wanted to speak or

think about Dean tonight. This night was supposed to be about Noah and her girls.

But as soon as the name was uttered, Olivia's thoughts went wild. As if that one mention of the man next door was all the permission her mind needed to start rolling all of the memories she'd been trying to suppress for the past couple of months. She'd been working so hard to keep thoughts of Dean out of her mind since she'd started dating Noah, but it had been difficult. Practically impossible. Especially with the big role Dean played in their lives.

Olivia's reflections went back to the morning after Olivia's first date with Noah, which had also been the night of Dean's breakup with Charlotte. Dean had come over to apologize about how loud the fight had been, and her girls had rushed in to comfort him. After he seemed sufficiently comforted, the girls then told Dean all of the details of Olivia's date with Noah, and Dean said he was delighted for them. He didn't say anything about Charlotte's accusation that he had feelings for Olivia, so Olivia ignored the issue as well. Probably because it was a non-issue. Either Olivia's mom had heard things wrong or Charlotte had thrown out a baseless accusation while upset. Either way, Dean was just a friend.

So that should make things easy, right? Dean was just a friend, and Olivia's only romantic future was with Noah. But it wasn't that easy. Because Dean was always there. Playing soccer with the girls, arriving home from his shirtless runs just as Olivia pulled into the driveway, dropping off Rachel's favorite dessert when she'd failed a test. He was just there. And Olivia, no matter how confused it made her, wanted him there. Did that make her a terrible person? Because she was really starting to like Noah too. And she was dating him. Possibly exclusively. They hadn't had a talk about it, but considering Olivia hadn't gone out with anyone else, she at least felt exclusive. She assumed Noah did too since they were together nearly every weekend and talking to one another on the phone most every other night.

But tonight was not the time for those thoughts. So Olivia pushed them away and focused on the people in her bungalow. Thankfully Noah made that a simple task by speaking again. As long as Olivia focused on Noah, her thoughts of Dean could stay in the background of her mind.

"Are you worried?" Noah asked, looking down at Olivia's lip which she didn't realize she'd been gnawing.

Was that where Noah thought her mind had gone? She guessed it kind of had. Along with a few other places.

"Yeah, a little," Olivia said honestly. She really hoped her girls would love Noah and he would love them. The alternative was too sad to even consider. She couldn't fall in love with a man unless her girls were just as head over heels for him.

"I'll love them. I already do just from the stories you tell," Noah said as he reached over the center console of his car to hold Olivia's hand comfortingly.

Noah was right. This would go well. It was Olivia's birthday, after all. Birthday magic would *have* to come into play.

"Surprise!" Pearl called out as she threw open the door, and Olivia let go of Noah's hand to hurry out of his car and up to her porch where Pearl stood waiting for her.

"It's not a surprise," Rachel reprimanded as she came out to join them. She gave Olivia a look that said something along the lines of *she's such a child*.

Olivia shot a warning look at her older daughter to be kind as Pearl hugged her arms around her mom's waist. "Yes, it is. Grandma told me not to tell mom about her chocolate cake."

Rachel rolled her eyes in the way only a preteen could. "You just told her, genius."

Olivia shot Rachel another warning look, and this one

seemed to hit its mark because Rachel nodded reluctantly and then gave Olivia a hug. "Happy birthday, Mom."

"Thank you." A grin stole over Olivia's face now that her girls were no longer fighting.

At the sound of Noah's footsteps approaching behind her, Olivia took a step away from both girls and stood next to the man she was eager to introduce them to.

"Girls, this is Noah," Olivia said as Noah took ahold of her hand again.

Rachel's eyes went from the joined hands to her mother's face, and she pursed her lips. Not the best sign, but Olivia wasn't about to worry. She did pull her hand away from Noah as a precaution, though.

"Hi, Noah," Pearl said with a friendly wave.

Rachel nodded at Noah, and for now Olivia felt that was enough. Rachel just took longer to warm up to new people.

"It's good to meet you, Pearl and Rachel," Noah said with a huge grin.

So far, so good.

"And this is my mom and dad," Olivia said as she pushed the front door open. Sure enough, her parents stood on the other side of the door, probably eavesdropping on recent events.

"Pleasure to meet you, Mr. and Mrs. Penn," Noah said as he shook both of her parents' hands and then turned to Olivia.

"You have raised an amazing woman," Noah added.

"We like to think so," Kathryn said with a laugh. Then she moved from the doorway so that everyone could enter the house.

So far, so good again. Now as long as the rest of the evening could go so well. The small successes were helping Olivia to relax a bit.

"Oh, did you make creamy chicken?" Olivia asked as she caught a whiff of the wonderful smells coming from the kitchen.

Kathryn nodded proudly. She knew it was Olivia's favorite.

"It was what I asked to eat for my birthday every year as a kid," Olivia said to Noah, who smiled in return.

Olivia had asked her mom to make dinner earlier that day and hadn't expected anything great because of the short notice. But she should've known her mom would knock the meal out of the park.

"It's a very basic dish, but it's Olivia's favorite," Kathryn said.

"Basically delicious," Olivia added with a pump of her eyebrows, causing the adults in the room to laugh.

"That it is. Happy birthday, Baby Girl." Olivia's dad used the same term of endearment he had for all of Olivia's life as he put an arm around her shoulders, pulling her in close and pressing a kiss to her head.

"I bet Olivia was an adorable baby," Noah said to Mr. and Mrs. Penn. Then he turned to Olivia's daughters, "Kind of like you girls." He grinned at Rachel and Pearl, the latter scowling hard. That wasn't good.

"I'm not a baby. I'm eight," Pearl said, her scowl somehow deepening as she crossed her arms across her chest.

Noah nodded quickly, knowing he'd stepped in it.

"Oh, I know that. You're definitely a big girl now. I just meant that when you were a baby, you were probably adorable." Noah tried to save himself, but Pearl didn't look convinced.

"Noah wasn't saying you're a baby, sweet girl," Olivia said as she walked away from her dad to give her younger daughter a hug. "But you will always be my baby. Just like I'll always be my dad's baby."

Pearl pondered on that and then appeared appeased before pulling away from Olivia and running into the kitchen.

"I'm going to help Grandma with dinner. Because I'm a big helper." Pearl said the last sentence to Noah, and Olivia realized it would take a minute for Pearl to forgive Noah. Which was unlike Pearl. She wondered what was going on.

"'That's a great idea," Kathryn said. "Let's get dinner on."

Olivia moved to go to her kitchen.

"Oh not you, birthday girl. No birthday girls or guests in the kitchen," Kathryn said as she ushered Olivia and Noah to the table.

Olivia's dad and Pearl went to the kitchen, ready to help, but Rachel followed Olivia and Noah to the table instead.

"But daughters of birthday girls are definitely needed in the kitchen," Kathryn said lightly to Rachel.

Kathryn knew Olivia was trying to get Rachel to help around the house more. Pearl loved to help, but Rachel usually preferred to be served. Olivia wasn't going to raise that kind of person.

"He doesn't have to help, but I do?" Rachel asked sassily as she pointed to Noah.

"Don't point, Rachel," Olivia reprimanded because she wasn't sure where to start with Rachel's rude behavior.

Rachel rolled her eyes yet again.

"Rachel," Olivia warned, and her daughter stood, pushing her chair back loudly as she did so.

"I'd love to help," Noah said, trying to stand. But Kathryn pushed him right back down.

"It's fine. Just a little preteen rebellion," Kathryn said under her breath as Rachel left and Pearl came back with a bowl of green beans.

Dinner was finally served a few minutes later, and Olivia breathed a sigh of relief when Rachel was no longer staring daggers in her and Noah's direction.

"I hear you love soccer?" Noah asked Rachel, and Olivia cringed. She was sure she'd told Noah Pearl loved soccer. But it must've been hard to keep track of the girls before meeting them. However, mixing her girls and their interests up was considered a high crime in their home.

"That's her," Rachel said curtly as she pointed her fork at her sister.

"But you play soccer too." Olivia tried to salvage the situation.

"Only with Dean. Because he's fun." Rachel said the last part like an accusation at Noah.

That wasn't fair. Rachel didn't even know Noah.

"Noah's lots of fun too," Olivia said with a forced smile.

"Oh yeah? What do you like to do for fun?" Rachel quizzed.

Olivia really hoped Noah knew how important these questions were. Olivia knew Rachel was behaving badly, but reprimanding her in front of Noah would only hurt things. Which seemed to be exactly what Rachel wanted, although Olivia wasn't sure why. She thought the girls liked Noah, or at least the idea of him, as recently as this morning. Something must've happened between then and now that was making her girls wary.

Maybe it was Olivia? She realized her meddling in every interaction might be hurting things instead of helping, so she decided she would let the conversation flow between Noah and her girls, allowing Noah to win the girls over. He was charming and trying so hard. How could he not succeed?

"I love biking. Especially in the mountains," Noah said.

Pearl leaned forward in her seat, obviously intrigued.

This was good.

"Have you seen a mountain lion?" Pearl asked, her eyes full of wonder.

"Um, no. Not yet," Noah said, trying to sound upbeat. But it was clear to see from the way Pearl slumped back in her chair that she was no longer impressed.

Okay. So maybe Olivia's meddling wasn't the problem. She needed to resuscitate this situation ASAP.

"Noah likes swimming. Just like you, Rachel," Olivia offered, and Noah nodded.

"I don't really like swimming anymore," Rachel said, and Olivia wanted to scream. What was going on with her daughters?

"The creamy chicken is so good, Mom." Olivia decided a different tactic was in order. She just needed to come out of this dinner with the girls not hating Noah. Evidently they weren't going to love him today, but she could deal with that. She'd let them warm up to him without any pressure, and things would work out eventually.

"I'm so glad, Sweetie," Kathryn said.

"Dad, did you know Noah knows Eldon Foster?" Olivia said about her dad's long-time friend.

"Oh yeah?" Olivia's dad asked.

"He's been a client for years," Noah said.

Olivia's dad nodded, and the conversation stalled. Couldn't anyone help her?

"You look just like your mom," Noah said quietly to Rachel, who sat to the left of him.

"Everyone says that," Rachel said, still unimpressed.

"It's a compliment," Noah supplied with a grin.

"I know," Rachel said as she crossed her arms across her chest and turned away from Noah to Pearl, who sat on the other side of her.

Olivia glanced over at Noah, who looked stung by this latest interaction. But Olivia didn't feel it was right to say anything at this time and decided to ignore Rachel's rudeness once again. Her daughter would be getting a good talking to the moment their guest left for the evening though.

Pearl slurped up the last of her noodles and then turned to

her grandma. "Now can Dean come over? I know you said he can't come to dinner, but how about dessert?"

"What?" Olivia asked. This was the first she'd heard about this.

"The girls wanted Dean to join us for your birthday meal, but I thought it would be a good idea for it to be just the six of us," Kathryn said.

Olivia felt she was beginning to understand. The girls were angry that this dinner with Noah had kept their beloved Dean from them. No wonder they were so mad. Anything that kept the girls from Dean made them upset. But fortunately, there was a simple fix. Dean could come over, the girls would be happy, and they could finally get to know Noah without this barrier. On second thought, it might be a mistake, considering Olivia's mixed feelings about Dean. But if he could save this meal? Olivia would greet him with open arms.

"Of course Dean can come over for dessert if he would like to," Olivia said, hoping Dean would serve to diffuse some of the tension in the room. He was Noah's friend. If anyone could help the girls to love Noah, it would be Dean.

"Yay!" Pearl shouted.

"I'll go ask him," Rachel said as she jumped out of her chair.

"I'm coming too," Pearl added, following her sister.

"Don't slam the door!" Olivia called out as Pearl was about to do just that. Pearl shot a grin at her mom right before closing the door softly.

Olivia smiled at her daughters' exuberant antics as she leaned back in her seat, relief filling her that this night could still turn around.

"Wow, the girls sure do like Dean," Noah said with his eyes on the door Rachel and Pearl had just escaped out of.

Olivia nodded. "He's been a good ..." Olivia was about to say male role model but that felt weird to say to the guy she was dating. So instead she said, "Friend." Olivia then added, "To them during a hard time."

Noah nodded. "You guys were lucky to have him around. Dean's a good guy," he said. The words were the right ones, but something about the strained way he said them worried Olivia.

But Dean and the girls were back moments later, so Olivia had no time to worry. She had to be focused and ready to help salvage this nearly desperate situation.

"I'm ready for some chocolate cake," Dean said as he walked in, rubbing his hands together.

The girls laughed at Dean, and Noah shot Olivia a look that she couldn't decipher.

"It was supposed to be a surprise, Dean," Rachel teased.

"Oh no," Dean said as he raised a hand to his chest in a dramatic manner. "Did I ruin everything?"

Pearl giggled. "It's okay. I already told Mom."

Dean nodded in exaggerated relief. "Phew."

Even Olivia joined the laughter this time. Dean was sometimes too much.

Kathryn moved to the kitchen and began to light the candles on the cake as Rachel pulled a desk chair up to the table to go in between herself and Noah.

"I want to sit next to Dean," Pearl complained, and Rachel reluctantly moved the chair so it was between herself and Pearl.

Olivia looked over to Noah, who seemed deep in thought. What was he thinking? She hoped it was all good things and that Dean was taking some of the pressure off him.

"Happy Birthday to you," Kathryn started singing, and Dean quickly took his seat. The group finished the song and then Dean and the girls added their silly rhyme that they added at the end of every birthday song they sang.

Olivia looked around the table at the people who meant the most to her. She was glad to have them all in one place, even if they weren't quite getting along yet. She drew in a deep breath, not feeling the need for a wish, and blew out the candles.

"Woo hoo!" Rachel cheered. The identical beaming smiles on Rachel's and Pearl's faces told Olivia they were much cheerier now that Dean had joined them. Thank goodness.

As soon as *Happy Birthday* had been sung, Dean took the cake back into the kitchen and began serving pieces that Rachel and Pearl took to the table.

"I thought guests don't belong in your kitchen?" Noah asked into Olivia's ear.

Oh. She hadn't even thought about how that would look. Dean had been there so many times, he hadn't been a guest in their home in forever. But she knew that wasn't the right thing to tell Noah.

"He owns the place," Olivia joked, knowing Noah was aware that Dean was her landlord.

"Right," Noah said with a tight smile as he sat back in his seat.

The rest of the evening went about the same. The girls no longer had any sort of attitude and were even kinder to Noah. Noah seemed gracious about the situation, but Olivia felt an underlying tension.

"It's time for bed," Olivia called to her girls after her parents had left.

Her daughters had been bouncing around the room, probably because Olivia had allowed them to each have an extra piece of cake, singing a song about all the things they loved in life. They'd added Noah to their song, so although things hadn't gone as well as they could've, the night had somewhat turned around. Olivia would count the song as a win.

"Do we have to?" Rachel asked as Pearl looked pleadingly at Dean.

Olivia saw that Noah didn't miss the look.

"You have to," Olivia said, earning a pout from both girls, who went to hug Dean good night first. She knew it was their way of punishing her for making them go to bed, but she was worried about how it would look to Noah. Olivia was too nervous to even glance toward Noah to see how he was taking this.

"Night, Dean." Rachel gave Dean a long hug and then turned to her mom to give a brief one.

Pearl gave Dean the same long hug and then a kiss on his cheek. She then gave her mother the same treatment.

Both girls took a step back from the group before looking at Noah, unsure of what to do. But what did Olivia expect? They had just met the man.

"Thanks for coming, Noah," Rachel said politely, and Pearl parroted her words.

That sweet good night had been better than Olivia had expected. She looked over at Noah with a beaming grin but saw a strained smile in return. What had gone wrong this time?

"Thanks for having me," Noah said, and the girls ran to the bathroom for their baths.

"I guess that's my cue as well. Happy birthday, Liv," Dean said as he came over to give Olivia a hug. She pulled away sooner than Dean seemed to want to, but she figured it was for the best with the way Noah had to be feeling. She was well aware that Noah felt second place to Dean in the eyes of her girls. She wouldn't let Noah feel that way about her as well.

"Good to see you, man," Dean said as he gave Noah a handshake, and he left.

The room filled with silence after the sound of the shutting door, and Olivia was unsure of how to approach. So she didn't.

"You and Dean are close," Noah said, breaking the quiet.

Olivia nodded. They were.

"He's like a dad to your girls," Noah stated.

Olivia swallowed. It was weird to hear someone say it out loud. But Olivia guessed that he was. The situation had kind of just happened because Dean had been the only male influence in their lives, other than their grandpa and uncle, since Bart decided he no longer wanted anything to do with them. Olivia had hurt for her girls and their lack of a father, so she may have encouraged them to really embrace their relationship with Dean. It had all made sense at the time. It still did. But she could see what it would look like to Noah. How hard it would be to carve himself a place in the lives of her girls. But he didn't have to make that place in one night. And Olivia thought they'd made some good headway.

"They don't like me," Noah said thoughtfully.

Olivia shook her head immediately. That wasn't true. "I think they were just mad in the beginning because they thought you were the reason Dean couldn't come to my birthday dinner," she replied, trying to smooth things over.

"But I was," Noah said with a confused cock of his head. "Why?"

Olivia shrugged, even though she had more than an inkling as to why her mom had kept Dean away from dinner.

"Is there something going on between the two of you?" Noah asked.

"No, nothing," Olivia said firmly. That she could answer with a surety.

"But he wants something," Noah said matter-of-factly.

What? How could Noah say that?

"Dean set us up," Olivia said, feeling ridiculous that she even had to state the obvious.

"Yeah, I'm trying to figure that out too," Noah said softly.

"Noah, I really wanted tonight to work. I wanted you to love my girls and my girls to love you. My mom probably didn't invite Dean so that that could happen. This whole night was

arranged for you," Olivia said quietly because she heard the
sound of the water turn off in the bathroom. This was the last
thing her girls needed to overhear.

"I know. I appreciate it. I really do."

Olivia nodded. Noah seemed sincere. But she could tell he
was still holding something back.

"Olivia, I like you."

Olivia wanted to close her eyes against those words. The
final tone with which Noah said them. Because she might not
have too much dating experience, but she recognized that line.
She'd seen plenty of rom-coms and knew what was coming next.
Her heart sunk. Noah was breaking it off with her. On her
birthday.

Noah dug his hand into his pocket and came out with a
small box, handing it to Olivia.

Okay, that was unexpected.

Olivia eyed the box.

Noah moved his hand closer to Olivia, making it obvious
that the box was for her.

"What is this?" Olivia asked as she held the box Noah had
offered.

"Open it," Noah said with a smile, so Olivia did so.

In the box was a thin, textured gold ring. It was beautiful.

"I really like you," Noah said as he moved onto the same
couch where Olivia sat.

"I like you too," Olivia said, still feeling confused. She had
been sure Noah was going to break it off. Now he was giving her
a gorgeous ring?

"I want us to be exclusive, Olivia. Will you be my girlfriend?" Noah asked.

Wait, what?

Olivia knew she had to look like a gaping fish with her wide
eyes and mouth open in shock, but she couldn't help it. With all

that had been said and done this evening, Noah wanted to take things to the next level? Olivia had thought they were over just moments before, so her mind was taking just a bit of time to catch up.

So the night hadn't been an utter failure? Noah was asking her to be his girlfriend?

"Is that a yes?" Noah asked with a chuckle.

Did Olivia want to be Noah's girlfriend? Sure, the evening hadn't gone to plan, but she did really like him. Her girls might not love him, but they were warming up to him. And hadn't Olivia just been hoping that she and Noah could be exclusive? This was much better news than what Olivia had been sure was going to come after the words, *Olivia, I like you.* There was only one answer for her to give.

"Yes!" popped out of Olivia's mouth as she couldn't help but grin. After all of that, Noah hadn't run. For that alone, Olivia admired the man. And now he was her boyfriend. A great guy who made her laugh and cared about her girls. This man had chosen her. And suddenly Olivia felt like the luckiest woman in the world. She guessed she had been served a bit of birthday magic.

CHAPTER EIGHTEEN

BESS HAD INSISTED that if she was going to go to therapy with Jon, they had to meet with Dr. Bella. If she was going to give their relationship one last shot, she wanted to do it with the best doctor she knew.

She still wasn't sure Jon deserved this therapy, but Bess knew she did. So that was why she was sitting with Jon in Dr. Bella's waiting room. It had been two months since Jon's lie and one month since Dax had declared his feelings for her. Bess was no closer to coming to a resolution for her dating life. But she'd put off an individual appointment for this couple's appointment, and she was so glad the time for the appointment had finally come. It had taken Jon, Bess, and Dr. Bella quite a bit of time to align their schedules, but they were here now. And she'd never needed Dr. Bella's help more.

"Jon, Bess," Dr. Bella greeted as she came out of her office and ushered them in.

Jon took a seat on the big couch in the middle of Dr. Bella's office, but Bess took the armchair that sat to the left of the couch, facing another armchair that was to the right of the couch. Bess knew sitting with Jon would probably be a better place, but she wasn't quite ready to take that seat. She wasn't sure why; she just wasn't.

Dr. Bella took her traditional seat on the armchair that sat across from Bess's and then looked from Bess to Jon.

"Are you uncomfortable, Jon?" Dr. Bella asked, and Bess looked over to see a look of surprise on Jon's face. Then he rubbed his nose, a telltale sign that he was indeed nervous.

Huh.

"I'm not sure uncomfortable is the right word," Jon said, and Dr. Bella nodded.

"What is the right word?" Dr. Bella asked as she crossed one of her legs over the other. Bess noted that Jon glanced down at Dr. Bella's legs during the shift. She didn't feel he was lusting after their doctor, but he was noticing that she was a beautiful woman. That much was clear. Before the affair, Bess wouldn't have minded that. She would've thought it was human nature. Bess had also noticed that Dr. Bella was a beautiful woman. But now? That was something she'd need to discuss with the doctor if this was going to work.

"I guess I feel like Bess has an unfair advantage. She's met with you many times before. This is the first time I've seen you in this capacity," Jon said.

Bess cracked her neck, first one way than the other. She assumed Jon's words meant he'd seen Dr. Bella around the island before, and she didn't like it because she hadn't known that Jon was familiar with Dr. Bella. It shouldn't be a big deal and Bess shouldn't be jealous in the slightest, but she was. Bess realized that would also have to be resolved. Bess couldn't bristle every time Jon talked about knowing another woman.

"Bess *has* met with me. And if you'd like to see a different doctor, I'd understand that," Dr. Bella said.

Bess immediately shook her head. She liked this advantage, and she wasn't giving it up.

"Well, I can assure you I've been doing this a long time. I can manage to be impartial," Dr. Bella promised.

Jon nodded, either convinced or knowing that he shouldn't fight Bess on this. Whichever way, the couple was resolved to work with Dr. Bella.

"I guess we can start with a formal introduction. Would that help to put you at ease, Jon?"

Jon shook his head, probably thinking it was a bit over the top since Dr. Bella obviously knew his name and he knew hers. "That won't be necessary. But thank you."

Jon turned his attention to Bess, and she swore she saw an accusation in his eyes. Dr. Bella was working hard for Jon to feel comfortable with this arrangement, something Bess hadn't worked to do. Something old Bess would have done for Jon in an instant. It was as if that look was telling Bess that the therapist had more concern for his feelings than she did. And Bess might've been annoyed if it weren't true. Bess wasn't feeling much concern for Jon at the moment. She was still angry. And she felt she had every right to be.

Dr. Bella must have felt the tension rise in the room because she turned to Bess as well.

"Bess, do you want to talk about anything?" Dr. Bella asked.

Bess had plenty she wanted to talk about. She just wasn't sure where to start. A thought suddenly came to her mind, and she went with it.

"I don't like that Jon was checking out your legs when you crossed them," Bess said. Might as well get right into it.

"What?" Jon asked, but Dr. Bella kept Bess's gaze, not the least bit embarrassed or rattled. The woman was good at her job.

"It happened," Bess said to Jon, and then she turned to the doctor. "And it's happened in our marriage for years, but I figured it was normal. Jon is a man. But now ... I just don't want to have to put up with it anymore." Bess was as honest as she could possibly be. And it felt good.

"Why do you feel differently now than you did before?" Dr. Bella asked.

That was an easy answer.

"Because the looks I thought were harmless might have been a precursor to his affair," Bess said as she put her elbows on her knees and leaned forward.

"That's not fair, Bess," Jon said as his head whipped from Bess to the doctor. Bess, too, looked at Dr. Bella, but the doctor didn't look as if she was going to intervene. So Bess spoke.

"How is that not fair? Why wouldn't I put two and two together?" Bess asked. It seemed only logical to her.

"Because it isn't two and two. It's more like two and two and two and two," Jon said.

Bess narrowed her eyes. "I'm not sure I understand that."

"I'm just saying there is no direct link," Jon defended.

"How can you say that? You were checking women out. Something that a married man shouldn't do. I let it go. You had an affair," Bess said.

"Bess," Jon said in his way that made Bess feel so little.

"Listen to me!" Bess shouted, and then she calmed her voice. Screaming would get her nowhere. She drew in a deep breath. "I feel like you aren't listening to me. That you aren't validating my feelings. I'm saying you checking other women out is not okay. You want to start over, but I can't do that when we haven't resolved our past. I can't do that when I'm not sure the exact same thing won't happen again because you are still checking out other women. Why did you cheat, Jon?" Bess asked. She hadn't even realized she'd been thinking those things until they all came out. But the last question had to be asked. If they were going to move on, Bess had to get an answer that made sense to her.

Jon opened his mouth but Dr. Bella cut him off with a hand in the air. "Jon, Bess just dug deep to what she feels is the crux of the matter. I don't think you should brush that off. Think and try to understand before you react. Or better yet, how can you act instead of react?" Dr. Bella asked as she put her hand back in her lap.

Jon shifted and put his ankle on his knee as he leaned back on the couch. Bess saw that he was really trying to think about what she'd said, so she gave him credit for that.

"I feel like I'm trying to listen. But Bess, I can't go back and change anything."

Bess opened her mouth, but this time Dr. Bella's hand cut Bess off, allowing Jon to go on.

"This is me. I want you to want me just the way I am. I've tried to explain why I cheated, but it's never enough for you. So we have to move on." Jon swallowed. "I want you to love me because of who I am today, not because of some man you hope I'll become," Jon said.

Bess took Dr. Bella's advice. She sat, she thought, and she considered. Jon didn't want to change. He didn't feel it was necessary. He thought he should be loved for who he was, and if Jon hadn't put Bess through their past, she could understand where he was coming from. But that was the thing. He had put her through their past. And there was just no getting beyond that. Changes had to happen. Or Bess couldn't stay with Jon.

"I get you feeling like you shouldn't have to change for a relationship. I would feel the same way. I want to be loved for me as well. But Jon, what you put me through, that kind of betrayal. I can't fully love you if I'm worried it would happen again. And to stay in this all while knowing I'll never put my whole heart into it? That would be torture for both of us," Bess said.

Jon nodded. He sat deep in thought as Bess moved from her armchair to the couch. She felt the need to be nearer to

Jon now. She was over punishing him. She had felt she was the one always taking steps for them to be closer, and she'd taken her seat as a stand against that. But after the conversation they were having, it felt like her stand wasn't going to matter much.

"I don't know if I can make all of the changes you need me to make," Jon said solemnly.

"Do you want to make them?" Bess asked quietly.

"I don't know," Jon responded just as softly. "What do you need from me?"

"I need more honesty. I need you to tell me the things you keep buried away. I need you to decide that our relationship matters and always put it first. I need you to take steps to close the gap between us."

"What gap?" Jon asked.

Bess couldn't believe Jon didn't feel the same distance that she felt. But she decided to swallow back her astonishment and explain.

"I have you back physically, but you're still so far away." Bess held her hands tightly in her lap as she spoke.

"I'm not sure I understand," Jon said, and Bess paused. How could she get him to comprehend what she was feeling?

"Like the lie," Bess began, and Jon shook his head in frustration.

"Hear me out, Jon," Bess said.

Jon didn't say what he looked like he was going to, but he didn't seem at all ready to hear Bess's words either. This was what was wrong.

"You don't want to hear me, Jon. You want me to just get over things. Sweep them under the rug. But I'm not okay with that. These problems fester in me, and that isn't fair. You get to forget about your wrongs, and I have to deal with my feelings about them forever."

"But I don't get what you want me to do!" Jon said as he threw his hands in the air.

"Tell me you're sorry," Bess said.

"I did." Jon lowered his hands.

"And mean it. Sorry means you're willing to change those things that hurt me. And you don't want to change. So tell me this, Jon. If you could've gotten away with your lie and not had to deal with talking about it, would you have? If it would make your life easier?"

Jon paused and then shrugged.

"See! This is the problem."

"The problem, Bess, is that you won't let anything go. You expect nothing less than perfection, and if I mess up even the tiniest bit, you hold it over my head for eternity," Jon said.

That was not fair.

"An affair isn't *messing up the tiniest bit*," Bess muttered, knowing it was a low blow. But Jon was driving her nuts.

"I wasn't talking about that. I had every right to be jealous of Dax," Jon said.

"But you had no right to lie to me about it. Do you have any idea how that made me feel? The only reason why you asked me out again was because of another man, not because of me. Not because you love me. I now feel like you are only wanting this relationship in order to keep me away from other men. But when another better woman comes along, I'll be history. You just don't want me to be the one to leave you," Bess said as she crossed her arms and leaned back in her seat. She was so tired of fighting for a relationship that she really, truly felt was over. Why did she keep giving her and Jon another shot?

Because of the history. She was too afraid to let go and start over. But holding on wasn't all that great either.

Bess noticed that Jon was looking up at the ceiling instead of at her. This was not going well.

"Jon, what do you think about what Bess said?" Dr. Bella asked, causing Jon to look down and meet the eyes of the doctor.

"That there might be some truth to it," Jon said.

Even though Bess expected as much, it was like a shot to the gut. Was Jon only keeping her around until someone better came his way?

"Do you even love me?" Bess asked, her eyes glistening with tears.

Jon nodded immediately. "Of course I do, Bess. You gave me three beautiful children. Thirty great years."

Bess nodded as she came to understand what Jon was saying along with what she was feeling. She wasn't crying because she was losing Jon, even though she knew that was what was happening. She was crying because it was finally done. After all of the years, all of the tears, all of the work ... they were over.

"I know. But that kind of love is different, right?" Bess understood what Jon was trying to tell her because she was beginning to realize she felt the same thing. She had so much love for Jon, but was she in love with him? She didn't think so.

Jon nodded.

Bess finally recognized that they'd both mistaken comfort and having love for one another as being ready to fall back in love.

"This isn't going to work," Bess said as goosebumps covered her arms.

Jon nodded, finally agreeing with Bess. "We can't say that we didn't try."

Bess had never figured they would come so far just to fail again. They'd worked their butts off, and still they'd failed.

Bess bit her lip because of her frustration at the situation. And the worst part was that she only had herself to blame. She had made her choices, and she was reaping the consequences.

"I'm tired of being angry with you ... and myself," Jon said.

Bess agreed. There had been some high points with dating Jon again, but too many days had ended in frustration that he was still the man he'd once been. Because she was a different woman. And these two versions of Bess and Jon weren't compatible. No matter how hard they tried to make themselves fit.

"I forgave you for the affair, Jon. I really did. But forgiving doesn't mean forgetting. And my fears will always be between us unless you make them go away," Bess said.

Jon nodded. "And I can't do that," he said.

Or won't. But Bess didn't add that clarification. That was up to Jon. She couldn't make him do this for her.

Bess looked at Dr. Bella. This was not what Bess had been expecting, but had the doctor known? Her face gave nothing away.

"Where do we go from here?" Bess asked Dr. Bella.

"That depends on you two," Dr. Bella responded, so Bess turned to Jon.

"We can try to be friends again. It may take a bit of work because you've changed a whole lot, Bess. And that isn't bad, but I'm still trying to understand this new version of you. My Bess was a bit easier to anticipate," Jon said softly and with no accusation, so Bess chose not to be offended.

But was old Bess easier to anticipate or better to manipulate? She felt it was more the latter. Bess had been all too willing to be anything and everything that Jon needed, molding to his needs. But Jon hadn't done the same for her.

"And we'll always be parents to three great kids," Bess said, focusing on the positive instead of pointing out the revelations she'd just had about their past relationship. She didn't need to share that with Jon, to tell him all the ways he had wronged her. And that was a huge relief. The idea that she could just coexist with him was a blessing. She felt lighter than she had in a long time.

"That's true. And you'll always be the woman I was stupid enough to lose," Jon said.

Bess laughed. Jon had always had a certain charm about him that Bess loved. She hadn't been able to enjoy it in recent days, for fear that that charm might be turned on other women as well. Now Bess could accept that.

She would've thought that would drive her crazy, but it didn't. Because Jon was no longer her Jon. She'd been letting him go little by little for the past two months. This was just the final string to be cut.

"Are you going to go back to Dax?" Jon asked suddenly.

"Is that any of your business?" Bess asked.

Jon laughed. "I guess it's not. Is it weird that I actually feel relieved that it's not?"

Bess shook her head. They might not be the same people they were when they were married, but it looked like they could still find the same wavelength. That bode well for their future friendship.

"That's it then?" Jon looked at Dr. Bella.

Dr. Bella shrugged. "Again, that's up to you two."

"I think it is," Bess said when Jon looked at her. They were done. And as much as part of her hurt to throw away thirty years, Bess realized she wasn't throwing those years away. She was putting them away. In a beautiful treasure box that she could one day go back to when she wanted to relive the memories.

Jon stood and stopped in front of where Bess sat.

"Can I get a hug?" he asked.

Bess stood, opening her arms and embracing Jon, then letting him go.

"I really wish you all the best, Bess," Jon said.

"You know I want the same for you," Bess replied.

And then Jon walked away. With him went all of the frustration, anger, disappointment, embarrassment, and fear that Bess had felt whenever she thought about Jon. She could still associate so many good things with the man, but now that the pressure of trying to regain what they'd lost was gone, so was the negative.

"Are you going to be okay?" Dr. Bella asked as Bess stared at the closed door Jon had left through.

"Yeah," Bess said with a smile as she turned to Dr. Bella.

"Is this what you want?" Dr. Bella asked.

Bess shrugged. "I'm still not sure about that. But I am sure that this is what I need. So I figure my wants will fall in line soon."

Dr. Bella grinned. "I have a feeling you're right."

CHAPTER NINETEEN

"ORDER UP," Dax called out from the grill that he and Levi had set up beside Bess's food truck. It was a monstrosity that Bess was a little jealous of. One side of the grill had the typical barbeque rack, but the other side had a griddle, making it possible for Dax and Levi to fry up and grill burgers all at once.

Bess sat at a table nearby, dying that she wasn't allowed to do the cooking for the end-of-summer party she'd planned for her community as a thank you. The food truck was doing so well, and it was all thanks to her friends, family, and neighbors.

But when Dax had gotten his invitation, he'd insisted on giving Bess a break, and Levi had hopped on that idea. So now Bess sat cradling Cami as Gen ran around after Maddie on the grassy knoll next to the truck that overlooked the ocean.

It had taken Gen a few months to warm up to being a mother of two—Bess would bet that postpartum hormones had done nothing to help—but she was now a pro. Bess knew Gen still had her rough days, but Cami had begun to sleep better, and that had helped Gen to turn a corner. It was amazing what one full night of sleep could do for a person.

"It's killing you, isn't it?" Deb asked as she slid onto the bench next to Bess.

"What?" Bess asked, trying to hide her irritation from her best friend.

"Oh give it up, Bess. I know you too well," Deb said, and Bess laughed.

"I should be cooking," Bess said, staring at the grill masters.

"No, you shouldn't. You should be taking a break and enjoying your friends, just the way you are," Deb said with a grin.

"Are you trying to say you know me better than I know myself?" Bess asked with a raised eyebrow.

Deb nodded. "And that man over there seems to know you as well," she said as they both looked over at Dax. Dax turned right at that moment, his bright blue eyes gleaming mischievously, shooting Bess a grin that made her knees go weak. Thankfully she was seated.

"What's going on with you two?" Deb asked. "I feel like between Luke, the girls, and the gallery, I never get to see you."

Bess did miss her best friend, but she knew Deb was doing exactly what she should. Luke deserved a woman who wanted to spend all of her free time with him. Not that Deb had very much to begin with. The gallery had just opened to the public at the beginning of the tourist season, and Deb was still keeping the place a one-man show. She hoped to hire someone in the near future, but for now, she didn't quite have the expendable income to make that a possibility.

"How are the girls adapting to life on Whisling?" Bess asked.

"I saw how you sidestepped my question, but I'll let it go for now," Deb said, giving her friend a warning look that Bess answered with an innocent look of her own. "The girls love it here. But Clara still insists that she wants to go all the way to California for design school," Deb said with a frown. "I thought it was hard when Wes and Bailee left for school in Seattle. But California? Do you know how far away that is?"

Bess smiled. She did. And she understood how hard this would be for Deb. Bess could only imagine how she'd feel if one of her kids decided to do the same. But if it was what was best for them, Bess would have to accept it. "She's growing wings."

"And I want to chop them off. But Luke won't let me. He says this is good for her. Whatever that means," Deb grumbled.

Bess laughed. "But you still have Grace for another year," she said.

"Until she goes to culinary school in New York. New York! I just can't," Deb said as she shook her head at the mere thought. It was easy to see the love Deb felt for her new daughters was growing by the minute.

"But traitor Luke is looking forward to an empty house," Deb muttered.

Bess laughed again. Her best friend was too much.

"Can you blame him? He wants you to himself."

"There's plenty of me to go around," Deb said, waving her hands over her curves and causing Bess to laugh once again. Man, it was nice to hang out with Deb.

"I beg to differ." Luke's voice interrupted them as he came to stand behind his wife. "I hate sharing. Speaking of which, do you mind if I steal her away, Bess?"

Bess shook her head with a grin. As much as she missed her best friend, she loved the way Luke adored Deb even more. Bess had noticed the way his eyes checked in with her when they were apart and then lit up when she approached him. And if that meant Bess got less time with her best friend, so be it.

"But I don't want to go with you," Deb teased. Bess and Luke both knew that Deb never wanted to be anywhere without Luke.

"I'll get you a burger?" Luke offered, and Deb stood up.

"Why didn't you say so sooner? Lead the way," Deb demanded, and Bess watched her best friend get wrapped up in the arms of the man she loved before she pulled away and made him get her that burger.

With Bess's attention free again, she looked toward the trees that grew a few yards from where the men had set up the grill. Gen and Maddie darted in and out of the trees where many families had set up picnic blankets while they enjoyed the delicious fare and the gorgeous day.

Bess's eyes landed on Alexis, sitting on one of those blankets with a handsome blonde man. He leaned over to push some of Alexis's hair behind her ear and she blushed at his touch. Bess had heard a whole lot about Dalton over the past couple of months, but this was the first time she was getting to see him in real life. Alexis had brought him over to Bess to introduce him as soon as they'd arrived at the picnic, but after that, Dalton had been sure to keep Alexis's attention to himself. Alexis seemed flipped over the guy, so Bess really hoped he was worthy of her attention. It was hard to gain any kind of impression of the man when Bess had spent so little time with him.

"So what do we think about Noah?" Lily asked as she took the open seat next to Bess.

Bess took a second to think about the new man Olivia was dating. Bess had gotten to know him quite a bit over the past few months. Noah had made sure to become friendly with all those who Olivia cared about, and Bess counted that as a point in his favor.

"I think he's good to Olivia," Bess said as she shifted Cami, who seemed to be waking up. The baby's nap was supposed to be a good twenty minutes longer, and Bess wasn't going to let Cami off her sleep schedule on her watch.

"And?" Lily asked.

Bess caught sight of the parking lot where Noah, Dean, and

Olivia's girls played soccer between the cars. The little girls both howled with laughter as Dean tried to retrieve the ball that had gotten stuck under a car. Noah stood back with his arms crossed over his chest, but he was smiling.

Olivia sat on a picnic blanket with Kate and Amelia, but her gaze kept drifting over to the others in her group.

"He's got some competition in Dean, right?" Lily asked, and Bess shot Lily a small smile. This happy-go-lucky woman looked nothing like the Lily who'd been followed by a dark cloud ever since Allen's accident. According to Gen, Lily had been working things out with her husband, and she was content enough with her circumstances for now. She'd somehow been able to rent the same little cottage she and Allen had shared before his accident, and Lily had told Gen she was waiting for Allen to come home. She'd have a place ready for him when he did. Bess admired that kind of faith in a man. She'd had that once. And she hoped she wasn't too jaded to have it again.

"I'm not sure," Bess said. "I think Olivia really likes Noah."

"But she loves Dean," Lily said with a shrug.

Bess had wondered the same thing but wasn't about to say it aloud. It wasn't fair to Olivia. Bess knew how hard it was to date, but to date with the pressure of knowing the whole island's eyes were on you? It was nearly impossible. Bess had endured it with Jon, and it was part of why she'd insisted she and Dax just be friends for now. But Dax was making that hard.

Anyway, Bess knew the island was just as curious about the Olivia and Dean saga as they were about Bess and Dax. So she wasn't about to add to the speculation.

"Momma," Amelia called out from where she stood, holding onto Kate's shoulder. The interruption saved Bess from having to say anything about Olivia and Noah or Olivia and Dean.

"That's my cue. Thanks for the party, Bess," Lily said as she stood and then jogged to her daughter, swooping her up in a big hug.

Bess's attention was pulled away to the parking lot at the sound of giggling, and she saw that Rachel and Pearl had linked arms and were running away from Dean together. Noah had joined Olivia on their blanket, and both of them watched as Dean caught up to the sisters, causing them both to squeal and hug the other tightly.

Kate nudged Lily, causing the latter to take in the scene as well. Lily laughed and then leaned her head on her sister's shoulder. Lily had told Bess more than once that she wouldn't have managed these past months without her sister and her ever-present help and grace.

Seeing the scene of sisters made Bess think about her own. Bess knew exactly what Lily was talking about because she felt the same of Gen. Bess would've fallen apart without her own sister.

"It's time to wake her up," Gen said as she slid into the seat next to Bess.

"Is it? But I love this so much," Bess said as she held the sleeping baby to her cheek.

Gen raised her eyebrows. "I do as well. But during the night. Wake her up, Bess," Gen commanded, and Bess grinned.

Gen began to tickle Cami, who wriggled in Bess's arms at the touch, and then Gen cooed in Cami's ear. Maddie noticed what her mom was doing and joined her, albeit a bit more aggressively. But it got the job of waking Cami done quickly. Cami awoke with a loud squawk, and Bess handed the baby to Gen. She knew Cami would be ready for her next feeding.

"Levi," Gen warned as Maddie ran toward her dad, and then Gen arranged Cami on her breast.

Levi turned around, understanding that he was now on

daddy duty. He called to Dean, who jogged over, seeming more than willing to man the grill in Levi's absence.

"I can do that," Bess offered to Dean, but she was answered with a chorus of *no*s, Dax's the loudest. Dean got to the grill before Bess could even stand up, and Bess realized she'd been beat.

Bess watched as Dean and Dax took over flipping burgers while Levi carried Maddie, all three men laughing at something the little girl had said. Bess tried not to notice the way Dax's broad shoulders shook, but she found her eyes always drifting to Dax these days.

"Dax likes you a lot," Gen said in a teasing tone.

Bess smiled. "Yeah, I think he does." Bess admitted to her sister what she wouldn't to anyone else. "And I really don't want to take that or him for granted, but I'm not ready to jump into anything new yet," Bess said as she watched Dax joking with Dean.

"You shouldn't. Doing that wouldn't be fair to you or to him," Gen said.

Bess nodded. She loved that her little sister was so wise. Bess often went to Gen for advice, and she never came away disappointed.

The sisters sat shoulder to shoulder as they quietly admired the lively time happening all around them. Just then, Maddie escaped her dad and ran to where Gen and Bess sat. She pulled herself onto the wooden bench and then leaned over her nursing sister's head.

"I love you," Maddie said as she kissed Cami on the head and then jumped off the bench, ready to terrorize her father again.

"That," Gen said as her eyes trailed after her older daughter. "You know, sometimes I wonder if I'm a good enough mother, and then that happens and I remember. No matter what I do wrong, I did one really great thing for my girls. I gave them a sister," Gen said as Bess felt tears prick her eyes. Gen was the very best gift her parents had given to her as well.

"Thank you, Bess," Gen said as she looked toward where Levi had caught Maddie and was tickling her while she cackled. "I don't know if I would've survived the first few months of this era of motherhood without you."

"Oh, you would have," Bess said. Then she added with a wink, "But it probably would've been a whole lot harder."

Gen laughed. "My sister. Ever the humble one."

Bess joined Gen in her laughter as she put an arm around her little sister.

"But in all honesty, I should be thanking you. These past couple of years have been ..."

"Enlightening?" Gen supplied optimistically.

"Sure, yeah. And a whole lot of other words," Bess said with a chuckle. Then she stopped as she gazed at her sister. "But I've known that with you, I can always make it through the darkness of the night."

"And then we have a sunrise," Gen said as she met Bess's gaze. "Sisters and sunrises. Sounds like heaven to me."

Sisters and sunrises. The surety of a new morning with the person she'd always been able to count on. That sounded about right.

"As long as we have sisters and sunrises ..." Bess began.

"We can survive anything," Gen finished.

"That we can," Bess said as she squeezed Gen's shoulders. They really, truly could.

Made in the USA
Coppell, TX
29 June 2021